CAR

THE SEVENTH CROW

TAMARA GERAEDS

FREE SOUL JUMPER ORIGIN STORY!

Looking for a series of stories with just as much action, twists, monsters and magic as *Cards of Death*? Look no further! *Soul Jumper* is the thing for you!

Subscribe to my newsletter now – through www.tamarageraeds.com – and you will receive a *Soul Jumper* origin story FOR FREE!

PREVIOUSLY, IN CARDS OF DEATH

Our fight with the Devil isn't over yet, but we're getting closer to the end. Whose end that will be—our or his—I'm not sure yet, but I have high hopes. You see, a couple of good things have happened lately. Dad visited me. Unfortunately, his transparent state confirmed that he is indeed dead, but he hasn't left us. The lingering fear that he might have turned evil before he died is gone now, because he told us what happened: He was under the influence of the White Horseman and was later killed by his black brother. These two have also held him captive since he died, but he managed to escape to tell me about the Devil's back-up plan to get out of Hell. There is a way to open the circles of Hell without having all of the souls. If they manage to make the chosen souls commit the sins of each circle, Lucifer can use that somehow to break through the circles.

Anyway, Dad went back to his prison, in who knows where, to see what else he could find out. He'll try to join our fight later, so I hope to see him again.

But not everything is going well. A while ago, we lost two members of my Shield: D'Maeo and Jeep. D'Maeo got sucked into the box we captured the Black Void in; the thing that killed him and took parts of his soul. Jeep was sucked into another world when we returned from Purgatory. And I haven't seen Mom since she fell into the pit to Hell. I knew we needed more power to keep fighting, so I added another ghost to my Shield: Kessley. After a hesitant start, she's turning out to be an excellent addition to the team. She can multiply herself *and* shapeshift into any living thing she chooses! And besides that, she's got a great personality, and she can be so funny when the alcohol takes over—since she died drunk.

With Kessley as extra back-up, we went to see Gisella's aunt, Kasinda, who put the curse on Dad (which jumped over to me when he died and caused Vicky to have the same Exorcist-like fits that Mom used to have). We managed to break the curse and transfer Kasinda's dark powers to Gisella, who is still working on learning to control all of them.

After that, we found out that Shelton Banks not only–probably–killed Vicky's grandmother and sent the pixie that killed Taylar's brother, but that he's also the one touching Vicky's grave, causing her to get pulled to the Shadow World. We took Taylar's adjusted memory to the police, and they brought Shelton Banks in for questioning. Meanwhile, we went to his house and killed all of his troll and pixie servants. We found some interesting things in his mansion: three books, evidence of a murdered angel, a Devil's shrine, and… Jeep.

CHAPTER 1

A couple of weeks ago, I would've considered what I'm seeing now impossible.

I'm in a secret room, looking into another secret room with a portal in it. That's weird enough to begin with, but it gets crazier. I'm surrounded by several ghosts, who are all part of my Shield, which means they protect me, because I'm the chosen one, the only one capable of keeping the Devil in Hell. Every time I think about this, I question my sanity. Maybe I fell asleep and got caught up in a really long, crazy dream? Did I get into an accident and end up in a coma? That could explain the unbelievable turn my life suddenly took. I mean, an angel as a friend? Two friends who turned out to work for the Devil himself? Making love to a ghost? Traveling to other worlds, meeting the ferryman of the Underworld, Saint Peter and the Four Horsemen? All in my head, right? I made all of this up in my dream to escape from Mom's horrible fits, Dad's disappearance and… a car accident? The weird things started happening after we all drove home from school in Quinn's car, so why not?

Sure, Mom's fits were also strange. And strange is an understatement here. At least once a week, she acted like she was possessed by a demon. Of course, demons don't exist, so we searched for some other cause. Brain damage? Severe epilepsy with something else on the side? It was none of that.

My mind short-circuited and came up with this explanation: The world is filled with magical beings. Humans with powers, monsters of all kinds, demons, and, to make the horror complete, Lucifer. Maybe Mom's lunacy is hereditary. That makes much more sense.

I shake my head to get rid of the images from the past that roll by before my eyes. I see Jeep, the necromancer of my Shield. He's trapped behind the portal in the secret room. Can a dream feel so real? Can you love the people you meet there? Because my heart breaks at the sight of Jeep suffering like this. Just after he died, his wife was attacked by a bunch of ghosts. He was able to fight them off and save his wife, but the only way to beat the ghosts was to trap them in his tattoos. He's been fighting to keep them there ever since, and now, they're escaping. Being trapped in the empty world behind this portal must have consumed the last of his energy.

The tattooed ghost doesn't look up when we call

out his name. He doesn't even seem to hear us, although that's hard to tell with only a faint, small light shining down on him in an otherwise completely dark world.

Vicky is the first to break the stunned silence. She dives forward before I can stop her. Then, with her nose inches from the portal, she comes to an abrupt halt. "No! Jeep!"

The ghost is on his knees with gritted teeth and closed eyes. He trembles violently. Stretched-out bodies rise from his tattoos. Bony, transparent hands push the bodies from the pictures that have been their prison for so long.

"Do something!" Taylar yells behind me.

My foot moves forward on its own. It bumps against an invisible wall. My heart stops beating when I hold out my hands to find the same obstacle.

"No…" I breathe. *Why is this happening? We finally found Jeep. The thing we've been fearing for a while has come true, and there's nothing we can do about it. There's no way of reaching him.*

I put my arm around Vicky and pull her close. All we can do now is watch in horror as our friend gets surrounded by the evil souls he trapped under his skin, souls that have been yearning for revenge for decades.

Vicky's hand clutches mine as we watch helplessly.

I ball my hands into fists and will myself to wake up. *Enough of this. I want my life back. I'm going to wake up now in a hospital bed. I will find Mom sitting next to my bed, with an exhausted, but relieved look on her face.*

"Dante?" Vicky's voice startles me.

I realize I'm swaying on my feet.

"Stay with us, Dante. We need you. We need to figure out a way to get to Jeep and help him."

She sounds desperate. There's a mixture of emotions on her face that I can't fully read.

Mom's voice comes to me from the corner of my mind. A Christmas memory. Me and Mom sitting at the dining room table. Me with my sketchbook, Mom with her sewing machine. "Winter Wonderland" playing in the background. Mom is staring at me, and I put down my pencil. 'What is it?'

She smiles. Pride and love shine through her eyes. 'You are so talented.'

I look down at my drawing. It's a portrait of a snow owl surrounded by trees covered in white bliss. I shrug. 'It's okay.'

'It's more than okay, Dante. Can't you see that?'

'Not really.'

'You should apply for art school. If you want to make a living with this.'

It's probably the tenth time she brings this up. 'I don't know. I'm not *that* good.'

'Yes, you are.'

'I'm good at one thing, Mom. Drawing animals. Nature.'

She stands up and walks around the table. With her arms wrapped around my neck, she studies my work again. 'You could draw something else. Practice with other materials, see what else suits you.'

'That's just it, Mom. I'm not really interested in anything else.'

She lets out a sigh. 'Try a fictional animal then, to start with. Do it for me.'

Of course I agreed to try it, but it didn't work out. Not enough imagination, like Dad would say.

With a jerk, I jump back to the present. *Not enough imagination.* Dad wasn't only talking about when I am awake. Even my dreams are much more realistic than those of other people. Even in my sleep I lack imagination. Which means I could never come up with all these powers and this whole crazy plot about the Devil wanting to escape the nine circles of Hell by myself. Which means… this is all very real.

I blink and see Jeep hunched over on the floor, alone and unable to defend himself against the angry souls that are still pulling themselves from his tattoos.

"This isn't right," I say, and I take a step back, dragging Vicky along. I turn my head to face my other friends: Charlie, Gisella, Taylar, Maël and several Kessleys. That last ghost is certainly something I could never have imagined myself. Someone with the ability to shapeshift *and* multiply? No way. "Everyone, hit the barrier with everything you've got, in three… two… one…"

It rains lightning, gel balls and weapons around me, but they all bounce off against the invisible wall. Gisella slashes away with her blade hands, but although sparks fly everywhere, they don't penetrate the barrier.

"Again!" I yell.

We hit it even harder, Maël with her staff, Taylar with his bare hands and Vicky with powerful kicks.

Nothing.

We cease our attempts, panting hard.

"Vicky, try going invisible," I suggest.

She vanishes instantly, and the wall lights up.

"Yes!" I cry out. But my excitement is premature. Vicky appears again, on our side of the portal.

We have some success though. Jeep looks up from his place on the floor. The souls still swirl around him, most of them attached to a tattoo by only a small sliver now.

"Jeep!" Vicky and I call out at the same time.

I move closer to the portal. "Can you hear us?"

"Guys?" Jeep's voice is hoarse.

"Yes, it's us!" Vicky shouts.

"We can't break through," I explain, although I'm not sure he can hear us. "Try to damage the wall from your side."

A glint of hope flickers in Jeep's eyes. He swats the souls away that try to wrap around his face. Two other ones grab his wrists, but his newfound hope makes him stronger. He frees his arms and reaches for his bowler hat, which is lying two feet away.

"Hit the wall once more with everything you've got when Jeep's hat connects with it," I order the others.

They all prepare, their faces contracted in

concentration.

Jeep's hand is an inch from the rim of his hat when one of the souls finally manages to pull free completely. The tail of the dark wisp frees itself from the tattooed skull and shoots up high into the emptiness of the world Jeep is in.

"Watch out!" I yell as it drops back down.

But Jeep is too late to avoid it because the other souls hold him down. The sliver of black mist slams into him, and he screams in pain.

I pound my fists against the wall. "No! Leave him alone!"

Vicky joins me. "Keep fighting, Jeep!" Tears stream down her cheeks while she moves her fists forward with all her might.

But Jeep stays down. One by one, the souls escape from his tattoos and slam down on him like bricks. They wrap around his wrists and ankles and pull.

CHAPTER 2

Jeep moans and screams.

"Make yourself invisible!" I tell him.

He flickers like a bulb that's about to die. It's no use; the souls keep him in a death grip. They will literally tear him apart, and we can only watch as they do it.

Vicky stops pounding and rests her forehead against the invisible wall. "If you can hear me, Jeep, I want to tell you something." Her voice is fragile and full of sorrow. "You mean the world to me. You watched out for me from the moment I was added to the Shield. You supported me, taught me how to fight, and had faith in me. You never failed me."

Jeep stops struggling and looks up at her. He wants to answer, but as soon as he opens his mouth, a dark sliver covers it.

"I want to thank you for the great time we had

together, Jeep," Vicky continues. "I never thought it would end like this, and I'll miss you terribly." She wipes her nose and looks Jeep in the eye. "I love you, Jeep."

For a second, Jeep's mouth is uncovered, and his lips form into a sad smile. "I love you too."

The ground rumbles, and a thin golden line trickles from Jeep's forehead. Vicky grabs her head as the same happens to her. Slowly, the two lines stretch toward each other. Vicky's travels through the wall unharmed. The moment the two lines touch, the rumbling gets louder. I jump back as invisible bricks hit me in the chest. The pain barely registers. *The wall is breaking down!*

Vicky reaches forward and steps over the shattered barrier and into the empty world. I follow her, afraid of the wall mending itself. The ground still shakes, and the souls loosen their grip on Jeep. Vicky has reached him and helps him up with both hands.

I bend over to pick up his hat before hitting the fleeing souls with lightning.

Balls of gel zoom past my head. Something tugs at my leg, but I kick it with my other foot, and it lets go.

Four Kessleys take their place behind us and fight off the souls that are trying to reach Jeep again.

Vicky and I swat the rest of the slivers away from him. Mouths appear at the end of one and snap at me. Others have blinking eyes, and I even see an arm.

"They are transforming back into their human forms," Maël says, smacking a half-formed head with

13

her staff.

"What happens after that?" I ask, throwing Jeep's arm over my neck.

"I do not know."

"I'd rather not find out," Gisella says while she cuts souls in half with her blades.

Taylar holds his shield up above Jeep's head as two souls dive down. "Can we lock them back inside this room?"

Maël and I answer at the same time, "I hope so."

Slowly but surely, we get closer to the portal. I try to ignore the feeling of oxygen getting sucked out of my lungs with every step I take. There's something off about the air in here. It's unnaturally dry.

The Kessleys, Taylar, Charlie, Vicky and Gisella try to block the souls' way back to Jeep.

Maël moves faster than me, unaware of the lack of oxygen flowing to my brain.

"Hurry, Dante," she says, and I urge my feet to keep going, and my arm to hold up Jeep. But the longer I am in here, the foggier my mind becomes. All strength floods from my limbs, and suddenly I'm falling. In the corner of my vision, I see Jeep tumbling to the ground as Maël loses her grip on him.

I gesture at her to pick him up. "You go... on. I'll... follow."

"No!" Jeep's voice is suddenly strong. He lifts his head and meets my eye. "You... safe..."

Maël hauls him back to his feet, and he leans on her heavily. "I'll take him out and come back for you.''

I nod and rest my head on the ground for a moment.

"Babe!'' I feel Vicky's cold touch on my cheek. "Don't give up. It's only three more steps.''

"I can't,'' I whisper without moving. All energy has left my body, as has the will to even try to get up.

"Vicky! Hurry up!'' I hear Charlie yelling.

Then Taylar's answer, "We'll never be able to trap them in here. Can you use the shadows, Gisella?''

Someone tugs at my arm. "Come on!''

My eyes have closed, and no matter how hard I try, my eyelids refuse to open.

Then, something wraps around my ankles and drags me along. Hurried footsteps follow me.

I force my eyes open and see shadows hovering in the air, diving left and right whenever a soul tries to pass. Fresh air flows back into my lungs, and I push myself into a sitting position.

Vicky is still on the other side of the portal with Taylar and Gisella. When I turn my head, I find Charlie next to me on the ground, gasping for air.

I pat him gently on the back. "Take it easy. You're okay.''

He takes another gulp of air and wipes the sweat from his forehead. "I couldn't… breathe… you know.''

Maël helps us both up. "It was the climate in that world. Hardly any oxygen in the air.''

I point at Gisella, who's directing the shadows

with some simple hand movements. "Why isn't she gasping for air?"

Charlie frowns. "Good question."

Maël steps forward and holds out her hand, sensing the air. "She is using her new dark powers to fight."

Charlie gasps. "What? No!" He dives forward, but Maël grabs his arm before he reaches the portal.

"Let her try."

Charlie pulls himself free. "And risk her life? No way!"

"That is her choice to make."

Taylar and Vicky reach the portal and step back into Shelton Banks' mansion.

As soon as Vicky sees that I'm alright, she steps past me to check on Jeep. He looks a lot better, sitting up and smiling at her, so I focus on Gisella again.

I nudge Charlie, who's still hesitating. "Now that the wall is gone, we should be able to attack from here."

He nods at me and starts throwing grease balls at the spinning souls. My lightning bolts follow quickly, illuminating the darkness. That's when I see a familiar face behind Gisella's shadows.

I grab Charlie's arm. "Wait, Kess is still in there too."

Charlie lowers his hands and shouts, "Kess! Get out of there!"

"Who's Kess?" Jeep says from behind me.

I hear Vicky answering, but her words are

drowned out by a roar that freezes everyone in place.

Charlie shivers. "What was that?"

The answer jumps out from behind the souls. An elephant-sized lion grabs a foot and launches the attached soul out of sight. Three fully formed heads turn to face the new threat, and Gisella seizes her chance. She raises her arms high above her head and brings them down with force. The shadows obey immediately and shoot down like rockets. Momentarily, all the souls vanish from sight.

The giant lion jumps over the mess of wriggling black, grabs Gisella gently by the waist and steps through the portal. As soon as the beast lets go of the werecat-witch, it changes form. Just in time, because we were about to attack it. When we realize it's Kessley, we lower our hands.

Charlie hugs Gisella tightly. "Why did you do that? You could've gotten yourself killed!"

She kisses him on the lips and smiles. "How is that different from any other day?"

He shakes his head. "That's not funny. I was really worried, you know."

"Incoming!" Taylar hollers, and we all turn back to the portal.

The souls have managed to break free from the whirling shadows. Slivers of black mist with arms, legs and heads attached to them slither our way. Vicky and I move closer to shield off Jeep, who is still on the floor. Maël holds out her staff and starts mumbling.

"Can we close the portal?" I ask.

Gisella shakes her head. "Not in time. Let me try something."

She steps to the edge of the portal and spreads her arms. We watch as the souls approach, our weapons at the ready. Gisella utters strange words and guttural sounds, and the shadows swerve around the souls. They cling to the sides of the portal. Gisella's voice rises in volume, and a wave of energy shoots through the swirling black. They moan in pain but push forward with more vigor.

Maël's mumbling rises in volume too, and the souls' movements stutter.

"Yes! Keep going!" I call out.

Hands reach out and mouths open in the chaos of black wisps. Red eyes glare at us angrily before disappearing again.

"Pulverucorvus volucurus!" Gisella yells, and she slams her hands together.

We all back up when the souls burst into a million pieces.

"Brilliant!" Kess exclaims, and at first, I agree. It seems as if Gisella has managed to make the souls explode.

Maël has fallen silent. The agate stone on the tip of her staff stops glowing as she watches with fascination.

"What did you do?" Charlie asks. "Was that an incantation?"

Gisella steps back without taking her eyes of the descending dust. "It was. I turned them all to ash."

The moment she finishes her sentence, the specks stop falling.

"What are they doing?" Kessley asks nervously.

Gisella raises her arms again and starts to utter her strange sounds. But the souls are no longer affected, and even the shadows grow restless. Bit by bit, they shrink back to where they belong, leaving the werecat-witch alone in the doorway.

"That's enough." Charlie pushes me aside and yanks his girlfriend back. Fast as lightning, he builds a grease wall that separates the souls from us. While he works, I watch the soul parts wriggling through the air. They form solid shapes with wings and sharp beaks. Their shiny black feathers reflect the light from the lightning ball I conjure in my hand.

Charlie stops building when the wall reaches his shoulders. He looks back at us. "I'm out of energy."

Vicky and I reach out to him at the same time. "Watch out!"

We drag him down and duck when the birds dive out of the portal. But they don't attack us and even leave Jeep alone. They caw loudly as they soar over our heads, straight for the hallway. I count them as they disappear. Seven crows with glowing red eyes.

CHAPTER 3

Before returning to Jeep's side, Vicky hands Charlie four chocolate bars. He manages to leave the wraps on until he's checked on Gisella.

I look around dazed. The portal has vanished, leaving an empty, white room behind. Gisella is fine, but as surprised as I am, and Jeep is hugging everyone.

"Dante?" He stands before me, a bit unsteady, but in one piece, and suddenly, I can't hold back my tears anymore. With a sound that's a cross between a sob and an exuberant cry, I fling my arms around his neck. He presses me against his chest as firmly as I hold him.

"I knew the Devil didn't capture you. I'm so glad we found you."

"Me too." He dries his cheeks and stares at me. "You're still standing."

I smile through my tears. "Barely. We've missed you."

He lets go of me and looks around. "Where are we?"

I frown. "You don't know?"

He rubs his face. "I don't remember much. All I know is I got sucked away when we left Purgatory. After that, everything is dark until I got stuck in that empty place, where I slowly went crazy."

I nod. "Which is why the souls were able to escape." Gently, I squeeze his shoulder. "I'm so sorry we weren't able to find you sooner."

He swats my apology away. "Don't worry about that, I knew you had more important things to do."

I lower my head, ashamed that he wasn't our first priority. "I wish we didn't."

He picks up his hat from the floor and places it back on his head. "No really, don't worry about it." With a sigh, he turns to face the others. "Can we get out of here? This house feels toxic. You can introduce me to the leopard girl on the way home and fill me in on what I've missed."

Kessley giggles. "Leopard girl, I like that."

Maël leads the way, and I close ranks, mostly because I want to keep an eye on Gisella and Jeep. The tattooed ghost hasn't fully recovered yet, no matter how hard he tries to hide his pain, and the werecat-witch seems ready to collapse.

We reach the ground floor without trouble and find no one stopping us outside either. When I glance over my shoulder, I see that every trace of us vanishes in a second. My spell worked.

Vicky has handed the books we took from the library to Kessley, who carries them with trouble, but proudly. Charlie hovers around his girl nervously. She's lost in thoughts and mumbling to herself now and then, thankfully not with the same voice she uses for incantations, but still, it worries me.

I catch up with them and lean over to Charlie.

"Is she alright?" I whisper.

When he shrugs, I clear my throat. "Gisella?"

She turns her head and blinks. "Yes?"

"How are you feeling? Are you okay? Using your dark powers and containing them afterwards must have cost a lot of energy."

"So that's what that was," Jeep calls out over his shoulder. "You're using your Black Annis powers now?"

I can almost see him thinking, 'they must have been really desperate.'

"Yes, plus Kasinda's dark powers. I can control them pretty well," Gisella answers.

"But something went wrong," I say gently.

She nods and scratches her head. "Yes, I was trying to turn them to ash and let that fly away, but I must've mixed up the words." She bites her lip. "I'm sorry I messed it up, but I didn't see any other way."

"It's fine," Charlie and I say in unison.

Jeep slows down and pats her on the back. "You prevented them from tearing me apart, and I'm grateful for that."

"Me too," Vicky says.

We reach the spot where I hid Phoenix. Once all the bushes have been removed, I'm glad to find my car unharmed. I pat her on the roof before stepping in.

Jeep takes his place next to me without hesitation. Thankfully, Charlie doesn't seem to mind. He slides onto the back seat, next to Gisella. The other ghosts have no other choice but to merge in the two remaining spaces. Even in his transparent state, I can see a blush rising to Taylar's cheeks as Kessley makes herself comfortable on his lap. Or in his lap. Maël and Vicky are both leaning back, their heads next to each other. They look like a two-headed monster-ghost. I grin.

"What is it?" Jeep asks.

I gesture at the back seat with my head, and he smiles too. "Yeah, you need a new car, man. I'm not sharing my seat with D'Maeo when we get him back."

"Sure you are," I answer, reaching for the ignition. "You'll have no choice if I order you to."

I start the car and pull out of the forest and onto the driveway. Jeep chuckles, but it's not until we reach the road that we all fully relax.

Halfway back home, I glance at the ghosts in my rearview mirror. Taylar and Kessley have found a comfortable position. Taylar has made his body solid, and she is sitting on his lap, a little slouched so she can rest her head against his shoulder. Her dress has moved up to reveal even more of her bare legs, and Taylar's hands rest on them. My throat clogs up. Now I'm even more sure I made the right decision by adding Kess to my Shield. Not only is she a great addition, she also makes Taylar feel better. I can count the times I've seen him this relaxed on one hand.

"Do you think we'll see those crows again?" Gisella asks when I turn into Blackford. She sounds worried.

Charlie squeezes her against him. "Don't worry about that. It's not your fault they got away. None of us could stop them, you know. And if you hadn't done that, someone would've gotten hurt."

I nod in agreement. "Without a doubt."

Jeep turns around in his seat. "If we see them again, we'll be prepared. I took them out on my own once. They've grown stronger somehow while they lived inside me, but now we can fight them together. We'll be fine."

Gisella nods thoughtfully. "You're right. Thanks."

I steer Phoenix onto the magical road and watch out for trouble. Blackford seems to be the center of trouble, so I wouldn't be surprised if we bumped into another monster, of the demon or human kind. Also, if Shelton Banks was taken to the Blackford police station, I sure don't want to run into him. He'd probably read what we've done from my face, which is why I speed up a little when we pass Pine Street with the police station to our right.

"Wait, slow down," Vicky says.

When I do, we all follow her gaze.

But I don't see anything.

"What is it?" I ask, speeding up again to escape whatever danger she's spotted.

"I thought I saw something weird moving around the Winged Centaur."

Charlie turns to look at the bar through the rear window. "Define weird."

Vicky closes her eyes in concentration. "I only saw a glimpse, but it looked like…" She struggles to find the right words. "A panda."

I frown. "That doesn't sound like a threat to us, necessarily."

"Well, there was something off about it." She shakes her head. "I'm not sure what though."

Jeep chuckles. "You mean besides the fact that it was running around free in a country where pandas don't live in the wild?"

"And where there are no zoos with pandas either," Gisella adds.

Vicky sighs. "Yes, other than that."

"So what do you think it was? Someone dressed as a panda?" I joke.

"Very funny. But I'm telling you, it was something dangerous."

My heartbeat goes up at the sound of the worry in her voice. "Like a demon?"

She meets my eyes in the mirror. "Exactly like a demon."

We spend the rest of the way home in silence. When we reach Darkwood Manor, Jeep lets out a deep sigh.

"Are you okay?" I ask him.

"I am more than okay." He smiles at me. "Very happy to be with my family again, and to be home."

"Don't cheer too soon," Taylar warns him. "You won't be that happy anymore when a swarm of demon pandas comes knocking on our door."

Vicky points at the sky. "Or a swarm of killer crows."

I follow her gaze and gasp. The crows must have followed us. I can't believe none of us noticed them before, but now, they are swarming above the mansion, ready to attack.

As fast as I can, I park Phoenix close to the front door. "Everybody out. Run or apparate inside."

They obey as one. Car doors slam as the non-ghosts make for the front door.

The crows dive down, their red eyes gleaming in the sunlight. I swerve to avoid them. One of them catches the hem of my shirt sleeve. I tear myself free, ripping the fabric. I'm the last to cross the threshold, and I slam the door closed. "Is everyone alright?"

They all nod, and we hurry to the window of the study, where Mona greets us. Her relieved smile widens when she sees Jeep, but we are all absorbed by the crows outside. They are trying to enter the mansion, but thankfully, the protection spell holds. Every time they hit a door, wall or window, they are propelled backward. But they keep trying. From up close, I can see their beaks are smeared with blood. I'm afraid to think too much about what or who they killed before they followed us here.

"Why do you think they came here?" Kessley asks, pulling her dress down for the third time since we stepped inside.

"To get to Jeep?" I suggest.

The tattooed ghost shakes his head. "No, if they only wanted me, they would've attacked me when they flew through the portal."

I watch the birds charge again and again like brainless zombies. The protection holds up, so I'm not worried anymore. "What is it then? They had someone to kill first?"

"Or maybe they needed to consult someone first," Vicky says.

I frown. "Like who? Satan?"

She shrugs. "Maybe. Or Shelton Banks."

Jeep takes the books that Kessley must have taken from the car. "Not every maleficent soul works for the Devil." He walks into the kitchen.

"Thank goodness," Kessley and I say in unison.

All lost in our own thoughts, we watch until the crows finally give up.

Charlie straightens up and stops munching on his chocolate bar for a moment. "They're leaving."

We relax a little, except for Maël, who looks like the guard of a palace, motionless and alert. "I do not think we will be that lucky."

"What do you mean?" I ask.

With her staff, she points at the retreating figures. "They are taking up their posts in that tree."

Taylar slams his fist against the wall. "Great. So we're trapped in here."

I turn away from the window. "Not for long."

Everyone follows me to the kitchen, where Jeep is flipping through one of the books we took from Shelton Banks' mansion.

"Now that everyone is safe, I'm going to run some errands," Mona announces, and she vanishes while waving goobye.

Vicky hurries over to Jeep and reads over his shoulder. "Anything interes—" She furrows her eyebrows. "What language is this?"

Kessley joins them. "Can I see? I studied the languages of the world in my spare time."

Taylar gives her an incredulous look, which she must sense, because she grins at him. "Yes, I'm a nerd."

The white-haired ghost shakes his head. "Not at all! I think it's cool. I always dreamt of studying ancient languages, although I knew I never could."

"Why not?"

I expect him to choke up, but he just swallows and explains it to her. "Me and my brother were homeless. The chances of me ever going to college were close to zero. And they dropped below zero when I died." He winks.

Kess giggles, and I can practically see the sparks fly

between them. "Well, I can always teach you, if you want."

Her radiant smile is answered by a deep blush. "I'd like that."

Jeep slides the book over to where Taylar has sat down. "Great. You two take a look at this one while I continue with the other two."

He opens the next book, and his shoulders sag. "Or not."

Vicky looks at the third book and shakes her head before sliding that one over to Taylar too. She walks around the table and sits down on her chair on my right side.

"More gibberish?" I ask.

She sighs. "Of course. Why would anything ever be easy?"

I scratch my head. "How is that possible? We could read at least one of them back at Shelton Banks' place."

With a shrug, she watches Jeep slam the book shut. "You know how magic works. It must be another form of protection."

I grab Dad's notebook and my Book of Spells from behind my waistband and put them in front of me. "Well, I'd better start writing a spell to get rid of those crows."

CHAPTER 4

Vicky shoots me a surprised look when I throw down my pen and lean back five minutes later. "You're getting the hang of this, aren't you?"

"Looks like it!" I lean over and kiss her.

Then I turn to Taylar and Kessley. "How are you getting along?"

I know the answer before either of them responds. I can read it from their faces. "Nothing, huh?"

They both shake their heads solemnly.

"This isn't a language I've ever seen before," Kessley says.

Charlie leans forward from his spot next to Jeep— since Kessley has taken his chair. "I think Vicky was right. It's not an actual language; the books must be protected by a spell."

I nod thoughtfully. "We'll try to lift it later. First, I want to get rid of those crows."

"Me too," Jeep says. He looks a lot fitter than he did when we found him. His eyes seem lighter too, and he's lost a lot of his creepiness now that his tattoos no longer move.

Heat rises to my cheeks when I look up and realize he's seen me staring.

"What is it?" he asks.

"You look different," I tell him honestly.

"Better or worse?"

I smile. "Definitely better."

Charlie turns and takes Jeep in from head to toe. "I agree. You look a lot less creepy, if you know what I mean."

Jeep laughs out loud. "You thought I looked creepy before?"

Charlie wipes a blond lock from his face. "Well, yes. Those moving tattoos freaked me out a bit, you know."

"Me too," I admit.

"I didn't like them much either," Jeep says, holding out his arm in front of him. "But to be honest, they look stranger now than they did before. I've gotten so used to the souls moving inside them. I didn't expect this, but I feel kind of incomplete without them."

Maël grabs his hand over the table. "It will take some getting used to, but you are better off without them living under your skin."

He smiles at her. "I know that. I'll be fine." He blows her a kiss with his other hand.

A feeling of joy washes over me at the sight of them. Everyone is so happy to have Jeep back. It gives us all new hope and strength, even though we're facing several new threats. My optimism must be working. Three more souls to save, two more loved ones to get back and we're done. *If we can also put a stop to Lucifer's back-up plan.*

Vicky's hand rests on my arm. "We'll be fine," she whispers.

I kiss her again before redirecting my attention to the ingredients for my spell. "I think this is it." I slide the book over to her. "Do you have all that?"

"I sure do." She digs into her endless pocket several times, and I crush the herbs and spices in a bowl.

"No salt?" she asks.

I shake my head. "I don't need a circle."

"Are you sure? Salt circles add extra protection and can help you build up your magical energy."

I study the contents of the bowl, repeating what I've added in my head. "Okay, I guess it can't hurt."

With a smile, she hands me a bottle of salt.

When I get up, I notice Gisella standing by the backdoor, looking into the garden.

"Is something wrong, Gisella?" I ask.

She points at the protective circle in the grass. "I was just wondering if we would be able to make it there."

"Why?"

She throws up her hands and turns around. "I hate

sitting around doing nothing. We could be training while you cast that spell."

"Sure, but how would you get back inside? Those souls will wait you out. You can't stay inside the circle forever."

The werecat-witch drops back into her seat. "We won't have to. You'll get rid of them while we train, right?"

I hold up the bowl and my Book of Spells. "I'm going to try, but you never know."

She folds her arms over her chest. "Okay, we'll wait here then."

"This won't take long." I turn and walk into the annex, where I have a clear view of the crows that are perched in one of the pine trees that line the lawn.

Vicky follows me with the candles I need.

I put everything down near the middle windows and take the salt to draw a circle.

Vicky walks up to the windows. "It's as if they know what we're doing. Look at them."

I do, and I agree with her. A minute ago, the crows were sitting quietly on their branches. Now, they are getting restless, hopping around, stretching their necks and cawing at each other.

"It doesn't matter," I say, turning back to my spell. "They can't do anything about it."

"I hope so," Vicky mumbles. "They give me the creeps."

I shrug. "Lots of things give me the creeps, but that doesn't mean we can't beat them. I'm actually glad those souls escaped from Jeep's tattoos. He's a lot better off without them crawling around under his skin, and so are we."

Vicky keeps staring at the birds and doesn't answer, so I put the candles in the right spots and read the spell one more time. "Here we go."

Vicky leans against the window pane. "I'll keep an eye on the crows."

"Let me know if something strange happens." I don't think anything will, but I also trust Vicky's gut, and that worries me a bit.

I shake the restless feeling off and light a match. I light the three candles. Brown ones, for animal-related spells. In the middle of the circle, I turn three times, spreading the herbs around me.

"Seven souls that changed to crows,
leave the bodies that you chose.
Go to where you're meant to be.
Leave this place for eternity."

After the third turn, the candle flames reach up before moving around the circle, following the line of salt. I watch them as they hover above the herbs for a moment and then swallow them up. The ash that's left behind floats up and tickles my nose.

"Is it done?" Vicky asks.

I rub my nose to suppress a sneeze. "Yes. Are they gone?"

"Not yet."

I join her at the window. The crows are going crazy. They hop up and down and shake as if they're having a fit. They shriek so loud that the rest of the Shield and Charlie and Gisella file into the annex to see what's going on.

"Did you cast a torture spell on them or something?" Charlie asks.

"No, I cast a spell to make them move on."

Maël leans on her staff. "It did not work." She sounds disgruntled.

I frown. "How do you know? They're obviously affected by it."

"Watch and see."

Jeep stays about two paces from the windows, as if he's afraid the crows will come soaring through the glass. He flicks his hat over and over in his hands.

The crows start to change form. Their necks are stretched, their tails get longer and their eyes bulge. Then the rest of the body follows. One by one, the parts grow. First the legs, then the bodies, the wings and the heads. The beaks are last. They grow wider, longer and sharper.

Why is this happening? I didn't put this in the spell.

"Are they growing to human size?" Charlie wonders out loud. "Maybe they change back into their true form before they move on?"

He sounds hopeful but scared, and I share his feelings. Seven ghosts in human form seem more dangerous to me than seven ghosts in bird form.

The mutation stops, and the birds shiver violently.

35

Old, discarded feathers float to the ground and turn to ash.

"Do you see that?" Vicky whispers.

I let out a sigh of relief. "It's working."

Dark shapes rise up from the large birds. The body parts seem to come out randomly. A hand here, a head there, a foot attached to a shoulder. They look like Frankstein's monsters, sewn together in the wrong order. A soft, pained moaning reaches us through the glass.

I grit my teeth. *Something must have gone wrong. They should've moved on already, and it should've happened effortlessly.*

I turn back to my salt circle. "I'll try again."

"No, don't!" Vicky calls out, and I freeze.

"Why not?"

She points at the birds. The body parts are pulled in again, and the crows stop shaking. "All you've done is make them bigger. What if they grow again if you repeat the spell?"

My shoulders sag. "You're right. Do you think they're protected by something?"

"They must be."

Taylar sighs gloomily. "Shelton Banks probably did something to them. He knows Jeep is part of your Shield, why else would he trap him in his house?"

I nod. "True."

"He must've known about the souls in his tattoos too. He thought they'd kill Jeep if he kept him in there long enough, but he built in a back-up in case he escaped."

"And now we did exactly what he hoped for." I press my temples to suppress the headache that threatens to push through.

Outside, the branches of the pine tree have trouble supporting the weight of the bigger crows. They're almost twice their normal size now, and they look pretty happy about it, with their glinting red eyes.

"How are we going to beat them now?" I ask.

"We aren't," Gisella answers.

I turn to face her with a frown. "What do you mean?"

"We can leave the mansion through the porthole in the secret room. They won't even know we're gone."

I tilt my head. "Okay, that's a good idea. But eventually, we'll need to kill them."

"And we will," she says cheerily. "Once we've had a chance to think about it."

Charlie presses her against him. "You're right. We'll work something out."

CHAPTER 5

We walk back into the kitchen and sit down again. My gaze falls onto the books we took from Shelton Banks' house. "It's probably best if we don't try a spell on these either."

Taylar rests his chin on his hands. "What other options are there?"

"You guys could check with other ghosts. Maybe someone else knows a way. Or maybe you can find someone who can read it."

Maël takes one of the books and leafs through it. "Maybe."

I lean back in my chair. "Maybe is good enough for now. But first…" I take a deep breath. "It's time to think about the panda creature that Vicky saw. If it *is* a demon, what was it doing there?"

Vicky flips her hair over her shoulder. "I say it came to get Shelton Banks out."

I shake my head. "That doesn't make sense. A demon stands out too much. Pixies are a much more logical choice to sneak in and free him."

Vicky tilts her head. "Yes, babe, but we killed all of his pixies."

"You don't know that. He might have back-up somewhere."

Silence descends on the table as we think it over.

"Hey," Charlie suddenly says. "Didn't you have a list of the circles of Hell somewhere?"

I turn my head to Vicky, who's already digging in her pocket. As soon as she pulls the list out, she reads it out loud.

"Circle nine, sin: treachery, punishment: ice. Circle eight: fraud, punishment: boiling pitch and excrement."

"That one was gruesome," Taylar whispers to Kessley, who's listening breathlessly.

"Circle seven: violence," Vicky continues. "Punishment: boiling blood and burning sand."

I close my eyes for a second when I remember the boxer we lost.

"Circle six: heresy, punishment: fire. Circle five: anger, punishment: water. Circle four: greed, punishment: smelting gold."

The troll that stole from Shelton Banks. Another lost soul.

Vicky pauses to build tension. "And now we have reached circle three. The sin of this circle is gluttony. Punishment: rain and black snow."

Jeep slams his hand on the table so hard that we all

jump. "That's it! That panda demon wasn't going to the police station. It was watching the next soul."

I frown. "Where was the next soul then?"

He smirks. "At the Winged Centaur. They also serve food there."

I grin back. "I think you're right." I rise to my feet and check my weapons behind my waistband and in my pocket. My fingers wrap around my athame. "Guess what? We're going out for dinner."

On foot, it's a lot further than it seems from the silver mine to the bar across the police station. Nervously, we look left and right. There's no sign of pandas or other strange creatures. Everything seems quiet on both sides of the street.

I miss the comfort and shelter of my car. Phoenix might not be as reliable as she once was, but she can take us out of here fast if needed.

I'm sure we'll attract attention when we file into the Winged Centaur. We must look like a weird collection of people: several generations, some very serious, some not so much. I glance at Charlie walking in after me and grin to myself. I'm glad he's sticking by me through all of this. Even though he's lost some of his carelessness, he still manages to lighten the mood when we need it most.

Once we're inside, my worries about attracting too much attention evaporate. But so do my hopes of finding whomever the panda demon is after. Almost every table is occupied, and the room is filled with chatter, music and laughter. I have no idea how to find the soul we're looking for amongst all these people. He might not even be in here anymore. He could've left while we were at Darkwood Manor.

I follow the others to the back of the bar, where we take the last two available tables. They are high tables—metallic like the rest of the interior—without chairs, but I don't care. I'm too restless to sit down anyway.

Charlie leans over to make himself intelligible. "Do you want a drink?"

I scan the crowd and sigh. "Sure, why not?"

"Goblin beer?"

The corners of my mouth move up by their own accord. It seems like ages ago that I was here for the first time, inside a bar that's only visible to magical people, drinking my first goblin beer and putting a spell on my 'friend' Simon to reveal his true nature.

I shove those images to the back of my mind and smile at Charlie. "Yes, please. I could use one."

Charlie checks with the rest of the group and makes his way to the bar. The rest of us eye the many faces around us warily.

I move around Maël and nudge Gisella. "Is it a special day or something?"

She shrugs. "Not that I know of."

"So, it's just bad luck that it's so crowded in here."

She grabs my arm and squeezes gently. "Don't be gloomy. We'll find this soul in time."

I ball my hands into fists. "Yes, we will."

"I've never been in a bar like this before," Kessley says. "Is it invisible to non-magicals?"

I chuckle. "Thankfully, yes. Can you imagine someone without magic walking in here? They would freak out!"

She stares at a man with spikes all over his body, dressed in nothing but tiny underpants. "I'm not too comfortable here either. What if the evil beings attack us?"

"They won't," I assure her. "There's protection here, some sort of spell, I think, plus a silent treaty that no one will attack another customer."

"Yeah, people know it's wise not to mess with the owner." Charlie plants a bottle of goblin beer in front of me. "Drink this. You'll feel better, you know."

At the other table, Kess refuses her beer. "I can't drink that. I'm drunk enough as it is!"

Taylar and Charlie try to convince her she'll be fine, but she holds her ground. Eventually, Taylar nods and makes his way through the mass to get her something else.

Maël seems to have forgotten her drink entirely. She's clutching the bottle tightly, but her eyes move around the room.

"Don't make it too obvious," I tell her. "We don't want to make anyone angry."

I remember my last visit to this bar and my encounter with the dragon girl that tried to seduce me. Goosebumps appear on my skin at the thought alone. I hope it's not her we need to save. That could become really uncomfortable.

"I have not seen any gluttony yet," Maël says without looking at me.

My eyebrows move up. "Really? I see a lot of it."

I gesture at the group of horned men devouring one chicken wing after another.

Maël finally relaxes a little and takes a sip from her beer. She pulls a face and puts the bottle down again. "That is horrible."

Before I can protest, she continues, "I see mostly hungry people and people with natural cravings. Nothing extreme yet."

"How can you know for sure?"

She pushes the bottle away from her. "We will know gluttony when we see it."

"I hope so," I mumble, and I work my way back to where Vicky is standing. She's enjoying her beer and moving her hips to the beat of the music. When I follow her gaze, I realize she's watching Kessley and Taylar. The white-haired ghost hands the blonde girl a glass of soda, and she takes it without pausing her sensual moves. His beer almost slips from his hand when Kess moves closer to him with a provocative shake of her chest.

"We should try to find the next soul," I say to Vicky. "With everything going on in Heaven, the next cards could be delayed or lost too. Like the ones that murdered angel was carrying."

She plants a kiss on my cheek. "I know, but I enjoy watching them."

I wrap my free hand around her waist. "Yeah, me too."

We watch until Taylar notices. A blush creeps up from his neck, and he takes a step away from Kess.

I raise my hands in a 'don't mind us' gesture, and Vicky averts her head with a chuckle. She clears her throat. "Okay, time to focus."

I agree. The loss of the last soul is like a huge weight on my shoulders, that I manage to ignore most of the time, thankfully. But I'm not about to hand Satan another win.

"What about that guy?" Vicky nods in the direction of a tall, but slender, thirtyish man with more hair than bare skin.

"Is that a werewolf?" I ask, lowering my voice in case he can hear me.

"No, I saw one once. It looked much more vicious. It had long fangs and pointy ears. I'm not sure what this is."

Charlie and Gisella move closer to us.

"I don't think it's the person we're looking for," Gisella says.

I take a swig from my beer when the hairy man turns his head in our direction.

"Why not?" I ask.

She tilts her head in thought. "He's too… in control. I think gluttony is an out of control craving. We'll recognize it when we see it."

"But…" I rub my forehead and struggle to recover the thought that just hit me.

"But what?" Vicky asks.

I push my fingers against my temples. *Come on. Don't run away. This is important.*

The thought drifts by, and I grab it forcefully. I say it out loud before it disappears again. "The Devil needs people who have no tendency toward the sins, right? It makes the sins stronger, that's why the souls can be used to open the circles."

Nobody even blinks.

"Right?" I ask uncertainly.

Vicky's head goes up and down fast. "Yes, you're right. I can't believe we forgot about that."

Gisella takes in the crowd around us. "So, we're looking for someone who has perfect self-restraint now, but will give in for whatever reason later?"

I down the rest of my beer. "Well, the demons will try to make them commit this sin. But maybe they will fail this time." I shoot my friends a hopeful look. "I mean, this sounds like a hard one. How do you make someone with perfect self-restraint eat like a pig?"

Maël's voice behind me makes me jump. "We have met someone who has the power to make that happen with one look."

My heart sinks when I realize who she's talking about.

The Black Horseman of Famine.

CHAPTER 6

I turn back to our table and beckon the others. When everyone is leaning toward me, I fill them in on our suspicions.

"We should go home to think of a way to beat the Horsemen," I conclude.

"But what if they take the soul while we're gone?" Kess says.

Taylar straightens up. "What if some of us stay here, to keep an eye on things?"

I shake my head. "We'll need all of our powers to defeat the Horsemen. Tricking them won't work anymore, which means our only option is to fight them. And we need a plan to survive that."

Charlie raises his empty glass. "Can't we make a plan here? I thought we were having dinner?"

I bite my lip and scan the faces at the other tables. "To be honest, I don't trust anyone except you guys. I can't discuss something like this here."

"What about in the parking lot? Or across the street?" Gisella suggests. "We can watch the bar from there and jump into action if needed." She throws Charlie a sympathetic look. "You'll have to wait for dinner. I'm sure Vicky has some chocolate or a couple of cookies stuffed away in her pocket for you."

Without a word, Vicky digs into her endless pocket and slides a packet of chocolate cookies in Charlie's direction.

His eyes start to glow, and he rips the packet open. "I think I can wait for another hour. After all, it's still early."

Meanwhile, I'm still mulling over what Gisella said. I don't like the idea of starting a fight with a Horseman without a proper plan, but it's better than letting them take another soul.

"Okay. Let's do that." I put my glass down on the table and start to make my way back to the entrance.

"Wait!" Vicky suddenly hisses behind me.

I instantly freeze. "What?"

"Panda demon at two o'clock."

My gaze swerves left, and I step back without thinking. The thing is horrendous. When Vicky told us about a panda demon, I pictured a fluffy black and white creature with long teeth and blood dripping down its fur. Like a rabid dog, but bigger. This is something else entirely. Something far worse too. Sure, it's black and white, but its skin is slick like a snake's, and its head is small compared to its overweight body. It has black spots around its eyes, just like a panda, but these eyes are bulky. There are no ears on the white head, and instead of soft paws, it has claws that remind me of Wolverine. Just when I wonder what rain and black snow have to do with this monster, the whole skin is suddenly covered in dark mush. A long white tongue shoots out of the small mouth under the protruding nose and licks the snow from every part of the body.

Even after fighting so many demons and other monsters, the sight of this demon makes my skin crawl. My instincts tell me to run. Normally I override those, but this time, getting out of its way might be the best thing to do.

I slap myself in the head—hopefully not too theatrically—and make a quarter turn. "I forgot to pay."

While we make our way to the bar, sweat forms on my back. I suppress the urge to look over my shoulder.

There are about six people waiting to order a drink, which gives us some time to think of a strategy.

"We can't attack a demon in here. It's too risky," I say.

Jeep nods. "Too many evil creatures around."

Charlie peers over his shoulder. "But it probably knows what we look like. If it sees us…"

"You think it will attack?" Gisella asks incredulously. "One demon against all of us?"

He licks his lips. "Maybe not. But they'll speed up

their plan if they spot us here."

"It is lingering near the door," Maël says. "We cannot leave."

My hands ball into fists. "Not through there, but I know another way out."

Charlie grins. "My secret passage in the bathroom."

He turns to walk to the back of the bar, but Gisella stops him.

"We can't let that demon leave with the soul."

Charlie swats away her objections. "It's probably just watching, you know."

She crosses her arms over her chest. "What if it's not?"

He looks at her for a couple of seconds and sighs. "You're right. We can't leave."

"Don't look so defeated," she answers cheerily. "This is our opportunity to find out who the soul is."

Without further ado, I take the lead back to our tables against the far wall. One of the waiters, a waist-high girl with yellow eyes, is collecting the empty glasses. She smiles up at us. "Can I get you something to drink?"

"Do you have something that gives us more energy?" I ask.

"Sure. We've got rum with a drop of dragon saliva. That will give you a nice boost."

My lip curls up in disgust before I can stop it. I quickly turn it into a smile. "Sounds lovely. We'll take six glasses." I search for my wallet. "How much is that?"

"Put it on my tab," Charlie calls out from the other side of the table.

The girl nods and walks away without asking his name.

I frown at my best friend. "You've got a tab here?"

"Sure, I used to come here a lot, before… you know." *Before our lives started to spin out of control? Right.*

"It's usually a really nice place," Gisella adds.

I snort. "You mean, when there are no demons among the customers."

"Actually, even when there are, although demons don't make a habit out of visiting bars." She throws her red locks over her shoulder. "The Winged Centaur is a place where everyone can have fun. Fights are rare here."

My cheeks heat up when I remember the last time I was here. I cast a spell meant for Simon, and it affected all the evil creatures inside. It was a mess. I'm glad the owner didn't recognize me when I came in. "I guess that panda demon is not likely to start a fight in here."

"Not at all," Charlie and Gisella say at the same time.

"But it probably has some friends waiting for it outside," Jeep says.

"Unless this is the head demon of the third circle." I turn carefully and take in the demon again. It is quite large, especially when it stands up on its hind legs and stretches its neck, like it does now.

"Watch out," I warn the others while I turn away.

I'm grateful when the waiter comes back with our drinks. It gives us something to do, something that looks natural. I can only hope the demon won't recognize us from behind, if it can recognize us at all.

When I raise my glass, Kessley changes into a gray-skinned girl without hair, so she can spy on the demon without being recognized. She thanks the waitress, who doesn't seem surprised or bothered by her sudden metamorphoses. She just smiles and walks to the next table.

"What is it doing?" I inquire.

"Don't worry, it hasn't seen us," creepy Kess answers. The skin around her mouth makes ripping sounds with every word she utters. "I think it has found the soul."

I turn my glass around in my hands nervously. "Who is it?"

"It's a slender girl. She's sitting at the third table from the door, near the wall, chatting with a friend."

I move my hand over the strangely soft metallic tabletop to give it something to do. "Can you tell what she is?"

Kess shakes her head. "I'm afraid I don't know every magical creature yet."

"Describe her to us," Jeep says.

She nods her bald head, averts her eyes for a moment and then looks at us again. "I haven't seen anything like her before. She looks…" she searches for words, "… frozen. Her skin is blue, as if she's hypothermic, but she has no shirt on and no shoes, just a ragged pair of dirty pants. She's all skin and bones. If she didn't look so scary, I'd offer her dinner. Still, she does have a nice smile. Her friend looks almost normal. Slender, lots of freckles on a kind face, but she does have moving hair."

I look at Jeep for an explanation. When I see his frown, I turn to Vicky, but her face is blank.

Eventually, it's Maël who gives us the answer. "I do not know what her friend is, but the blue girl you described is a Mahaha."

"Sounds like some sort of clown," Charlie jokes.

"It is a phantom of cold and hunger. A person that starved to death and then froze. It can be brought back from the dead by a warlock, to work as a slave. It is neither good nor bad and eager to follow orders of those who offer it shelter."

"Or food." I take a swig from my glass and immediately energy courses through me. Without thinking, I gulp down the rest of the mixture.

"No, not food," Maël says. "The will to eat has left them."

I bring my glass back to my lips only to realize it's empty. Disappointed, I put it down again. "Then it can't be the soul the demons are after."

I eye Maël's drink, and she pushes it toward me. "There is a way to awaken the hunger of a Mahaha."

Charlie grabs her glass before I can take it and lets the contents slide down his throat.

I groan but focus on Maël again. "How?"

"By making it relive its final hours."

Charlie puts down the empty glass. "Wait, does that mean the Devil doesn't need the Black Horseman to make the Mahaha so hungry she'll commit the sin of gluttony?"

Maël's face lights up. "I think it does."

I hold up my hands. "Let's not get too excited yet. We pissed off all of the Horsemen, so I'm pretty sure we'll run into them again. We should be prepared for any kind of attack, by creepy pandas, Horsemen or both."

"She's leaving," Kessley informs us casually. "And…" She purses her lips. "Yes, the demon is following her."

With my hand on the athame behind my waistband, I turn. "Then we're leaving too."

Kessley slips around the table. "Let me go first. That thing won't recognize me."

I let her pass, and once again, we make our way through the crowd.

Halfway to the door, Kessley turns around and grows two inches. "I think I forgot my purse."

We all come to a halt, and I peer past her. The demon is on its hind legs again, scanning the room. Its pale tongue slips from its mouth and licks its knees. I lower my head and scratch my cheek to hide my face.

The panda demon drops back on all fours and hurries to the front door.

I give Kess a gentle push. "Okay, we're good to

go."

At the door, Kessley stops again, and I bump into her. I touch her bare, gray arm and pull back in disgust. The skin feels dry and dead.

"Couldn't you have turned into something less gross?" I whisper.

She grins at me over her shoulder. "This was the first thing that came to mind. Sorry."

She pushes the door open and peers outside. "The coast is clear."

The door creaks when Jeep closes it behind us, and we freeze, our eyes locked onto the demon that's making its way down the street after the Mahaha and her friend. It doesn't seem to notice, focused as it is on its prey.

We all scan the street carefully before setting off after them. There's no sign of other demons, and, thank goodness, also no Horseman waiting for us.

I bend over to Vicky, who's walking next to me. "This must be some sort of scout, sent to follow the girl home, or prepare something."

Vicky wipes invisible dust from her black leather sleeves over and over. "Maybe. I have a bad feeling about this."

Charlie catches up with us. "A 'this is a trap' kind of feeling?"

With a sigh, she lowers her arms. "I'm not sure. But something isn't right."

I tell the others to be on guard, and we speed up as the demon rounds the corner. Soon, we reach it too, and Vicky makes herself invisible before peering around it.

She beckons us immediately, and when we follow, we see the panda demon sneaking up to a small house. I've never seen it before, so it must be one of the magical houses, invisible to non-magicals and those whose veil hasn't lifted yet. It looks more like a small storeroom than a house. It's high and square, like a wooden box. Paint peels off everywhere, and thick curtains block the windows. The front door looks as solid as that of a vault, and there's a wired fence around the small garden. I get the feeling that this girl does not lead a quiet life.

A light goes on behind the curtains, and the demon moves toward it.

"We should take that thing out," I say, conjuring a lightning bolt in the palm of my hand. "Kill it before it can do whatever it's planning."

Vicky takes her sword from her boot. "I like that plan."

CHAPTER 7

I look at the others behind us. "Let's approach it quietly. Take it by surprise."

We move forward as one. The demon left the gates open, giving us an easy way in. Charlie and I lead the way, our hands raised, the lightning and grease ready.

We've almost reached the demon when the gates slam shut behind us. Charlie whirls around in a reflex, but I won't be fooled. Without hesitation, I aim my lightning bolt at the demon and release it.

There's a lot of cursing behind me, but I'm not turning around until this demon is down.

Another lightning bolt comes to life in my hand, and I bring my arm back to throw it.

Then I freeze.

I blink several times.

This can't be real.

The monstrous panda flickers like a broken

television and disappears.

"Well, that was easier than I thought," a familiar voice booms.

I turn on my heels and throw my bolt at the sound.

The Black Horseman steps aside with a lazy grin. "You fell for that way too easily, Dante. Looks like we overestimated you."

"Don't count on it," I say through gritted teeth.

He takes a step forward, and my friends move away in unison.

The Black Horseman raises his hands. "No horse this time. Just you and me."

Carefully, I reach for my Morningstar in my pocket.

"Not even your brother. I'm impressed," I mock. "We must have messed with your brain more than we thought."

It may not be wise to provoke him, but I can't help myself. Anger rages through my veins and makes me clench my fists over and over.

The skinny legs of the Horseman don't look like they are able to support his weight as he takes another two steps toward me.

My friends gather around me to form a cordon of protection.

The grin of the Black Horseman widens, and his sunken eyes narrow when he chuckles. "How cute and predictable."

Predictable? What does he mean?

Before I can figure it out and respond, the Horseman slams his hands down on the ground. The earth beneath us starts to tremble. I try to step away from the moving ground, but I'm stuck.

I fire several lightning balls at the cracked garden tiles around me, but it doesn't help one bit.

Maël clutches her staff and mumbles her spell to slow down time.

The booming laughter of the Horseman vibrates through my body.

"Don't bother," he says. "Your powers won't work against my trap. Farewell."

Panic rises to my throat when he disappears.

"Don't listen to him," I say, my voice hoarse with worry. "Use everything you've got to get out of here."

A millisecond after I utter my last word, the ground goes from vibrating to shaking. Cracks appear under our feet, and we stumble to stay upright.

"I wish I had the power to fly," Charlie mumbles.

Then the ground disappears completely, and we fall into darkness.

I throw out my arms for support, but there's nothing.

"Grab each other's hands!" I yell, but the words die as soon as they leave my mouth. There's no response. There's only emptiness around us. Sounds are muffled in here, which makes it impossible to communicate.

I reach up and to the sides, but I don't feel anyone. *Did we get split up?*

I grit my teeth. *We should've taken Vicky's ominous feelings more seriously.*

I'm still falling and starting to wonder what will happen when I reach the bottom of whatever this is. *Will there be a devastating impact with the ground that breaks every bone in my body and pushes the last bit of air from my shattered lungs?* I shiver at the thought. *Maybe a collision with water will break my bones, causing me to drown? Or I'll keep falling like this forever, with no knowledge of anything or anyone around me.*

None of those options sound comforting, but I need to know anyway, so I conjure two balls of lightning and shine down.

Below me, I see Maël and Kessley. Maël with a resigned calmness, and Kess frantically waving her arms and kicking her legs.

They both look up and blink when they see the lights I created.

Kessley shoots me a relieved smile when she sees me. She holds out her hand to Maël, who takes it reluctantly.

"Can you see what's down there?" I call out, but again, the sound is cut off immediately.

With a sigh, I look left, right and up. To my left, I see Jeep, clutching his hat in his hands, ready to throw it at whatever enemy we encounter on the way. Above me there are some vague forms, but it's too dark to make out who is who. At least everyone seems alright. *For the time being.*

I turn my gaze back to whatever we'll find below.

Now that Kessley is no longer moving frantically, I can throw my lightning balls past her. I aim carefully and release them.

Kessley cringes, and I see Maël pulling her closer.

I watch the descending lights. Around each ball a space of about ten feet is illuminated. There seem to be no walls. No sand and no rocks in sight. Then I see something below.

A large cube made of glass.

A second before the lightning dies, I spot the Black Horseman standing next to it.

So, he wants to trap us. Why doesn't he just kill us?

We reach the cube sooner than I'd thought. Taylar and Maël land softly. They move out of the way when I land, and soon the others follow.

I'm glad to see everyone is in one piece, and that we didn't lose anyone on the way, but I don't spend too much time checking them all. I don't want to let the Horseman out of my sight. He might have more surprises in store for us.

He waits until we're all sitting up before speaking. "How nice of you to drop by." The skin around his mouth moves with every word he utters, as if it can fall off at any second. His leather jacket slides off on one side to reveal a bony shoulder with frayed skin. He opens his arms. "Welcome to your prison."

I jump to my feet and walk up to the glass between us. "Why didn't you just kill us?"

His body shakes with laughter. "Yes, you'd like that, wouldn't you?"

I frown. *Why would I like to be killed?*

He shakes his head. "What good would it do me to kill you? You'd come back as ghosts to annoy us some more."

Annoy us. As if that's all we've done.

Vicky puts her hand on my arm.

"Don't fall for it," she whispers. "He's mocking us."

"I know."

"Enough talking." He licks his barely visible lips. "I've got work to do."

With a twist of his hand, he lowers a glass ceiling on top of the cube. It shuts with a loud click.

"Don't worry," he says. "There's enough oxygen in there to last a couple of lifetimes, and most of you don't need it. I'll make sure you get food and drinks later."

"Great," I mumble.

With a mocking bow, he says goodbye. He turns and walks away, vanishing into the darkness around us.

CHAPTER 8

"What now?" Charlie asks solemnly. "I mean, we can try to shatter the glass with our powers, but I have a feeling that won't work, you know."

I scratch my head. "I agree, but we should try it anyway. He might have underestimated us."

Carefully, I place one hand against the cold surface that makes up our prison. I expect electricity to spread through me or an invisible force to throw me back, but nothing happens.

"Let's focus all of our powers on this point," I say.

We form half a circle, and I count back from three. On one, we release all the power we've got. Lightning, grease, blades, hat, sword, time bending, everything hits the glass at the same time.

The noise is deafening, and for a moment, I think it will work. A sound of cracking glass answers our efforts, and I throw in some ice for good measure.

There's a loud bang, and we're all blown backwards. I hit the other side of the cube hard and blink several times to clear my blurry vision. Before I even manage to stand up, I know it didn't work. Despite the noises, there's not even the slightest crack in the glass.

It's only when we all stumble to our feet again when I realize we're one person short. I scan inside and outside our prison. "Where's Taylar?"

Kessley shoots me a radiant smile. "He managed to grab an overhanging branch when the ground opened beneath us."

"Wait." I shake my head in confusion. "What do you mean? I saw him land in here."

She shrugs. "When I saw the Black Horseman standing there, I knew I had to convince him we were all here. I think he doesn't know me yet."

I remember Taylar and Maël landing, and realize even I fell for it.

Charlie slaps her on the back. "Way to go!"

She blushes and mumbles a thank you.

A spark of hope ignites in my chest. "So Taylar is at Darkwood Manor with Mona right now, trying to figure out a way to get us back."

"That's what I assumed," Kessley says.

Charlie sits down with his back against the glass. "They'll probably call Quinn. The three of them should be able to think of a way to free us, right?"

I start pacing. "If they can reach Quinn. He's really busy, remember? A dead angel is a serious thing."

"But even if it's just Taylar and Mona," Kessley

says hesitantly, "they'll still be able to think of a solution, right?"

I take three steps and turn to walk back. When I reach the other side, I turn back. And again. My legs are restless; they want to run, far away from here. "Of course." Those are the words that escape my mouth. But do I really believe them? Sure, Taylar and Mona are smart and resourceful. But what powers do they have? Mona can heal, she can move from one place to another with her sparks, and she can check in on Mom and me because she's our fairy godmother, but can she also track people into other worlds? I don't think so, or she would've been able to track Mom to Purgatory or Hell, and me into that world I ended up in with Maël. And Taylar... his power hasn't even woken up yet, and he doesn't know much about spells. Neither does Mona. Vicky and I are the experts in that department.

Still, Taylar and Mona do have a lot of knowledge. They're both older than you would guess if you saw them. Taylar might look like a fourteen-year-old boy, in reality he's years older. And Mona isn't exactly in her thirties anymore either.

"We have to trust in them," I say, more to myself than to the others. "But we should also keep the possibility that they won't be able to reach us in consideration."

Vicky places both hands on the glass and stares at the empty world around our cube. "There is always a way out."

Kessley steps up next to her. "And we will find it."

Vicky looks up. "Hey, maybe we can lift the roof?"

I shrug. "We can try."

She spreads her arms. "Lift me up."

Jeep, Charlie and I immediately step over to her.

"No need," Gisella calls out while she runs past me.

She leaps against the wall and pushes off hard. I gasp as she soars to the middle of the ceiling gracefully. She hits it hard, but it doesn't budge. There's not even a creak of protest.

Gisella lands on her feet without trouble. "It's locked tightly." She wipes a stray lock of bright red hair from her face. "Let me try something else."

She sets off again. Halfway up, her hands change into blades, which she slams into the ceiling. The blades slide into the glass. Cracks run in all directions. Gisella drives her blades in as far as she can.

Next to me, Kessley is bouncing up and down with wide eyes. "It's working! It's working!"

I yank her out of harm's way when the werecat places her feet against the ceiling and pushes off. She plummets face-down to the floor, but at the last moment, she manages to turn and land on her feet, like a true cat.

We all look up hopefully. When nothing happens, Charlie scratches his neck. "I think you need to hit it again."

Gisella grins. "No problem."

This time, she runs along the other three walls

before catapulting herself at the cracked glass. In the air, she turns several times, speeding up like a drill rig, with her feet aimed at the ceiling.

I hold my breath when her boots connect with the glass.

A deafening bang splits my ear drums in half and makes the whole cube tremble. Gisella is hurled away by some sort of force field that glows red. She lands on her side with a groan. Charlie kneels down next to her, and I bend over to check on her while I try to ignore the pounding of my head.

"Are you okay?" I ask and frown when I don't hear my own words.

Apparently, Gisella and Charlie don't hear anything either, because they don't look up.

I put my hand on the werecat's arm and repeat my question.

She gestures at her ears, and I nod and point at mine too. "I can't hear a thing!"

Charlie's mouth is moving, and he shoots me a concerned look.

"It will pass in a few seconds," I try to assure him, but he only gives me a questioning look.

I turn to Vicky and pretend to write something in thin air. She nods and digs up a pen and a piece of paper from her endless pocket.

Jeep walks over to Kessley, who's frantically slamming her hands against her ears, as if that will bring back her hearing. He eases her arms down and turns her toward me.

Maël is slowly making her way along the walls, calmly sliding her hand across the surface.

Stay calm, I write. *I'm sure it will pass soon.*

I hold it up for everyone to see, and they all nod, although Charlie's expression tells me he's not so sure of this.

Are you okay? I write, and I hold the paper up to Gisella, who's still sitting on the floor.

"Fine," she mouths, and she pushes herself to her feet.

When I look up at the ceiling again, the cracks are gone. My shoulders sag. *We'll need to think of another way to get out of here.*

Just to be sure, I put my hands around my mouth and yell, "Quinn!"

My ears pop open, and my voice reverberates around the room.

"I can hear again!" Kess calls out.

Jeep massages the unmoving tattoos on his arms. "Let's not do that again."

I gently rub my ears to drive out the painful throbbing that has dropped down from the sides of my head. "I second that idea."

Charlie looks up. "No answer from Quinn."

"I didn't expect him to hear me, but I figured it couldn't hurt to try."

Jeep turns to Maël, who has come to a halt. "Did you find something?"

She pushes her cape back. "No, but I have an idea."

"As long as it doesn't involve going deaf, I'm all for it," Kessley jokes.

"I cannot guarantee anything," Maël answers.

After a quick look around to make sure nothing is approaching, I walk over to where the African queen is standing. "What do you have in mind?"

When her eyes meet mine, I read fear in them. She takes a deep breath. "Do you remember the remnants of the tree from the Shadow World inside me?"

"Of course."

"I think this box is designed to keep benevolent beings trapped. It might let out something malevolent though."

I hold up my hand. "No way you're going to let that evil overtake you."

She shoots me a loving smile. "That is not my intention. But I might be able to guide it to my hand to make an opening."

"And get stuck halfway? I don't think so."

Vicky joins us. "What about Gisella? She can help, using the shadows. That's also a malevolent power."

I turn to face the werecat-witch. "That's not a bad idea. You have those shadows under control, right?"

She wipes some non-existent dust from her red catsuit. "Sure. There's only one problem."

"What's that?"

She points at the space around us. "There are no shadows here."

I raise an eyebrow. "What do you mean? Of course there are shadows. There's light, so there are also shadows. That's how it works, right?"

She shrugs. "Not in this world, apparently."

I squint at the corners of the cube and groan. *She's right. I can't believe I didn't notice that before.* And when I look down, my own shadow is missing too.

Vicky follows my gaze and bites her lip. "They prepared this well."

"But they don't know about the remnant inside Maël, do they?" Charlie asks. "So it might work."

They all look at me expectantly. It doesn't bother me anymore. Although I have no clue how to get us out of here, I know one thing… "I think you're right, which is exactly why we can't use the remnant. By giving away the element of surprise, we'll screw ourselves later."

Maël glows with pride.

"Next time we face the Horsemen, we'll have no choice but to fight them. We won't be able to trick them again, which is why we need to keep this a surprise. It might tip the balance in our favor."

"I hope you're not betting everything on that," Vicky says. "She might not be able to control it at all."

I start pacing. "I know. A solid plan would be great. Or a way to get D'Maeo back."

Vicky lowers her head. "That *would* be great."

The pain in her voice is obvious, and I squeeze her arm. "Soon." *Soon we'll free D'Maeo, and Mom too.*

CHAPTER 9

Vicky flexes her arms. "How about some training? Focusing on a battle tends to clear my head."

Gisella throws out her blades again. "I'm always up for a good fight."

Jeep's eyes narrow as he looks through the glass. He folds his fingers around the rim of his hat tightly. "Be careful what you wish for."

We whirl around as one, ready to attack. A ball of lightning sparkles in my hand. When I see what's wriggling closer to our cube, my mouth drops open. "Is that…?"

Maël steps up next to me, her staff held in front of her. "A chaos residue."

"How did it get here?" I back up as the green smoke suddenly speeds up and hits the glass between us.

It writhes around the corners of the cube, banging

against the glass every few seconds.

Gisella changes her blades back into hands. "Looks like it can't get in."

"Which probably means evil can't get out either." I sigh. "Good thing Maël didn't try. It would've been for nothing."

Kessley steps closer to the glass and grabs my arm firmly. "Look!"

At first, I see only the green smoke. It blocks our view in its attempts to get to us. But then, it slithers to the top of our prison, and I gasp. "There are dozens of them!"

A cluster of creatures made of smoke soars toward us. Strings of yellow, brown and black pull at each other while a purple sliver dives under the rest and creates a ditch in the ground.

"How did they all get here?" Vicky wonders aloud. "I though chaos residues came to life in a place of complete disorder? This world looks empty to me."

"Maybe it was a world full of chaos, which created all of these mist creatures. They must have killed everything in here, until there was nothing left," Charlie suggests.

Maël shakes her head and lowers her staff. "No, I think…" She hesitates. "I think they are imprisoned here, just like we are."

Vicky turns to her so fast her hair slaps me in the face. "That means we can send the chaos residue we trapped to this world, right? It won't be able to escape once it's here."

71

"I am not a hundred percent sure, but that is what I think."

"That's great!" Vicky beams at me.

"It would be, if we had the box with D'Maeo and the chaos residue with us."

She doesn't stop smiling. "You can try calling him to you, with the spell to call your Shield."

"That would bring Taylar here too."

"I'm sure you can change it, so it only applies to D'Maeo."

I kiss her on the lips. "You're brilliant."

She grins when I straighten up. "I know."

I grab my Book of Spells and turn to the page where I jotted the spell down.

"This should actually not be too hard."

Instead of five, I yank only one hair from my head. Then I take off my right shoe and sock and press my athame against the skin of my big toe until a drop of blood appears. With the wet tip of my weapon, I draw a small circle in front of me and place the hair in the middle. I dip my finger in it and touch the hair, thinking of D'Maeo.

"Let this subject hear my call.
Bring him here before I fall.
Keep him safe through time and space.
Transport D'Maeo without a trace."

I lift my finger and conjure a bit of lightning in my hand. When I hold it above the circle, the hair catches fire. The ash is lifted into the air and evaporates.

I clench my jaws when nothing happens. My new-found hope goes up in smoke.

But then there's a soft whoosh, followed by a triumphant cry from Vicky. "It worked!"

She bends down to pick up the glass box with the green and brown spots.

Relieved, I rest my head against the glass of our prison. I breathe in and out slowly several times. My hope and confidence return, and I straighten up. "Okay, now that we know spells work in here, I'm going to try another."

"Brilliant," Kessley says, rubbing her hands. "Which one?"

"The one that opens a portal."

"A portal home?" she asks eagerly.

"Not yet. First I want to open a portal to the other side of this cube."

Vicky stares at the moving shapes around us. "Opening a portal is a heavy spell. A lot can go wrong, especially in an unknown world like this one. What if you only created a hole in the glass?"

Jeep puts his hat back on and nods. "That would actually be a good idea. A hole through which only evil can pass. That way only the chaos residue will be able to leave the cube, and D'Maeo will stay inside."

"That will work!" Kess calls out.

I smile at her. "Thanks for the confidence. I hope you're right."

Maël taps her lightly on the shoulder with her staff.

"Give him a little room."

"Oh, right." With a blush, Kessley jumps back.

I put away my Book of Spells and flip through Dad's notebook in search for inspiration. There are a lot of herbs and spices I know the use off, but not all, and I really don't want to mess up this spell. I remember what that chaos residue did to D'Maeo. How it pulled parts of his soul from him. And of course, I haven't forgotten that it killed D'Maeo in the first place. Apparently, that wasn't enough. It came after him when he turned into a ghost. I don't want all of us to end up with the same problem.

Vicky blows me a kiss. "We'll be fine, stop worrying. You're a great mage. You'll have no trouble with this spell."

"Thanks," I whisper, and I slam the book shut. *She's right. I know what I'm doing.*

She hands me a couple of basic things: salt, black candles and thyme. Then I list the herbs I want.

"See," she says. "You know how it works."

I shrug. "There's still a lot to learn. Herbs and spices I don't know about. Other ingredients maybe."

"There are tons of possible ingredients. But we don't need any of them now. Your magic and your words will do most of the work."

When I've set everything up, I realize something is missing. "Do you have sodium hydroxide?"

"For cleaning? Sure."

She digs into her pocket again and takes out a pot.

"Not for cleaning this time," I say with a wink. "In

liquid form, it dissolves glass."

"I didn't know you were such a chemical genius."

I snort. "Far from it. This is one of the few things I remember."

Gently, I add a little to the bowl and hand the pot back to Vicky. Then I hesitate.

My foot taps in sync with the thoughts that tumble through my head. "You know what? I think I'll put a circle of protection around us first, just to be safe."

Vicky winks. "You're a fast learner." She puts down some more ingredients from her pocket.

It's nice to work together like this. A handful of words is enough to get ready. She knows what I need, sometimes even before I do. And I'm not just talking about spells.

A couple of minutes later, the protective circle is in place.

"Make sure you stay in it, no matter what happens," I tell the others. Then I take a deep breath.

"Stay back a little, give him some room," Vicky says, backing up herself too.

I place the glass jar with D'Maeo and the chaos residue in it against the glass, and push the tip of my athame into my finger. With the blood that wells up, I draw a circle, half on the ground, half on the wall. The mist outside moves away, as if the creatures know something is about to happen. *They're waiting for their chance to attack. No room for mistakes in this spell.* Not that there was any to begin with. I wouldn't want to make things worse for D'Maeo.

Quickly, I jot down the words that roll through my mind to make sure I don't screw them up. Ignoring the swirling forms on the other side of the glass, I place two black candles on the spots where the line on the ground meets the one on the glass. Next, I rub half of the herb mixture on the glass jar and half on the wall inside the blood circle. I flex my stiff fingers before lighting both candles.

"In this circle, make a hole,
but keep both sides under control.
To evil access is denied,
and all that's good will stay inside.

Once the good is safe inside,
open the hole and make it right.
Break the glass jar on the floor.
Release the souls inside once more.

Pull the evil through the gap,
but keep the good inside this trap.
Once this job has been completed,
let the full hole be deleted."

The candle flames flicker and hiss. Smoke rises and clings to the wall. The residues outside slither closer curiously, the red eyes narrowing as if they know I've got something in store they won't like. But a tiny fault in my spell will be enough for them to enter the cube and kill us all.

My gaze drops to the floor, where the jar wobbles from the weight that slams against the sides.

Slowly, the smoke from the candles works its way along the line of the blood circle. With another hiss, it swoops up again and starts drilling through the glass. The chaos residues on the other side soar restlessly from left to right, their gazes fixated on the spot where a small hole appears.

Once it's complete, the creatures dive at it at full speed.

My breath catches in my throat, and I'm unable to move. All my limbs go cold.

CHAPTER 10

No matter how hard the chaos residues hit the hole, they can't get through. The spell is working.

I jump when the jar shatters at my feet. Two distorted figures rise from the shards. I recognize a bit of gray hair and a foot; the rest of it stretches too far to make sense of.

A loud roar makes me cover my ears. The swirling forms that escape the jar are separated. One changes into an old man bit by bit, the other remains amorphous, except for a large mouth and glowing red eyes.

The residues outside go wild. They hit the hole with all the force they can muster. Mouths and claws become visible as they try to grab the edges. But it doesn't work. My spell holds out; the gap is impenetrable.

Suddenly, D'Maeo's voice rings out from the

cluster of mist and limbs. "You will… never… win this!" He sounds exhausted but unbending.

The smoke that created the hole pushes off from the wall and clings to the chaos residue in front of me. I clench my fists, wishing there was something I could do to help. *Come on, get that thing out of here,* I urge the smoke silently.

A hand reaches up from the mess of mist and smoke and tugs at a sliver that's clinging to part of a human back.

"Let go!" D'Maeo bellows.

Another roar shakes the whole cube, and I stumble to stay upright.

Behind me, I can hear Vicky sucking in a frightened breath.

The candle smoke pulls harder and finally manages to tear the residue from the broken form of D'Maeo. It wriggles and moans in protest, but the smoke has it in a firm grip now. It is dragged to the hole and pushed through bit by slivery bit. The other residues move out of the way and seem to calm down. I guess they realize it's useless to try and get inside.

Once the smoke has pushed the last of the residue through, the hole closes rapidly. A gust of wind blows out the candles, and the smoke vanishes.

"Dante?" D'Maeo's voice is as distorted as his body. He floats in front of me, only half of his face visible, red gashes running over his nose.

I gulp at the sight of his torso, that has limbs attached on the wrong sides. A leg without a foot sticks up where his arm should be while there's nothing on the other side. His legs are just a vague form, and a hand floats above his head.

He shows me half a smile. "Thank you for freeing me."

My voice trembles when I answer. "I'll fix you, D'Maeo. Don't worry about it."

There's a sob behind me, and the old ghost's gaze moves over my shoulder. "It's good to see all of you again."

He tries to make his way toward them, but his barely visible make-shift legs are unable to hold him. Mist takes over most of his form, and I hold up my hand. "Stay here. Give me a minute."

I hold out my hand behind me. "A piece of cloth, please?"

Vicky pushes it into my hand only seconds later, and I quickly wipe the blood circle from the floor and wall.

"Light blue candles?" I feel like a surgeon getting ready for a difficult operation.

Vicky takes two candles from her pocket.

"Light blue stands for health, right?" I ask her when she holds them out to me.

"Yes," she says hoarsely.

I squeeze her hand before I take the candles. "Don't worry, he'll be fine."

Of course, that's only wishful thinking. *What if I can't fix this with a spell? What if he stays like this forever? Or worse, if he's pulled apart until there's nothing but floating parts of him left?*

I suppress a shiver. *Don't think like that. This can't be harder than getting the chaos residue away from him.*

The torn-up form of D'Maeo still hovers in the same place, although his limbs float around him, as if they're searching for where they belong. There's not a glimpse of worry in his one visible eye, which gives me the bit of confidence I need to continue.

I scratch my head. "Let me think… Rosemary for healing…"

Vicky pushes some bright green leaves into my hand. "Use mugwort, it's stronger." She adds some dried, dull green stuff. "And horehound, to balance personal energy."

I blow her a kiss with my free hand. "You're the best."

She agrees with the rest of the herbs I choose, and after mixing them, I waste no more time hesitating. I'm doing this, and it will work.

I scribble the words that pop into my head onto an empty page in my Book of Spells. I'll add the instructions and ingredients later. When I look up again, D'Maeo shoots me an anxious look. *Is he having second thoughts?*

I hold up my thumb, not prepared to let his fear throw me off balance. Then I light a match and throw it into the mixture I made. With what remains of the herbs, I draw a new circle around D'Maeo and myself. With another match, I light the two blue candles. Then I push my hand with the remains of the mixture against D'Maeo's misty forehead.

"Take the parts that linger here,
and make the spaces disappear.
Whole again this man will be,
from now until eternity.

Change him back, but without pain.
Let his confidence remain.
He will come back as he was.
Let him now return to us."

D'Maeo's face and torso stretch. The limbs around him come to a halt. Then he is twisted by an invisible force, like a cleaning cloth that's being wrung. It looks painful, but the one eye that I can see only expresses surprise. I guess putting something in about the process being painless wasn't such a bad idea.

The old ghost is pressed into a ball of body parts and mist. The candle flames burn bright, and one by one, the legs and arms pop out from the ball. This time, they're in the right place. Hands and feet follow and then the head. The nose appears, and after a slight shiver, the mouth and eyes become visible. Slowly but surely, the leader of my Shield is build up before us. Eyebrows and sideburns are added, then the matching gray beard.

D'Maeo flexes his fingers and shakes his shoulders loose. Then he smiles at me and opens his arms wide.

I fall into them and hold him tight. "It's so good

to have you back."

"It's good to *be* back. I was starting to think the fight with the Black Void was never going to end."

He lets go and catches Vicky. The force of her embrace nearly pushes him over.

"I'm sorry it took so long," I say.

"It's fine, Dante. I understand."

They all welcome him back with a hug, even Maël, who isn't fond of hugging.

Kessley hesitates, but when D'Maeo beckons her, she greats him enthusiastically. "It's an honor to meet you. I've heard so much about you."

"Oh dear," D'Maeo chuckles. "I hope I can live up to your expectations then." He winks at me, and I grin.

We fill him in on everything he's missed. Everything I've felt since he got sucked into that jar passes his face in only minutes. He lets out a heavy sigh when we finally get to the point where we got trapped inside this cube.

"So, to summarize…" he says slowly, "you've had some luck and some bad luck."

I snort. "That's one way to put it."

He shrugs. "Well, if you add it all up, I'd say we're still ahead. Lucifer has, what? Two souls?"

"And Mom."

Charlie slaps my back. "We don't know that."

"Two souls and maybe your mother," D'Maeo recaps. "That's not a lot. He can't win with that."

I start pacing again. "Maybe not, but he also has a

plan for which he doesn't need the souls."

The old ghost scratches his beard. "Sure. A plan that's hard to execute, or he would've done so already."

"Still, I would not think of it too lightly," Maël interrupts.

"Of course not. All I want to say is…" D'Maeo pauses to look at us. "We're doing great. *You* were doing great, even without me and Jeep. Keep the faith, because the odds are in our favor."

"Hear hear!" Kessley yells, making us all jump. She does a pretty good impression of a cheerleader, but without the pompoms, and I end up in a laughing fit when I see D'Maeo's frown.

"Don't mind her," Vicky says with a smile. "That's normal."

"Oh right, the alcohol."

Kessley stops hopping and blushes. "Sorry."

"Don't be sorry," I say. "You make us laugh. That's important too."

Charlie bends toward D'Maeo. "And she can do some awesome things."

CHAPTER 11

After Kessley's demonstration of her powers to D'Maeo, we sit down and watch the residues outside. I don't need words to know that everyone is thinking about the same thing: how to get out of here.

After a long silence, I stand up. "I'm going to try another spell."

Vicky pushes herself up too. "What kind?"

"A reverse spell. One that will put the chaos residues in the cube, instead of us."

Charlie stares past the swirling forms. "What if there's more in this world than these creatures? We don't know what we'll run into, you know."

I pick up the bowl and wipe the remains of the last spell from the bottom. "Then we fight them."

He shoots an incredulous look. "Just like that?"

I hold up my hands in surrender. "What other choice do we have? We can't wait here forever."

Gisella hops to her feet and throws out her blades. "I'm in. I'm already sick of being stuck here."

"Me too," Jeep says. "I've been locked in an empty place long enough recently." He rubs his arms and shivers.

D'Maeo watches him thoughtfully. "But because of it, you got rid of the souls inside your tattoos."

Jeep smiles at him. "True, but it also added a problem to our list."

"Don't worry about those crows," I say. "We'll get rid of them."

D'Maeo is still studying Jeep. "How does it feel?"

The tattooed ghost stares past him. "Good. Weird." He pauses. "Empty."

Vicky puts her hand on his shoulder, and Jeep pats it gratefully. "It takes some getting used to, but I'm fine. Really."

We all nod in understanding.

I look down at the circle of herbs. "Some new candles and I'm good, I think." I pick up the light blue ones and meet Vicky's equally blue eyes. "There's no color that strengthens something like relocation, is there?"

She shakes her head.

"Then I'll take white ones, please."

With a smile, she hands me two. "White represent any color."

"Yep." I go over everything I put into the mixture to free D'Maeo. "I'd better add some knot weed, to control movement. It's the best I can think of."

Once again, she digs into her pocket. "I'll run out of ingredients if you keep this up."

"Don't worry. Hopefully you'll be able to restock after this spell."

"I'm counting on that," she says with a wink.

"Okay, get ready," I warn everyone. "Something might attack once we're out of this cube."

I add the knot weed to the mixture that forms the circle. Then I light the white candles. The flames reach up eagerly.

"Surround the creatures in this place
with this glass-encompassed space.
Free us of this cube of dread,
and lock the monsters in instead."

The glass around us starts to shake, and the candle flames dance, casting shadows upon the moving glass. I want to tell Gisella to call the shadows to her, but they vanish as the flames rise from the wicks. They float to the bottom corners of the cube, where they split into two. The new flames move to the other two corners, and the cube slowly starts to rise.

I hold my breath as the chaos residues dive forward. Gisella steps up next to me with her blade hands held out. Vicky's sword appears on my other side, the tip pointing down as the shreds of mist slither closer. *I should've put something in the spell about keeping us safe.*

As I conjure a lightning bolt, the cube rises farther

and farther up, lifted by the flames. The chaos residues form into balls and launch themselves at the gap. I'm about to throw my first bolt when one of the creatures hits an invisible barrier.

I lower my hand. "They can't reach us."

Everyone relaxes again, and we watch in silence as the cube rises above our heads and starts to move away from us.

It grows to encompass all of the residues. I wait for the flames to lower it over them, but the cube keeps growing. Soon, it stretches so far I can't see the back wall anymore. When it finally moves down, we're standing in the only uncovered space. The cube has locked in everything around us.

The flames die, and the residues snake around us, hitting the glass on each side over and over. Eventually, they give up and slither out of sight.

"That didn't go as planned," I say when no one speaks.

"Maybe because you didn't make a new circle," Charlie offers.

I look down at the herbs. "Maybe. Or I should've been more specific."

Gisella cracks her knuckles. "It doesn't matter." She points at the bland sky above us. "We're no longer trapped. I'll jump onto the glass ceiling and pull you up."

I frown. "Are you sure? That's pretty high. How will you reach us?"

Vicky's hand slips into her endless pocket and she

holds up a rope. "With this?"

Gisella nods approvingly and takes it from her. She wraps it around her waist and breaks into a run. After only a couple of paces, she leaps, hitting the glass and climbing the wall as if it's not vertical.

We all cheer for her until she reaches the top. There, her head hits an unseen barrier. She cries out in pain and falls down.

She lands on her feet but falls onto her knees, cradling her head. We all hurry over. Charlie is the first to reach her. He lifts her head and forces her to look at him. "Are you okay? How many fingers am I holding up?"

"Three."

"Can you move everything?"

She gently moves her head to both sides, then wriggles her shoulders. "Yes, but it hurts."

I crouch down next to her. "Of course it hurts. You hit your head hard there."

She leans against Charlie's shoulder and rubs the top of her head. "I think this world ends there. We can't get on top of the cube's ceiling."

Vicky takes her sword out again and holds it up. "Then we dig."

She lifts the weapon and brings it down with force. It bounces off, sending a ripple through Vicky's arms. She lets go with a pained cry and rubs her arms. "Ouch."

While I step up to her to see if she's okay, Jeep takes off his hat and throws it at the ceiling. It bounces off and returns to his hands. The glass is his next target, but there's no getting through that either.

I screwed it up. Now we're really stuck.

But I can't think like that. We've been in difficult situations before. And we've been trapped in strange worlds before too. We always find a way out.

I let go of Vicky and gesture at the circle. "I'll do another spell."

Vicky shakes her head. "We barely have any ingredients left. And what if we really get into trouble? What if something attacks us here?" She gestures at the chaos residues that come circling back.

With a shrug, I shake her objections off. "What we have will have to do. And if we're attacked, we'll use our powers, like we always do."

She doesn't look convinced, but she starts to dig into her pocket anyway. "I'm not sure…" She pauses, her gaze locked on something behind me. "What is *that*?"

All eyes turn to the figure that makes its way through the giant cube, passing the residues without even glancing at them.

"Looks like a boy," Vicky says.

Kessley sucks in air abruptly. "It's Taylar!"

I recoil. "What? No way."

The ghost in the leopard skin dress places a hand over her mouth in horror. "It *is* him. But something is wrong."

I clench my fists. "Something must be wrong if he can walk past those creatures without getting hurt."

Jeep strokes the rim of his hat. "Remember what happened in the Shadow World, when we were all in there?"

"When Taylar's copy tried to trick us?" I ask. "You think this is something similar?"

"I'm not sure."

Kessley uneasily shifts her weight from one foot to the other and back. "Maybe it's his brother."

"Lleyton? I don't think so."

"Why not? People come back as ghosts all the time. Look at us."

"No, it is Taylar," Maël interrupts. "He has the same hair, the same clothes and even the same walk."

"But his eyes and his skin..." Kessley turns away from the glass. "I can't look at it."

I find it difficult myself, but I want to know what he's going to do.

The closer he gets, the clearer it is to me that this is indeed Taylar. Maël is right, he looks exactly like him. Sure, this could be a copy sent here to torture us, but with all the luck we've had recently, I was expecting a setback. Taylar gave in to his hatred toward the gravity pixie in Shelton Banks' house. We all saw him turn evil. He seemed okay after that, but deep inside, I knew the darkness never really left him. It was only a matter of time before his dark side would show up again. I was hoping for better timing though.

Taylar comes to a halt inches from the glass that separates us. From up close, I can see the evil swirling around his irises. His skin has that unnatural gray shade again, and his mouth is a thin line.

He raises his hands and bangs on the glass. Kessley backs up with a soft yelp while Vicky only moves closer. For a moment, she and Taylar stare at each other, unmoving.

"There's so much anger inside him," Vicky whispers after a deafening silence.

"Do you think he's working with the Horsemen?" Kessley asks, her voice barely audible. "Is that why he stayed behind?"

My heart almost breaks at the sadness in her voice. But there's no time to comfort her. Taylar will make his move any second now.

CHAPTER 12

Taylar shows us a wide grin that makes my skin crawl, but still, I don't move. If he has truly turned against us, he won't be able to get through the glass. My spell made sure of that.

Taylar takes a burlap sack from his trouser pocket and shakes the contents into his hand.

"Are those...?" Charlie starts, but he doesn't finish his question, because the answer is clear when Taylar throws a handful of sparks against the glass. The tiny lights form a rectangle. They burn even brighter than they already did, and I shield my eyes with my arm. When the light dies down, there's a large hole in the glass. Taylar steps through, and the sparks close the hole again before disappearing.

As soon as Taylar sets one foot outside the giant cube, he starts to sway.

Instinctively, I reach out to catch him, but Vicky

stops me. "Wait."

Taylar places his hand against the glass for support and takes a couple of deep breaths. When he opens his eyes again, the swirling darkness inside them is gone. His skin slowly returns to its normal shade of see-through white. Color seeps back into his clothes.

He straightens up and shakes his upper body, as if to get rid of something that clings to him.

"That was intense," he says. Then he smiles his normal smile, sincere but with a hint of sadness. "It's good to see you all. I'm glad you're—" His voice falters when he catches sight of D'Maeo. In a blur, he moves over to him and flings his arms around the old ghost's neck. "You're back!"

The surprise on D'Maeo's face is replaced by tenderness when he holds Taylar close to him.

"It's good to see you, Taylar," he says. He pushes him away gently and holds him at arm's length. "Are you okay?"

The young, white-haired ghost nods. "I'm fine now. I'm not sure what happened when I got here, but it got me past those mist creatures."

"Chaos residues," I explain.

"Really?" Taylar shakes his head as he stares at the swirling shreds outside. "I guess I got lucky."

I wouldn't call turning evil lucky, but I'm grateful that he's okay.

"How did you get here? And what is the plan now?" I ask while Taylar and Kessley hold each other tightly.

Jeep mumbles something about keeping it short, and Taylar agrees. "I managed to hold on to a branch when the Black Horseman activated his trap. I called for Quinn when I was pulled back to Darkwood Manor. While Quinn searched for clues about your whereabouts, Mona and I came up with a plan. Quinn came back to tell us where you were, and Mona's sparks brought me here." He digs up another burlap sack from his pocket and holds it up. "I brought a bag full of sparks from Mona and her friends. They should be able to get us out of here, but Mona stayed behind in case it doesn't work."

"Sounds great," Jeep says, louder this time. "Let's give it a try."

Taylar beckons us. "We need to stay close together and think about Darkwood Manor. Try to imagine traveling there, picture it in your head. Hold up your thumb when you've got it. I'll count down from three when everyone is ready."

I smile, content about the ease with which he takes the lead.

After a last look at the world around me, I close my eyes and picture Darkwood Manor.

The image of the old mansion pops into my head immediately: the three steps to the double front door, the large windows of the annex, the dark roof with the small windows, all covered in dirt. The blistering white paint I still need to fix. And then I'm in the kitchen, sitting at the table. The eleven chairs around me are empty, but when I concentrate, my friends appear in their seats one after the other.

I hold up my thumb and hold on to the image of the kitchen. I see Mona making breakfast while her sparks move plates and cutlery from the kitchen counter to the table. Through the window in the back door, I can see the protective circle. Behind that, more pine trees than I can count.

"Three, two, one."

Something warm tickles my cheeks and neck. I'm lifted from the ground and hold out my arm to find Vicky's hand. It's not there, and when I open my eyes, she's looking up at me. Gisella lands next to her. In front of me, Maël is floating, but the pink sparks that support her are losing their glow fast. The green ones that hold on to me are crawling across my arms like rabid ants. With every second, they grow more restless. Maël is already back on the ground when the green sparks start to lower me.

"It's not working," Jeep says with a sigh. "Something is blocking them." He takes off his hat and watches with regret as the last of his red sparks extinguish.

As soon as they set me down, my green sparks vanish into thin air too.

Taylar peers into the burlap sack and shakes his head. "That was all I had."

I straighten my back. "It's fine. I can cast another spell."

"What kind?" Vicky inquires.

"Our best option is to open a portal to Earth, I

suppose."

She lowers herself onto the ground. "I have no ingredients left for that."

"What *do* you have then?"

She pulls out some thyme, a bunch of candles, an incense stick and a bottle of salt.

"That's it?" I ask when she looks up at me.

She nods solemnly.

"That's not enough to cast any kind of spell."

"I know." She sounds defeated, but I refuse to give up. We've come this far already. And if Taylar was able to join us, it means that there is a doorway somewhere.

I turn to the young ghost. "You said Mona stayed behind in case this didn't work. Is there a back-up plan?"

He avoids my gaze. "There is… but if we execute it, even more lives will be at stake."

"What lives?"

He twists a green ring around his finger. "The lives of Mona's friends and their protégées."

My heartrate speeds up. "You mean the fairy godmothers that helped us before?"

"Yes. We can summon them here with the rings they gave us."

We all look at the rings around our fingers. The rings the fairy godmothers gave to us when they created our disguises to make sure Trevor and the Devil's other helpers wouldn't know we were still trying to stop them.

"If we call them to us, they might be trapped in here too," Maël states the obvious.

I turn my attention back to Taylar. "How certain was Mona about them being able to transport us back?"

He tilts his head. "Pretty certain."

D'Maeo rubs his beard. "You know, without a spell, it might be impossible to get out of here. Meanwhile, Satan is closing in on the next soul, if he hasn't got her already. We might risk the lives of the fairy godmothers by bringing them here, but if we get stuck here, all lives on Earth will be lost."

I press my temples hard, as if that will force out the right choice. *Is there really no other way to get home?* "What if we call the Black Horseman, capture him and force him to take us home?"

Vicky snorts. "Capture the Horseman in a world he controls? I believe in our strength, babe, but that does not sound like a good plan."

I drop down next to Vicky and bury my head in my hands. "I know! But how can I risk the lives of seven fairy godmothers? If they die, I will never forgive myself."

Maël squats down beside me and pulls my hands away from my face. "Listen to me. I know all about hard choices and regrets. The important thing is to remember that you can never control the actions of other people. Some will try to hurt us; some will try to help. We cannot stop either of those. If an offer of aid falls into your lap, it is wise not to decline it. Not many people have the courage to stand by the chosen one. The ones that do, understand the risks."

I stare at her for a while. She smiles at me, and finally, I manage to smile back. "Well, if you put it like that…"

She holds out her hand, and when I take it, she helps me up.

"Okay, everyone," I say. "I hope you all still have the ring your temporary fairy godmother gave to you?"

Everyone except Jeep and Kessley raises their hands, where the faded rings start to shine again.

Charlie frowns at his. "I forgot I was wearing it."

"Me too," I say. I focus on Taylar. "Now, you're sure they want to help?"

"Positive."

Charlie is still looking at his ring, which is blue. "I thought we only got these for the duration of the disguise spell?"

I hold up my hand to study mine. "True. But we never gave them back. They must still work."

D'Maeo gives his yellow ring a longing look. I can guess what he is thinking. If we summon the fairy godmothers, he'll finally see Mona again. It hasn't been that long since he saw her, but it sure feels like it, and I can sympathize with his longing. I can't imagine spending even one day without Vicky, let alone getting sucked into a box and fighting for my life for days on end, not knowing whether you're going to see the love of your life ever again. Or the love of your afterlife, in his case.

"How did it work again?" Charlie asks, interrupting my thoughts.

"Turn the upper part of the ring left three times and right two times," D'Maeo says without hesitation.

I lift my other hand and grab the upper part of the ring between my thumb and my index finger. "Okay, on one. Three, two… one."

We all turn at the same time. The ring heats up under my touch, and hope flows through my veins.

All around us, sparks in different colors appear. The residues approach curiously, restlessly moving as if they know something special is about to happen.

As if on cue, the sparks turn into beautiful women. They look like supermodels, but older and with normal weight. My heart jumps. The fairy godmothers answered our calls.

CHAPTER 14

While we all hug our fairy godmothers, Mona falls into D'Maeo's arms with a sob. "When the box disappeared, I hoped it meant you had escaped. I was so afraid to lose you."

He smothers her tears with kisses. They lose themselves in each other for so long that I turn away and introduce Jeep and Kessley to the other fairy godmothers.

When everyone is up to speed, I thank them for coming.

"Of course!" they say in unison.

Flora, the one whose ring I'm wearing, shrugs. "We were born to protect, so that's what we're here to do."

"But not to protect us," I object. "You all have your own protégées to take care of. We can't ask you to protect us too."

"Sure you can," Bella and Donna say in unison.

"You just did," Hanna adds with a wink. She spreads her hands. "And we came."

"You're actually our last hope," Kessley confesses. "Dante cast a spell to get us out of the cube, but we're still stuck, and we're out of ingredients for more spells."

Mona finally lets go of D'Maeo and squeezes my shoulder. "You did the right thing. Don't worry, we'll get everyone out of here."

I gesture at the emptiness around us. "Do you have any idea where we are?"

Mona nods. "This is a corner of what is known as The Nothing."

"Very appropriate," Jeep mumbles.

Mona points at the chaos residues floating in and out of sight. "It is a world where nothing grows or lives. No sky, no ground, except for a thin layer you can move on. This whole world is empty. Or it was, until someone decided to use it as a place to hold creatures they can't control. Entities that can be used as distractions, for instance."

"Or to kill someone," Kara adds.

I clench my fists when I remember the trap the Black Horseman set up for us. "Or in our case, to trap people you don't want to kill."

Mona nods thoughtfully. "That works too. The Nothing is a good prison. But some beings are able to move through the most dense atmospheres."

"Beings like fairy godmothers?" Kessley asks,

barely able to stand still from excitement.

Mona grins. "Exactly."

D'Maeo rubs his hands together. "Well, show us the magic. I'm ready to go home."

Mona exchanges a look with the other godmothers. They start to glow from head to toe and form a barrier, holding out their hands to us.

"Make sure you're all holding hands with one of us," Mona instructs.

We join the barrier, and soon, the sparks from the fairy godmothers also cover our hands and arms. Dots of light jump from one person to the other, the colors blending as they cover more and more of our bodies.

Kessley watches it all with her mouth open in awe.

The sparks start to stretch and form a bubble around us all. It looks like a giant rainbow folding around us. The residues behind the glass suddenly look a lot friendlier with all the colors dancing across their foggy bodies.

My gaze moves to Vicky, holding my right hand. Yellow and purple lights hit her transparent form. Her lips seem to turn from green to orange. I wish I could kiss all the colors on her face, but I can't break the circle.

"Close your eyes," Mona warns.

I've learned from my mistakes, so I obey immediately.

There's a bright flash, and I feel weightless. But then, my feet touch the ground again. Even without looking, I know it didn't work, and fear trickles into every corner of my body. It cuts off my breath, and I gasp for air.

"Stay still. We're going to try again," Mona says, her voice full of confidence.

When nothing happens for a while, I can't resist the urge to open my eyes any longer. Carefully, I peer through my eyelashes. All the fairy godmothers have lifted their faces to the empty sky. Their mouths are open, and from them, strings of light shoot up. The strings twist together to form a drill, which rises until it can go no further. I hold my breath as the tip hits the invisible ceiling, the end of this world. *Will it be strong enough?*

"Everyone, try to picture a hole in the sky," Mona says.

I close my eyes again and imagine the drill creating a hole that gets bigger and bigger until we can all float through it. I try to ignore the feeling of not being able to breathe properly.

My feet no longer touch the ground. Vicky folds her fingers tighter around mine, and for the first time they don't feel cold. My heart skips a couple of beats when I consider the possibility of her becoming alive. But I shake that thought off quickly. *I shouldn't fantasize about impossible things. I'm happy to have her as she is.*

Even through my closed eyelids, I can see flashes of bright light as we drift higher and higher.

"Now think of Darkwood Manor," Mona

instructs.

It's not hard to picture it again, especially since my longing to get home has grown in the last minutes. This world is slowly suffocating me. It's sucking up all of my energy. All I want right now is to get out of here, and Darkwood Manor is where I prefer to end up.

The kitchen, garden and my bedroom whirl through my head. Memories come back: my first time in the mansion, me lying on the bed, Vicky popping up next to me. I smile as she shoots me that provocative look I've come to know so well.

Then, something pulls at my stomach. I suck in my breath so fast I almost choke on it. I start spinning fast, as if I'm on a rollercoaster that has gone berserk. The contents of my stomach rise and fall, and I swallow countless times to keep everything inside. I feel things yanking at me from all sides. Soon, my arms, legs, shoulders, everything hurts. The light seeping through my eyelashes gets so bright I want to turn my head away from it. But I can't; it's everywhere.

Somewhere in the distance, I can hear Charlie moaning. Vicky squeezes my hand. And then, finally, everything stops moving. My feet touch solid ground. I try to stay upright, but my legs collapse under me. I can feel Vicky tumbling over too. The light fades, and carefully, I open my eyes.

I think I hear Quinn's voice drifting toward me, but I can't make out the words. I'm too worried about Vicky, who is lying on the kitchen floor motionless.

It takes all of my exhausted strength and concentration to drag myself to her. Gently, I touch her face. "Babe? Can you hear me?"

There's no response.

I shake her shoulder. "Vick… please wake up."

My arm is heavy, but I keep shaking her. Then I carefully turn her head and kiss her lips. "Wake up, sleeping beauty."

Still, she doesn't move.

From the left, I see a dark blur approaching. I blink, and Quinn comes into view.

"Give me some room," he says softly.

I push myself away from my girl, feeling weaker by the second. *What if she never wakes up? What if I never see those gorgeous blue eyes again?* A heavy weight lands on my chest when I try to imagine my life without her. Unable to look at her still form any longer, I turn my head. Only then do I notice the others, lying just as still on the floor around me. Except for Maël, who watches me with a worried frown.

Flora blocks my view before I can find the words to ask Maël what's going on. The fairy godmother with the long blonde hair bends over me and places her hand against my forehead. "Don't worry, you will all be fine. We needed more energy, so we drew some from your power cores."

"You… w-what?" I stutter, getting dizzy again.

"Shh, it's alright. We'll heal you."

Pink sparks jump from her hand to my head and spread over my body. I lean against her, wishing I could sleep for days and wake up to a safe world. That is, until I hear Vicky's voice saying, "Thanks, Quinn." I'm sitting next to her, holding her hand, before I even realize I've moved.

The little pink lights are still crawling over my skin, healing the spots that hurt and replenishing my energy.

I kiss Vicky again, and this time, she kisses me back.

I want to say I thought I'd lost her, but the words get stuck in my throat. It doesn't matter anyway, because she can sense it. With tears in her eyes, she wraps her arms around me. "I love you so much."

"I love you too," I whisper back.

When we let go of each other, the last of the pink sparks extinguish. Vicky rests her head against my shoulder while we watch the sparks from the other fairy godmothers heal our friends. One by one, they wake up, and the heavy feeling in my chest fades.

Mona lets out a sigh while she strokes D'Maeo's hair. "That was close."

I push myself up, my legs still trembling a bit, and hold out my hand to Vicky. "Can you stand?"

"Shh," she whispers. "I'm watching the show."

"What show?"

She points at two intertwined bodies leaning against the back door. They look magical, like a collection of body parts put together by blurs of green and red. I only recognize them by the white hair and the leopard skin dress. It's as if halos of bright light have come down and pressed them together. They're so close they almost look like one person. But when the godmother sparks start to fade, Taylar and Kessley break up their passionate kiss and look at each other breathlessly.

I tear my gaze away from them for a second and take in all the relieved and smiling faces around me. D'Maeo winks at me, and I grin.

The two love birds finally notice everyone staring at them. Simultaneously, a blush creeps from their necks to their cheeks.

Vicky taps my leg. "Okay, you can pull me up now. Show's over."

We all pretend to need all of our concentration to stand up and drag ourselves to our seats. Except for Jeep, who slowly shakes his head. "There's way too much porn going on in this house, and way too little of me involved."

Charlie snorts in response, and soon we're all laughing hysterically, even the decent fairy godmothers. It feels great.

CHAPTER 15

We give the godmothers their rings back, thank them a thousand times and say goodbye.

Once they're gone, Charlie gets up and does a couple of squats and stretches. Then he walks around the kitchen table, touching the wood and then the counter behind him. "Man, am I glad to see this house again. I thought we'd be stuck there for eternity, you know." He walks into the annex. "I don't even mind those crows anymore. If we can get out of The Nothing, we can do anything!" He comes back and turns around immediately. "Anyway, I really need to pee."

"Good to know," I say, shaking my head at his retreating form.

D'Maeo follows Charlie's example and goes to the annex. He pauses in the doorway, where I join him. We watch the crows for a while. They have spread to different trees. All heads turn to us, and they start cawing viciously.

"They look mean."

I nod. "I'm not as convinced as Charlie is that we'll be able to get rid of them."

"Eventually, sure."

"That's good enough for me."

"I feel the same way as him though," D'Maeo continues. "About getting back here. For a while, when John was still here, all I wanted was for it to be over. But now, thanks to you and Mona, I am quite happy here."

"And it's good to have you back." I move to slap him on the back, but instead, he embraces me.

"I was so worried about you all. It's such a relief to find you all in one piece."

Mona's voice interrupts us. "The coffee is ready."

D'Maeo lets go and wipes a tear from his eye.

I follow him into the kitchen and watch Mona's sparks put steaming cups on the table.

I lower myself onto my chair and wait for Charlie to pass between us before I say, "You know, Mona, there's something I don't understand."

The fairy godmother puts a cup of coffee in front of me. "What's that?"

"When Maël and I were stuck in that memory and in those worlds we travelled to, why didn't you come and get us?"

She takes her seat next to D'Maeo. "There are some paths you need to travel. That was one of them."

"What about Mom? Did she need to go to Hell?"

Sadness falls over her face when I mention her best friend and protégée. "I don't know. I tried to find her, but she was outside my reach." Her finger follows the crack in her cup. "The Devil is strong, and so are some of his accomplices. They blocked my view of her."

Her voice trembles slightly, and I feel sorry for her. "Don't feel guilty. I know you'd do anything to keep us safe. I don't blame you for what happened to her, and we *will* get her back."

She nods sternly. "Of course we will."

I turn to Quinn, who has stuck around and is sitting between Jeep and Gisella. "How are things in Heaven?"

I almost chuckle at the weirdness of that question, but Quinn's expression stops me. There's a frown on his forehead that I haven't seen often, and his lips are stuck in a downward position.

He entwines his fingers on the table in front of him, searching for words. "Another three angels are missing."

Mona's hand flies to her mouth, and Kessley lets out a shriek of surprise while the rest of us shift in our seats uncomfortably.

When Quinn remains silent, I exchange a quick, worried look with Vicky. She nods, and I ask the obvious question. "Do you think they were also killed?"

The angel keeps staring at his hands. "Maybe. But we suspect something else is going on."

My throat goes dry, and I gulp down the hot contents of my cup. "Can you tell us?"

Quinn licks his lips. "I was ordered to tell you. That is why I stayed."

My eyebrows move up. "Ordered to tell us?"

Quinn shakes his head. "To tell you, the chosen one."

"Ordered by who?" Jeep interrupts.

"By God himself."

I gulp and put my cup to my lips again, but there's nothing in it anymore.

Mona flicks her wrist, and several yellow sparks pick up the coffee pot and take it to the table. It refills my cup, giving me time to pluck up the courage to ask the next question. "Why?"

I've never seen Quinn like this. His confidence seems to have gone, and his words come out in a hesitant whisper. "Because you were not only chosen to save Earth, but also Heaven."

The coffee works its way back up, and I run to the sink to spit it out. Wiping my mouth, I turn back to my friend. "Can you repeat that, please? I think I misheard you."

He still doesn't look at me. He fidgets with his fingers and seems to shrink a little. After a short silence, he sighs. "I'm sorry, Dante, but it's true. You're meant to save Heaven and Earth."

I wipe my face over and over, then splash water

over it. It doesn't help. It still feels as if someone smashed a wall against it. My breathing is shallow, and spots drift through my vision. *Just when I got used to the idea of me saving everyone on Earth… Now I need to save everyone in Heaven too? Including the angels?*

Someone touches my arm, and I open my eyes. I hadn't even realized I'd closed them. I must have slid to the ground too, because I'm sitting with my back against the kitchen cabinets. My head is pounding. Vicky caresses my cheek and whispers something while Mona sends over some sparks to heal me.

When the spots have cleared from my vision, I see Charlie throwing me a tormented look over his shoulder. "So, what message do you have for him?" he asks Quinn. "What do you know about the three missing angels?"

I hold my breath, afraid of the answer, but Quinn doesn't say anything.

Mona's sparks take away some of my fear, and I stand up, helped by Vicky.

"It's okay, you can tell me," I say.

Quinn shoots me half a smile. "We think they've crossed to the other side."

I walk back to my chair, feeling a bit better. *If I was chosen to do this, I should be able to succeed, right? I'll just take it step by step.*

Nausea rises again at the thought of being responsible for the destruction of Heaven, but I push the thought back and focus on Quinn. "By the other side, you mean…?"

Of course, I know what he means, but I need him to say it out loud.

"We think they're working for Lucifer." He looks sort of relieved now that he's gotten it all out.

Kessley shakes her head in confusion. Her hand is still entwined with Taylar's. "I don't get it. Why would angels side with the Devil? Angels are good, and Lucifer is evil, right?"

"Angels have free will, just like humans," Quinn explains. "Which means we aren't necessarily good. Although, our benevolent side usually dominates. And we're very loyal beings."

"And don't forget that Lucifer is an angel too," Gisella adds.

"But why?" Kessley repeats. "Why would an angel want to destroy the Earth and kill every human being on it?"

Quinn shrugs. "Why does anyone want to destroy?"

"For power," Vicky says, anger in her voice. "Everything is about power."

"Not with me," I object. "I don't want to rule over anyone."

D'Maeo smiles. "Which is exactly why you are the chosen one. Not a single molecule inside you would even consider suppressing someone else."

"Of course not. But that doesn't mean I can save everyone."

"Not everyone," Quinn says. "But most of us."

A shiver runs from my lower back to the top of

my head at his use of words. *Us.* The gravity of the word hits me hard again. *It's not just the human race that depends on me, but the whole of angel kind too. How lovely.*

Quinn sits up straight and looks me in the eye for the first time since we started this conversation. "There's a reason why you were chosen, Dante."

I sigh. "Yes, yes, I know. I'm awesome."

Vicky slams her hands onto the table. "I can't argue with that," she says cheerfully. "Now let's hear the plan."

Mona stands up again and rummages through the cabinets in search for some comfort food.

Quinn rakes his hand through his frizzy hair. "The plan is that I try to locate the traitors from Heaven and contact you again when I succeed."

"And then what?" Taylar asks, sounding a bit grumpy. "We get back-up?"

"I'm afraid not. Heaven is still under attack. And there are a lot of souls there that need protection." He pushes his chair back and stands up. "Which is why I should be going." He pauses, guilt falling over his face. "I'm sorry I couldn't bring you better news. And I wish I could do more to help, but all I can promise you, is that I'll do whatever I can to keep you all safe and that I'll send help if I can."

I stand up, walk over to him and pull him into a hug. "I know. It's not your fault. We'll come up with a plan to catch or kill those angels. You be careful up there."

He slaps my back hard. "I will. You too. All of

you."

I want to say more, but suddenly, my arms are grasping nothing but air.

I walk back to my chair and fall into it.

Vicky takes my hand. "He feels really bad about it."

"Why? It's not his fault that I'm the chosen one, is it?" I suddenly freeze. "Is it?"

She smiles. "No, I don't think so. The prophecy has been around longer than he has. But he knew about this."

"And he didn't tell me because I wasn't ready for it," I verbalize her unspoken thought.

"And he was right," I add when I see Mona approaching and opening her mouth to say something. "I wasn't ready for this kind of pressure. I'm not even sure I'm ready now."

D'Maeo leans forward. "Which is another reason why you have been chosen. You have exactly the right amount of confidence to pull it off."

I snort. "If you say so. Personally, I think I have exactly the right amount of awesome friends to help me."

"Hear hear!" Charlie shouts, and he raises his cup. "Now, can we please order something to eat? I'm starving."

We all burst into laughter, and the mood lightens a bit. Slowly, a sense of pride awakens in my chest. Who would've thought a simple boy from Blackford, Idaho, would be the one to save us all. I certainly didn't. But saving everyone is what I *will* do, even if it means giving my life for it.

CHAPTER 16

Darkness seems to fall faster than usual, but I don't mind. I don't think I've ever been this tired. Even my worries are overshadowed by exhaustion.

Everyone around the table starts to yawn.

I push my chair back and stretch my arms above my head. "I suggest we all have a good night's sleep. Tomorrow, I want to go back to that Mahaha girl. We might still be in time to save her. After all, it can't be easy to let a Mahaha relive her death and make her eat so much it could be called gluttony."

Vicky scrutinizes me. I can tell she's reading my emotions. "You don't seem worried anymore."

I rub my eyes. "Of course I'm worried, but I don't want to give in to that feeling of desperation anymore. Think of what we've accomplished already. Think of what I'm destined to do." I make quotation marks in the air at the word destined and place both hands on the back of my chair. "It's hard not to worry, and sometimes I lose faith in our chances to win this fight. But if Quinn believes in me, in us, and God does too... we should trust in that." My arms are getting tired, so I stand up straight again. "And I think..." I hesitate. "... maybe... maybe we should stop counting only the souls we've saved. We've done more than just that. We met Charon, made friends in other worlds, beat the Four Horsemen, killed dozens of demons *and* saved four out of six souls. That's a lot, right?"

"It is," Maël confirms.

Charlie takes a whole packet of cookies from Mona when she offers him only one. He stuffs the first cookie into his mouth whole. It's gone in seconds, and he sighs delightedly. "I needed that."

Mona chuckles and takes another packet of cookies from the kitchen counter.

Charlie holds up his finger. "Hey, you know what else is cause for celebration?"

I smile at the sight of his crumb-covered lips. "Please tell us."

"Well..." He pauses when Gisella wipes the crumbs from his mouth. "If you compare what we achieved to what Satan did, it sounds even better." He holds up one hand and starts counting. "Okay, he's got two souls out of six. That's more than we hoped for, but not nearly enough to get through the nine circles and reach Earth. Other than that, what did he get?"

"Mom, Jeep and D'Maeo," I say.

Charlie shakes his head. "No, he didn't. We don't know if the Black Void, or chaos residue, or whatever you want to call it, was working for the Devil. I'm not sure those things ever obey anyone."

I nod slowly. "True… but—"

"No buts. Even if it was working for him, we got D'Maeo back." He gestures at the old ghost. "Jeep was captured by Shelton Banks, who is probably working for the Devil, but…" He points two fingers at the tattooed ghost. "We got him back too! And Trevor has your mother, but he won't harm her."

I bite my lip. "No, but Lucifer will."

He grins at me. "Not if we get her back first."

I stare at him for several seconds before I respond, "I like the way you think. I always told you, you should become a motivational speaker."

He throws his hair over his shoulder dramatically. "I know. I'm awesome."

Gisella pushes him, and his chair almost tips over. "Hey! I wasn't finished yet." He wipes a stray lock from his forehead. "Where was I?"

Kessley leans forward on the table. "You were talking about what the Devil got, besides two souls."

"Right. So, he's got two souls, your mother—if he gets really really lucky—and he killed an angel, and maybe got three angels on his side. That's it."

A sharp pain shoots through my chest at the thought that he may have gotten to Mom already. "That's still more than he should have gotten."

Charlie's face clouds over. "I didn't mean to make it sound insignificant."

Briefly, I close my eyes. "I know. And you're right. He hasn't gotten much success up till now. And that's what I meant. We need to focus on the bigger picture. We'll keep trying to save as many people as possible, but the fight won't be over if we lose another soul, or even two. Although I would prefer if we didn't."

Jeep rubs his tattoos, more out of habit than need, I think, since there are no more souls trapped inside. "I'm proud of how much we've accomplished already. And don't forget the pixies and trolls we killed at Shelton Banks' house, and how much you've helped all of us with our struggles. Thanks to you, we're all a lot saner and happier, Dante."

I feel a blush creeping up from my neck. "I didn't do any of that on my own."

"Yes, you did," Maël interrupts. "You helped me find peace with my past. So thank you."

I think back to our trip into her memories and realize she's right. I did do that on my own. "Well, you're welcome. I'm glad I could help."

Charlie walks over to me and slaps me on the shoulder, sending crumbs everywhere. "You should become a therapist."

With a snort, I wipe the crumbs from my clothes. "No, thank you. I've seen enough shit to last a lifetime."

"I hear you, man. Listen, I'm going to crash at home. My mom was complaining about how little she sees of me. And Gisella is going home too anyway." He salutes me with half a grin. "Stay safe and call if anything happens."

"I will."

They say goodbye to the others, and I walk them to the front door.

"Wait!" Vicky calls out when I reach for the doorknob.

I freeze. "What?"

She apparates to my side. "The crows!"

I let go of the doorknob immediately. "Oh, right. I forgot."

Charlie's shoulder sag. "So how are we supposed to get home? I'm not walking all the way back from the silver mine, you know. My feet hurt enough as it is."

"I can take you," Mona says from behind us.

My best friend lets out a sigh, and Gisella looks relieved too. "That would be great."

We say goodbye again, and they disappear, surrounded by yellow sparks.

I walk back and lean against the kitchen door post. "And now I'm really going to bed. Goodnight."

Vicky says goodnight too, and we drag ourselves up the stairs. I'm halfway through taking off my clothes when I collapse on the bed. "You know what? Screw this, I'm too tired to undress."

Vicky lifts my feet onto the bed and snuggles up beside me. Her kiss on my lips is the last thing I feel and hear.

Terrible heat. It burns my neck and cheeks, and if I stand still for too long, blisters form on the soles of my feet. So I do the only thing I can think of: run to find shelter.

For miles there's nothing but bare, scorching rock. No trees, no water and no living thing. There aren't even insects or birds here. Not that I'm surprised. Not much could survive here.

After what feels like an hour of running, I can no longer go on. My legs refuse to obey any longer, and my heart has gone into overdrive. The heat makes it difficult to think, but I have an idea of where I am. I was here before, although only in my mind.

I come to a sudden halt and try to ignore the pain in my feet.

"This isn't real," I tell myself. "It's a dream."

Or… No, not a dream. A premonition. Another peek into Satan's plans.

As soon as the thought hits me, the pain in my feet fades. Nothing here can hurt me.

I squint in all directions in an attempt to find something other than smoldering rock. There's a shift in the air, a temporary blur, and three figures appear. I recognize all three instantly. The one towering over the other two with a menacing grin sends a shiver down my spine. Satan. He's in his human form: tall, dark-haired and handsome. The fire in his eyes burns bright as he addresses the man standing next to him, dressed in a familiar burgundy suit that has dark stains all over it. "I've had enough of this, Trevor. You have this woman, and still I don't see any progress. The boy escaped The Nothing, so it's up to you to deal with him. For good this time.

Am I clear?"

Trevor bends his brown-haired head. "Of course, master."

Mom stands beside Lucifer, still with that dazed expression on her face. She barely notices the intimidating figure or the venomous words that escape his lips. I'm relieved to see it, because it means she has no idea what's going on. Trevor's love potion—or should I say mine, since I made it—seems to be a blessing in disguise. Not only does she feel no fear, Trevor also makes sure she won't be harmed.

But that thought is quickly crushed when Satan grabs her arm and turns her with her back against his chest. She responds with nothing but a quick intake of breath while my stomach is turned upside down and every part of me freezes. I no longer feel the heat, yet sweat trickles down my spine.

Satan brings his hand to Mom's throat and forces her chin up. "If I'd known your son would cause me so much trouble, I would've made sure he was never born."

Trevor shifts his feet uncomfortably. "I can still beat him, master. We've trapped him before; we can do it again."

The Devil sticks out his forked, black tongue. It glides slowly over Mom's cheek, and I ball my fists. If I was really here, I would knock him over and rip his heart out. If he even has one.

But I'm not, so there's nothing I can do except watch and make sure I remember everything.

Trevor's growing unease pleases me. I was right to trust him with Mom's life. He'll do whatever he can to keep her safe. I just hope it will be enough.

Satan buries his nose in Mom's neck. "No fear at all. How boring."

I bury my fingernails so far into the palm of my hand it would bleed if this was real. I let out a cry of frustration and wipe the sweat from my forehead.

Lucifer lifts his head and sniffs. He lets go of Mom so suddenly that she stumbles. Trevor catches her and strokes her arm before shoving her half behind him.

The Devil grows even taller. The scales under his skin become clearer, and horns grow from his skull. He turns his head and breathes in deeply. "He's here. I can smell him."

"Who is?" Trevor asks carefully, following his gaze.

"That damned boy."

I smother a cry with one hand and duck at the same time. He can sense me? How is this possible?

Trevor changes into his stone form in the blink of an eye. "I'll take care of him."

Lucifer leans closer to him, his horns touching the top of Trevor's head. Smoke rises from Trevor's skull as the heat from Satan's skin turns his hair to ash. "Consider this your last chance."

"Yes, master. I won't disappoint you." After another bow, he turns and drags Mom with him.

Satan slowly changes back into his full human form. "Oh, and Trevor?" he says sweetly.

The earth elemental comes to a sudden halt. I can see him sucking in air before he turns back to the ruler of Hell. "Yes, master?"

"Use everything you've got to trap the boy. Your crush too."

Trevor's shoulders go rigid. "Crush, master?"

"DON'T PLAY ME FOR A FOOL!" Satan bellows, turning red all over. He takes two steps closer, leaving burn

125

marks on the rocks. "You think I haven't noticed your sickening love for this woman?"

Trevor gulps. "Eh…"

"I'm the king of Hell; you can't hide anything from me."

Trevor bows his head. "Of course not, master. I never thought I could. I… I mean I didn't want to—"

"SILENCE!" Lucifer is suddenly only inches from Trevor, and he grabs Trevor's ear between his fingers. Smoke rises from it as it turns bright red.

Trevor moans but manages to stay still. I almost admire him for it. "Make sure you use these. Now, listen carefully. I'll repeat it one more time." He lets go and waits for Trevor to look up at him. "This is your last chance to take care of the boy. If you fail, you will suffer for eternity, and you will take your crush with you. Do you understand?"

For the first time I see Trevor trembling. His teeth even chatter a bit.

"Do you understand?" Satan repeats.

"I understand, master. I will make you happy."

"You have served me well up till now. I would be sad to lose you. And I don't think you'll like me very much when I'm sad, Trevor. Especially not if you're the one responsible for it."

Trevor shakes his head. "Yes, master. I mean, no, master. I won't make you sad."

"Good." The Devil straightens up. He pats Mom, who has been standing next to Trevor like a statue, on the head gently. "Use her to get the boy, and I'll see what I can do to keep you together."

Trevor bows deeper than humanly possible. "Yes, master. Thank you, master."

"Go. He's close. This could be over before the end of the day." Lucifer cracks his knuckles and grins. "Everything will soon be ready for the last phase."

He disappears in a cloud of red smoke, and Trevor breathes in and out a couple of times. He touches Mom's cheek gently. "Don't worry, I won't let anything happen to you."

She smiles her hypnotized smile at him and bends over to kiss him.

That's when I can't stand it any longer. I veer upright, shouting, "Hey! Get away from her!"

There's a weird echo, and Trevor's gaze turns to it. The corners of his mouth move up to form a content grin. "Well well, looks like Lucifer was right. You are here."

I watch as my future self walks up to him with big, angry strides. He stops two feet from Trevor and Mom when steam rises from the ground.

"Break the spell on my mother and give her back."

Trevor is still grinning, but even from a distance, I can tell he's not happy. Sadness falls over him as he turns back into his human form. "I will."

My future self recoils. "What?"

Curious and now confident that they can't see me, I creep closer. Now I can see that Trevor not only looks sad, but also tired, exhausted even. He doesn't seem as confident and strong as he did the last time I saw him.

"You heard the master, didn't you?" he continues. "I've got orders to do whatever it takes to stop you from interfering with our plans. I'm to use Susan to get what he wants."

"So you're going to hurt her?" my other self asks incredulously.

"Of course not," Trevor huffs. "She means the world to me."

"Then why are you dragging her through Hell and forcing her to like you?" Dante makes quotation marks in the air at the word 'like'.

Trevor lowers his gaze and sighs. "I was so desperate to have her. To spend time with her. I wanted to know what it felt like to be loved back."

The other Dante crosses his arms. "And what did it feel like?" The smug expression on his face leaves no doubt about the expected answer.

"Good and awful at the same time." Trevor's voice has become hoarse. He rubs his forehead. "I know I was wrong, and I hope she'll be able to forgive me one day."

My other self is as stunned as I am. What has happened to the cold and cruel Trevor we know? Has he come to his senses, or is this a trick?

"Whatever," future Dante says, coming to the same conclusion I do. "Do you really think I'll fall for this? There's not a decent bone in your body. If there was, you never would've put that spell on Mom or kidnapped her, and you never would've sided with the Devil."

Anger flashes across Trevor's face, his dark eyebrows knit together. "You can think whatever you want, Dante, but I really love your mother. Taking her and influencing her was wrong, I admit that. We all make mistakes sometimes. Me working for Lucifer is not one of them. My master is powerful,l and he can make the world great again. Earth will be cleansed, and only the truly strong ones will survive. It is the only right path."

Dante snorts. "Are you serious? You think wiping out most of humanity is the right thing to do?"

Some of Trevor's attitude returns as he straightens his back. Part of his face turns to stone. "The human race is the foulest of all. We ruined the beautiful things that God made; we have no respect for any form of life. The world will be a better place with less of us around."

I nod and so does my other self. "True," he says. "But now that all of those people are alive, you can't just kill them. How does that show respect for life?"

Trevor shakes his head impatiently. "You don't get it. If we get rid of the biggest part of human kind, we will save countless other species. Plants, animals, Earth itself. It is how God intended it."

Dante raises his hands in despair. "I don't get it? Listen to yourself! If God wants us all dead, he would kill us himself. I bet he could do it with one twirl of a finger. So why doesn't he do it?"

Trevor sighs dramatically. "God has grown soft."

"Right." Dante taps his foot on the rock in front of him. "So you join his arch enemy. Sounds logical."

Trevor presses a hand against his forehead. The stone parts turn back to normal skin. "Look, we don't have to agree on this. Let's just agree on the need to take Susan somewhere safe."

My other self tilts his head and narrows his eyes. "I'm not going anywhere with you. I'm not falling for any of your tricks. If you want to fight me, fight me. If not, get out of my way."

Trevor's mouth forms a straight line. His hands ball into fists. I want to hurry over and snatch Mom away from him, but

I know I can't. I'm only a spectator here; I can't change anything.

"Okay," Trevor says, his voice trembling as he tries to stay calm. "I'm going to say this only once, so listen carefully." He points at my copy. "We are enemies. I will do what I can to take you down. But I don't want Susan to be stuck in the middle. Lucifer wants me to use her. If I don't, he'll torture her himself until you give in. I can't let that happen, so I need you to take her somewhere safe. I'll make sure I have the injuries to prove I tried to stop you."

Once again, we're both speechless. He's letting me go? He's letting Mom go?

My future self holds out his hand before my brain gets a chance to process what it's just heard. "Deal."

With a weak, relieved smile, Trevor copies the gesture.

But before their hands meet, the rocks between them explode.

From the depth below rises the monstrous form of Satan. Fumes escape his nostrils, and the fire in his eyes burns bright. He towers over us, and we all back up in horror. Even Mom seems to wake from her catatonic state a bit.

"Traitor," Satan hisses at Trevor. "You really thought I wouldn't find out about your betrayal? You think I ever trust anyone completely?"

Trevor's whole body trembles as he bows. "No, master. I was merely trying to win the boy's trust."

Flames erupt all over the Devil's body. "DO NOT LIE TO ME!"

His burning arm pushes Trevor so hard he's thrown back several feet. Then he reaches for Mom, and my future self and I *call out in unison. "Nooo!"*

CHAPTER 17

"Wow, calm down. You're alright." Vicky's soothing voice seeps through the noise of screaming and the roaring of fire.

I open my eyes, but I still see Mom disappearing into the flames. Shiver after shiver runs across my back while Vicky holds me close. Tears fall upon her leather jacket. Her soft hair touches my cheek, and her hand moves to my neck.

"You're alright," she repeats.

I wait for the inevitable 'it was just a dream', but it doesn't come. Vicky knows as well as I do that this phrase is rarely true for me.

Slowly, my breathing steadies, and the images go up in proverbial smoke.

I pull myself from Vicky's embrace and lean against the bedpost. "Holy shit."

Vicky almost crushes my hand. "I shouldn't have

left you alone."

I recoil. "You left? Where'd you go?"

She pats her endless pocket. "To refill my supplies." She strokes my neck. "What did you see?"

"I saw Mom… and Trevor. In Hell." It takes several breaths to be able to continue. "The Devil… he wants Trevor to torture my mother to get to me." I press my fingers against my temples to drive out the images drifting back in.

Vicky waits silently for me to continue, stroking my arm gently.

"Trevor wanted to send Mom back with me. But Satan was listening. He tossed Trevor aside and grabbed Mom."

"Wait." Vicky frowns at me. "You were also there? In Hell?"

I nod and wipe the tears from my cheeks.

"And Trevor didn't try to kill you?"

"No, he was only thinking of Mom's safety."

To my surprise, Vicky smiles broadly. "That's great! I knew his love for your mother would come in handy someday."

I shake my head. "Not really, babe. Satan still got her, and Trevor couldn't do anything to save her."

Vicky bends over me and pokes me in the chest. "But you can."

She stares at me, waiting for her words to sink in.

I go over them again in my head. "You mean…" I sit up straight. "You mean I can prevent this from happening, because I've seen it."

It's not a question, but she nods feverishly. "Exactly."

I slip to the end of the bed and slide out. "So, this is actually good news?"

I peer through the curtains. The sun is rising, and the seven large crows are already up, sitting silently in the trees, watching the house for any sign of movement. When they get a glimpse of me, they peck each other. Soon, all heads are turned toward me, the red eyes gleaming in the early light.

Vicky startles me when she presses her body against mine from behind. "It certainly is good news. You were right about Trevor. He really loves your mother, and he will do anything to save her. We can use that."

I drop the curtain and turn to face her. "Have I told you how amazing you are?"

Her eyes twinkle. "Constantly. But I can't remember the exact words."

I laugh and grab her butt. "You are super super amazing. More amazing than anything and anyone in the world."

She tilts her head. "Only in this world?"

"Of course not, I meant in any world."

She brings her head closer to mine. "I can live with that."

Our lips meet, and electricity flows through me. The ache in my heart and the restless feeling pressing on my shoulders evaporate. All I can feel is warmth and…

The door is thrown open, and we both look up.

"Oh, good, you're both awake. I'm sorry, I forgot to knock. I almost apparated in here, but I wouldn't want to interrupt..." Kessley falls silent. Her hand moves up to gesture at us. "... well, something like this." She blushes. "Sorry."

"It's okay," I say, letting go of Vicky with a pang of longing. "What's wrong?"

"I thought it wasn't that special, but Maël and D'Maeo, and even Mona, seemed shocked, so I offered to go and get you before we went to check it out ourselves," she goes on in a flurry of words. "Not that we can step outside with those creepy birds ready to rip us apart, but—"

"Just tell us already!" Vicky exclaims.

Kessley cringes. "Right. Sorry. This is all just so exciting for me. Being on the chosen one's team, fighting by Dante's side, and..." She slams her hand against her mouth when Vicky throws her an angry look. "Right. The reason I came up here..." She takes a deep breath. "There's someone at the door."

I frown. "That's all?" *Sure, that doesn't happen often, but still, it's not world news.*

"No." Kessley nervously rubs her hands together. "It's someone we've seen before. We're not sure..." She hesitates, and Vicky takes a step closer. "It might be a trap again," Kess finishes quickly.

I pat my hair and straighten my clothes. "Let's check this visitor out then."

Kessley takes the lead. As we hurry down the

stairs, I can see the others standing in the study, looking through the windows.

"Who is it?" I say, pushing past them to reach the window. I'm half expecting Trevor to be standing there with that smug grin on his face, but it's not. It's the Mahaha's friend, the slender one with the moving hair. Only now do I understand what Kessley meant by that. While the girl is pacing up and down between the steps at our front door and her car, her hair seems to have a will of its own. Instead of flowing naturally with the wind, it winds and unwinds around her upper arms constantly.

"She looks desperate," Vicky comments.

I tear my gaze away from the girl's hair and focus on her face. "Why haven't the crows attacked her?" I can clearly see them sitting in the trees, watching our every move.

"Because it's a trap?" Jeep offers.

Mona shakes her head. "Maybe not. They might be smart enough to wait until we open the door for this girl. After all, they're not really birds."

I take the girl in from head to toe again. "And if we don't?"

Mona turns to face me. "Then they'll probably torture her until we do."

"Great," I mumble. I don't want her to get hurt, but after what happened at the Mahaha's house, I'm not inclined to trust strangers anymore. On the other hand, she might've had nothing to do with the trap.

With a grunt, I walk over to the front door. "We

have to let her in. Or at least find out whether she's able to cross the line of salt. That should tell us enough, right?"

"What about the crows?" Kessley's voice rises in panic.

I shrug. "It doesn't make a difference whether the door is open or closed. They can't get past our protection."

"Are you sure? Your spell didn't work on them either."

I bite my lower lip and walk back into the study. "Good point."

Maël bends closer to the window. "We cannot leave the girl out there. Eventually, the crows will attack."

Jeep waves at her, and I frown. "What are you doing?"

"Telling her to run. Get ready to open the door."

As I walk back to the front door, Jeep points at the large birds, and the girl turns to look at them. She nods to let us know she's seen them. Then the tattooed ghost gestures to the door and holds up his hand. One by one, he drops his fingers. My hand folds around the doorknob.

"Three, two…" Jeep counts out loud. I can't see the girl anymore, but on 'one', Jeep's head turns with her movements.

A furious screeching fills the driveway, followed by the loud flapping of wings.

I keep my gaze locked on Jeep, who's counting

back on his fingers again. "Two, one…" I open the door, and the girl nearly trips over the threshold. The first crow is only inches behind her. I slam the door closed in its face. There's a loud thump as it hits the wood. More banging follows, plus a lot of scratching and pecking. It sounds as if an army of killer rats is trying to get through the door.

"Thanks for letting me in," the girl pants, her arms resting on her upper legs.

The banging on the front door stops, and the crows return to their branches, from where they continue to watch the house intently.

"What are they?" the girl asks, her lip curling up in disgust.

"It's a long story." I make sure the door is closed properly before beckoning everyone back to the kitchen.

CHAPTER 18

"Tea?" Mona asks. "Or coffee?"

We all go for coffee, and I gesture at Charlie's empty chair.

The girl sits down and stares at the table for a while before speaking. "I'm sorry to barge in here like this, but I didn't know where else to turn."

"It's okay," I assure her. "I'm Dante by the way. These are my friends Vicky, Kessley, Maël, D'Maeo, Jeep, Taylar and Mona."

"It's nice to meet you," she says, shrinking a little under our inquiring stares. "My name is Ginda. I'm a chlorokinetic witch."

I frown. "What does that mean?"

She smiles and holds her hands above the table. "It means I can create and manipulate plants." Out of nowhere, a green stalk grows. Tiny white flowers pop out of it. She raises one hand and moves her fingers fast, as if she's trickling salt onto a dish. Pink, purple and yellow roses grow from the table.

Kessley's mouth has fallen open, and with a chuckle, Ginda makes a throwing motion toward her, showering her with roses.

"That is amazing," Mona says, putting a steaming cup in front of Ginda. "Such a beautiful power."

"Thank you," Ginda says.

I wrap my hands around the cup that Mona gives me and lean forward. "So, how can we help you?"

Ginda takes a large swig of her coffee. "I came to ask you to help my friend."

"Your friend the Mahaha?" Taylar asks bluntly.

"Yes."

I try to hide my surprise behind my cup. "Why did you come to us?"

"We saw you at the bar. When we left, I didn't want to worry Chloe, my friend, but I knew you were following us. I saw you disappear at Chloe's house. At first, I thought someone saved us, but soon, Chloe started to act strangely. I think she's in trouble."

"Why do you think that?"

Ginda's fingertip follows the edges of the small white flowers, and a blue glow spreads across them. "Mahahas normally don't eat much, but lately, she's been gulping down food as if she's afraid to starve."

I exchange a meaningful look with the others. *So the Mahaha is indeed the seventh soul.*

"That still doesn't explain why you came to us. And how did you find us?" D'Maeo enquires.

"I took a picture of you through the window, in case you were the enemy and we needed to fight you later." She sends us an apologetic smile.

Jeep shrugs. "Sounds reasonable to me."

"When Chloe's behavior started to change, I figured you probably weren't the bad guys. I showed the picture to some people in town. The owner of Rodney's DIY-Shop gave me this address. Told me to be careful, that this place was cursed. But it was the only thing I could think of. Chloe and I don't have any family left, and people are generally not fond of helping a Mahaha in need."

"Can't blame them," Vicky mumbles. "Mahahas usually aren't much fun to be around."

Ginda nods. "True. But not all are evil. Chloe is kind and caring. She looked after me when my parents and brother were killed in an accident."

I look at Vicky, who's watching the flower witch intently. Ginda meets her gaze without fear or hesitation.

There's a long silence in which Mona's sparks pass around chocolate cookies everyone declines.

Finally, Vicky turns to me. "I think she's telling the truth. She's genuinely worried, and I also picked up a glimpse of hope. Nothing even resembling hate or anger."

"Good." I hold up my cup to Mona. "It's time to fill Ginda in on our mission. I think more coffee won't hurt."

Mona lowers herself onto D'Maeo's lap and sends

more sparks to fetch the coffee can. While it goes around to refill our cups, I give the chlorokinetic witch the short version of our adventure. I tell her about the Devil's plans, the nine circles, me and my Shield, the souls we lost and, of course, the souls we saved.

Ginda keeps shaking her head, as if she can't believe it. When I finish my story, she stares into her coffee. "So, Chloe is the seventh soul Lucifer needs to escape Hell?"

"Exactly."

"And someone is making her hungry…" She scratches the side of her head. "Why again?"

"Because to break through the circles of Hell, the Devil needs the sin to be strong," D'Maeo explains. "He needs souls that aren't prone to committing the sin. In this case, someone who never eats enough. Convincing that person to switch to over-eating isn't easy, but it can be done by making her relive her death."

Ginda's eyes grow wide. The flower she's touching withers and falls apart. She withdraws her hand quickly. "Someone is pushing Chloe to eat herself to death?"

That does sound horrible, but there's no use in sugarcoating, so I give her a simple 'Yes'.

When she moves her fingers above the table again, only black flowers bloom. She looks defeated. Her brown locks stop moving, and her face goes pale.

"We'll do what we can to save Chloe," I promise

her.

She keeps staring at the flowers she created. Her hand hovers above them, and slowly, the black gets lighter. "Thank you." With a gentle touch, she adds some gold to the gray of the petals. Gradually, the whole flowers turn gold. She picks one up and holds it out to me. I have to stand up to grab it.

"It's beautiful."

"It's a peony. It brings luck to the receiver. Gold is the color of success."

I bring it closer to my face to study it. "Thank you. We can use all the luck we can get."

She sends me a hopeful smile. "What will you do now?"

I flop back into my chair. "Now we have breakfast, and after that, we're going to find your friend, or the person trying to kill her, whichever crosses our path first."

Once we're all satisfied, I call Charlie to tell him about our plans.

"I'm picking up Gisella as we speak," he says. "Where do you want to meet?"

"Ginda says her friend is a regular at the Winged Centaur, so I guess that's our best shot. And if we don't find her there, we'll go to her house. Ginda can lead us around the back, in case another trap is set up at the front."

"Sounds good to me. See you in a bit."

Charlie's cheerfulness gives me energy and hope,

even though we don't have a plan to defeat the Black Horseman yet. If we end up in The Nothing again, getting out will be even harder than last time, since we gave the godmothers' rings back.

"Are you ready?" I ask Ginda. Since we don't want to walk from the mines to the city center again, we came up with a plan to reach the car.

The flower witch folds her hands around the edge of the table and squeezes hard, breathing in and out deeply. Then she pushes back her chair and stands up. "Yes, I'm ready."

"Is there anything we can do to help?" Vicky asks.

Ginda nods. "Can you stand there? As a model?"

"Sure." Vicky walks around the table and stops in front of the back door.

I peer through the windows in the annex to check on the crows. "One, two… four… six, seven. They're all there; they can't see you."

"Good." Ginda sizes Vicky up and starts to move her hands and fingers.

She looks as if she's playing the piano and doing magic tricks at the same time. With every movement, vines, stems, leaves and flowers appear. Slowly, she guides them into a human shape. The vines form the outline, and she colors the figure in with the rest. Skin-colored leaves for the head and hands, black flowers for the clothes.

"That is brilliant," Kessley whispers.

I silently agree. The figure next to Vicky is an exact copy of my girlfriend but made of plants.

Kess hops from one foot to the other. "This is going to work!"

Ginda drops her hands and takes some more deep breaths.

Vicky reaches out to her. "Are you okay?"

The chlorokinetic witch smiles wearily. "A little tired, but fine." She stretches her fingers a couple of times and moves her arms around. Then she cracks her neck and rolls her shoulders. "I'm ready."

Vicky hurries back to my side of the kitchen table, and the others follow, except for Ginda.

"On three," she says, her hand resting on the door handle. "One…"

I peer into the annex again.

"Two…"

The crows are still watching the house intently, waiting for movement.

"Three."

As soon as Ginda pushes the doorknob down, all the crows' heads turn to the back of the house.

I leap past the doorway to the annex and hurry to the front door as quietly as possible. The others follow, producing almost no sound either.

I reach for my car keys in my pocket and wrap my fingers around them tightly. I wish I could look through a window here. Not knowing where the crows are makes me nervous.

After a 'go' from Mona, Ginda joins us. Jeep pushes her next to me at the front door. "You and Dante go first. We can turn invisible, so they won't be able to see us. You can't."

I shake my head. "Don't be too sure about that. These crows are different from the other enemies we've faced. They might be able to see and hurt you, even in your invisible state. Stay close and get into the car as fast as you can. I'm not taking any risks with these birds."

Ginda has closed her eyes in concentration. We all wait for her signal.

She holds out her arms and moves her hands and fingers again. She twirls them, twists them and moves them back and forth. The back door creaks. Ginda makes a pushing motion and turns back to me. "Now."

I open the front door, and we spill out onto the driveway like a bunch of prisoners on death row set free but with a gun aimed at our backs.

I reach Phoenix first and fumble to get the key into the keyhole. From behind the mansion there's a loud screech and a ripping noise.

"Hurry up," Vicky hisses at me, sliding sideways through the car door.

Finally, I manage to get the key in. The door swings open with a soft creak, and I jump in. While I turn the ignition, Ginda drops down beside me. The back seat is flooded with ghosts. They tumble over each other through the closed doors, legs and arms sticking out on all sides.

"Close the door!" I yell at Ginda, who is moving her fingers again to create some sort of vine net between the side of the house and the forest.

When she doesn't respond, I lean over to shut the car door. Ginda keeps moving her fingers and arms. Her gestures are even faster than Jeep's when he's waking up the dead. But somehow, hers are more elegant.

"Start the car!" Taylar calls out, fumbling to sit up straight.

When I place my hands on the wheel, I realize the engine has stopped running. I turn the key, and Phoenix splutters.

"I told you you needed a new car," Jeep says matter-of-factly, pushing Vicky's legs down so she can sit up.

"She always starts at the right time," I mumble, patting the dashboard gently with my free hand. "Don't you, girl?"

A quick glance in the rearview mirror tells me Ginda's vine wall is almost as high as the house. Behind it, the angry caws of the crows grow louder. The first large black head appears above the wall. A vine reaches for it, but the crow swerves left to avoid it and swoops over the wall.

I turn the key again, and Phoenix roars to life. I hit the gas hard, just as the crow dives down. It misses the roof of the car, but its nails scratch the trunk. With a curse, I turn the wheel. Phoenix spins but finds grip, and we lunge forward. I almost hit a tree. At the last second, the car swerves back onto the dirt road, leading us away from Darkwood Manor. In my rearview mirror, I see the other crows catching up with the first. They let out frustrated cries, that almost sound demonic, but then they turn around and fly back to the mansion.

I slow down a bit. My hands are sweaty, and my heartbeat has gone mental.

"Why aren't they following us?" Kessley voices my thoughts.

D'Maeo turns to look back. "They know we'll come back."

While I steer Phoenix through the forest, I rub the steering wheel soothingly. "I'm sorry you got hurt, Phoenix."

I can feel Ginda's frown before I see it.

"Are you talking to your car?" she asks.

"Yes, I am," I say stiffly.

"Why, is it magical?"

I hear Vicky snorting behind me, but I ignore it. Phoenix is special to me, and I don't care if other people don't understand that.

"Not magical like you and me," I answer after a short pause. "But she's very special to me. She belonged to my father, and I feel like some part of him still lingers inside."

I swallow the emotions that rise to the surface.

"Besides," I continue, "we've been through a lot together, and she always comes through. Sure, it's a bit small in here for us, but we manage. It might sound crazy, but she's like a friend. A companion."

Ginda nods. "If you put it like that, I'd say she is

sort of magical."

Phoenix roars as we leave the forest, as if she agrees with Ginda.

I smile. "Yep. Definitely magical."

CHAPTER 19

The roads are busy with morning traffic. I use the magical lanes, but in the end, I think it takes us longer that way, since we constantly need to stop or slow down to avoid running over pedestrians or hitting cars crossing the street. They can't see us, after all. But once we're on the magical lanes, it's not easy to get off unnoticed, so I decide to stick with them until we reach the Winged Centaur.

I park Phoenix at the side of the bar and reach for the door handle.

"Wait!" Taylar calls out, and my hand drops back down.

"What? Did you see Chloe?"

Taylar turns a bit more transparent. "No, it's… it's Shelton Banks."

Vicky breathes in sharply. "You're right."

They both disappear from sight, and I exchange a

worried look with D'Maeo.

"Vick? Are you still here?"

"I am," she answers. "You should hide too."

Her words don't really get through to me, or maybe it's my curiosity overruling my fear that keeps me upright.

Finally, I see the man who has made the afterlife so difficult for two of my ghosts. Vicky described him pretty well when she had her vision. He does look average, and pretty boring, with his gray suit and blue tie and his dark hair combed to one side. His round face would be friendly if it wasn't for the heavy eyebrows that point down in constant anger. His chin is turned up slightly, as if he wants to show everyone he is above other people. The air around him seems to move every time he does, as if it wants to get away from him.

There's a hand on my head, pushing me down. "If he sees you…"

I know Vicky is right. We can't risk this man noticing us, but my eyes are glued to him, and my head is spinning with the possibilities of what he can do. Is he an air elemental, like our former friend Simon? Or something stronger? Something worse…

Suddenly, it's as if Shelton Banks senses us watching him. He turns his head toward us. Instead of ducking, I freeze.

Vicky pushes my head down harder, but it only moves an inch. I'm still in full sight of our enemy. If he turns his gaze a little to the left, it will fall on me.

And then… well, I guess we'll find out how powerful he is.

I try to duck, but my body won't cooperate. Shelton scans the parking lot inch by inch. Two seconds, and he will notice Phoenix.

My head is starting to hurt from all the pushing Vicky is doing.

"Get down!" she whispers urgently.

But not a single muscle obeys my brain.

Then, something blocks my view: flowers that match the red of my car and black vines wrapping around them to form something resembling a sunshade.

I shake my head and blink several times. "What the hell was that?"

"I have heard of this power," Maël says from somewhere in the back seat. Like the others, she has turned invisible, even to me. "He immobilizes the people he is searching for when they are close-by."

I scratch my head, that's suddenly itching like crazy, as if Shelton's magic has left a mark on it. "So he's searching for me. He knows what we've done. Great."

"That was only a matter of time," D'Maeo says calmly, blinking into view again. His hand is still raised from trying to block Shelton Banks' powers. "He's gone."

When I'm done scratching, I turn to Ginda. "Thanks for your help."

Her body tenses in fear, and I place a hand on her

arm. "Hey, are you alright? Did he curse you or something?"

Slowly she opens her mouth. "Do you… do you think that man is after Chloe too?"

"I'm not sure. It might be a coincidence." I bite my lip when the worry on her face doesn't disappear. "Either way, we'll do everything we can to save her."

Ginda nods and balls her fists. "I'll help you."

I give her a grateful nod. "That would be great."

Kessley pushes her nose against the window. "Do you want to go after him?"

"No, I don't want to provoke him, in case he's not after Chloe. And I'd rather avoid him altogether, if we can," I confess.

"How did he get out of jail anyway?" Taylar asks, anger seeping into his voice. "Why didn't they arrest him?"

"He's probably out on bail," Jeep offers. "Until the trial starts."

I turn to face the white-haired ghost. "I can go ask later, if you want to."

He nods, but it's not convincing.

Vicky leans over to him from the other side of the back seat. "I can run over to the police station to hand over the list of victims now."

Taylar mumbles something incomprehensible, but I think it's a good idea.

"You should," I tell her. "We need to make sure Shelton is gone before we go into the bar anyway. We'll wait for you here. Make sure you stay invisible as long as you can."

She shakes her head. "We'll all have to go, or we'll get too far away from you. I don't want to be pulled back to Darkwood Manor."

I grit my teeth. *Right, I hadn't thought of that.*

"Okay, we'll go together then." I turn to Taylar and wave a finger in front of his face. "But don't do anything stupid in there; that's an order. Vicky and I will be the only ones visible. Understood? I don't want to risk anyone even thinking we might not be who we say we are."

"Fine," he pouts.

Jeep puts his hat on firmer. "I'll go see if that Banks guy is still there. I'll wave if the coast is clear."

I give him a thumbs up, and he steps through the car door into the parking lot.

It always makes me nervous if they claim to be invisible, but *I* can still see them. I tell myself Jeep has plenty of experience going invisible. He knows what he's doing.

Nevertheless, I can tell I'm not the only worried one. Vicky is leaning through Kess to keep an eye on the tattooed ghost. She's probably afraid to lose him again. They've known each other for so long they're like family. When he got stuck inside the portal in the silver mine, it must have felt as if she was losing her favorite uncle. Or worse, probably.

"He'll be fine," I tell her, and she throws me a quick smile.

Ginda lowers the vines and flowers a bit so we can

see more.

Jeep walks around the corner without even stopping. Vicky leans back to give Kessley and Taylar some room.

We wait.

After about a minute, Vicky sits up again. "Is he coming back yet?"

"Not yet," I say. "Be patient. He has to make sure Shelton Banks isn't anywhere near anymore."

"Right."

She sits back and fumbles with the hem of her jacket. I've never seen her this nervous before.

After another thirty seconds or so, she sighs and moves through Kessley and Taylar. "I can't stay here."

"Wait." My heart leaps to my throat at the thought of my girl getting close to Shelton Banks. He's the one that cursed her. He's the one that keeps touching her grave to make sure she gets pulled closer and closer to the Shadow World. Who knows what he'll do when he sees her.

She's out of the car before I can grab her arm. I open the door to follow her, ignoring the protests from the others.

"Vick," I hiss. "Stay here. Jeep can take care of himself."

She stops in the middle of the parking lot.

"Please come back. I don't want that Banks guy to see you."

She turns her face toward me. Tears slide down

her cheeks. "I can't leave him, not again, Dante."

"We're not leaving him. He'll be back any second."

As if on cue, Jeep rounds the corner of the bar. When he sees us, he shoos us back to the car with panicked gestures.

Without hesitation, I dive forward, grab Vicky's arm and drag her along. She steps into the back of the car, and I drop onto the driver's seat. Carefully, I close the car door. It produces only a soft click.

Ginda directs the vines and flowers back up to block the view.

Jeep doesn't follow. He stays close to the wall, as if he's afraid Shelton Banks will be able to see him if he doesn't.

Vicky sucks in her breath when Shelton Banks strolls by. He's muttering to himself, looking very displeased. I mean, more displeased than he did before. This time, he doesn't pay attention to anything around him. He must no longer be looking for us, because none of us freeze this time.

Jeep follows him as he walks out of sight, and we all watch the road closely.

Soon, the sound of a heavy engine starting echoes through the street. The driver pulls up angrily.

Jeep appears on the sidewalk. After one last look in the direction of the fading noise, he beckons us.

Vicky hurries over to him and hugs him so hard he nearly topples over. When I reach them, I check the street for any sign on Shelton Banks. Of course there is none, or Jeep wouldn't have beckoned us, but the guy gives me the creeps, so I want to be sure he isn't hiding in a corner somewhere.

"What did he do?" I ask when Vicky finally lets go, wiping tears from her cheeks again.

"He went into the Winged Centaur and talked to the bartender. He didn't seem very pleased with the answers he got."

I snigger. "I could tell."

CHAPTER 20

Charlie's car rounds the corner. He stops next to us and rolls down his window. Gisella is sitting next to him, dressed in her usual red catsuit.

"Sorry we're late," Charlie says, holding up a bar of chocolate. "We had to stop for supplies."

With a grin, I slap him on the arm that rests on the car door. "It's fine. We're going to the police station to deliver the hitlist we found at Shelton Banks' house first anyway. Maybe Ginda can stay with you until we get back?"

"Sure!" He reaches into his pocket and holds up a flash drive. "I transferred the pictures I took of that Devil's shrine at Shelton Banks' house from my phone to this drive. Added some pictures of dead bodies, which I found in one of his drawers. You should hand that in too."

My mouth falls open. "You found pictures of his other victims? That's great! Why didn't you tell us before?"

He shrugs. "We found Jeep and then I kind of forgot. We had more important things to think about, you know."

Taylar gives him a relieved smile, and I slap my best friend on the back. "I know. It's fine. This is great news." I introduce him and Gisella to the chlorokinetic witch, and Charlie turns into the parking lot.

"We'll be right back," I tell Ginda, and she walks over to Charlie's car.

I turn back to my Shield. "Is everyone, except Vicky, invisible?"

They all nod, so I cross the street to the police station.

At the door, Vicky stops me. "We forgot something."

I frown. "We did?"

"Yes, when we delivered the footage of the murder, we were dressed as FBI agents, remember? Mona disguised us."

I slap my hand against my forehead. "You're right. We can't walk in looking like ourselves. But it'll take too much time to do a spell. Chloe probably needs us now." I turn to Taylar. "I'm sorry, we can't do it now, but we'll come back as soon as possible."

Instead of the depression I expect to appear on his face, I find anger. His see-through skin goes dark, and I take a step back.

"Shelton Banks is walking around a free man," he

hisses. "He should be punished."

It takes a lot of self-control to stay calm. "I agree," I say, "which is why we can't afford to mess it up. He might never be convicted if they don't take this evidence seriously."

Taylar is about to reply when Kessley holds up her hand. "I can help."

We both turn to face her.

"How?" we ask in unison, me sounding hopeful, Taylar with impatience in his voice.

Kess raises her chin proudly. "I can transform myself, copy the way you guys looked. I can even disguise myself as both of you at the same time, if you remember what you looked like."

"Great plan," Taylar responds, his color returning to normal.

I glance through the glass front doors of the police station. "I don't know, it sounds risky."

"All I have to do is deliver the note, right? I can go in disguised as one of you, tell the woman at the counter that I'm in a hurry and that she should put the list and the flash drive with the footage of the murder. It's no problem, really. I can do it."

Vicky nods. "I think it's a good idea. I can go with her, invisible, and tell her what to say if the woman has any questions."

I take some time to go over the risks in my head and decide they're not much bigger than when I would go myself.

"Fine," I say. "You'll go in as Vicky, since you'll be

more convincing as a woman than as a man."

Kessley changes into an exact copy of Vicky before I can even blink.

The corners of my mouth move up. *This power of hers is so cool. We're lucky to have her on our side.*

I describe Vicky's FBI disguise, and Kess changes easily.

"Like this?" she asks, adding some wrinkles to her eyes and forehead without moving.

"Not that many," I say. "And her hair was a bit shorter."

Kessley changes again, and I hold up my thumb. "Perfect. Add a black suit and you're good to go."

Vicky's leather and lace outfit is replaced by an expensive looking suit.

I chuckle. "Don't make it too fancy, you're FBI, not a movie star."

"Right." She adjusts the fabric. "Like this?"

"Exactly."

The real Vicky takes the list from her pocket and hands it to her older self. I give her the flash drive. "This is weird," Vicky says. "I never thought I'd see an older version of myself. Now I finally know what I would've looked like if I hadn't been..." She falls silent, but we all know what she means. It's as if we're getting a glimpse of a future she'll never have, a future in which she could grow old with me.

I wrap my arm around her and kiss her temple. "I'm sorry. It's only for a couple of minutes."

She shrugs. "It's fine. I made peace with my fate a

long time ago." She frees herself from my grasp and steps toward the glass doors. "Let's do this."

Kessley straightens her shoulders and follows her. She opens the door and walks to the counter with confident strides.

I try to peer inside discretely. It's quiet, so they can walk right up to the counter. I can see the police officer behind it smiling at Kessley and saying something. Kessley puts the hit list and the drive down and starts explaining. Vicky stands beside her, invisible, and tells her what to say, like a prompter in a play, except that lives depend on the right words now.

The receptionist picks up the note and studies it. She nods and writes something down on a piece of paper. Then she hits a couple of keys on her computer and smiles. I think I can read a 'thank you' from her lips. Kessley nods, says goodbye and walks out with firm strides. She goes left, takes a good look around and changes back into herself with a shake of her head.

I can barely stand still, and I can tell by the way Taylar's hand keeps moving through his hair that he's nervous too.

"How did it go?" I ask when neither of them speaks.

Kessley shakes her arms and hands and hops up and down. "It went great!" She turns to face Vicky. "Right?"

Vicky smiles. "Yes, you did very well."

Taylar walks over to Kess and buries his face in her neck. "Thank you," he mumbles.

"No problem."

They kiss, and we all avert our gaze.

When I feel like they've had enough time to themselves, I beckon them. "Come on, time to save another soul."

We cross the street again and join Charlie, Gisella and Ginda in the parking lot of the Winged Centaur.

"Ready?" I ask Ginda, who has turned paler since we left her with Charlie and Gisella. Her brown locks seem restless too. *I wonder if the werecat-witch scared her or something.*

But it turns out something else is bothering her. "What if the Black Horseman is inside? He'll know I went to get help."

"True…" I tap my foot on the ground in thought. "You can stay in the car, if you like."

"But if you need me—"

"We will come and get you," I promise.

With a sigh, she stares at the ground. "I don't want you to think I'm a coward."

"We would never think that," I assure her. Kessley and Jeep respond with a unified 'never'.

She raises her head and her jaw sets. "If you really need me, I will help."

I nod, and she hurries over to Phoenix, as if the Horseman is already on her heels. I can't blame her. If I could, I would rather run away too and stay out of sight until this whole fight is over and done with.

Unfortunately, I've been chosen as the lead character in this battle. Peace and quiet won't be on the menu for a while, and—

My thoughts are interrupted by Charlie, who slaps me on the back. "I don't know about you, but I could use a drink. And a snack or two." He shows me a wide grin, and I answer it.

"You always know how to cheer me up."

He throws his hair over his shoulder with an exaggerated flick of his head. "I know, it's a gift. I can cheer up anyone."

"Even that gloomy Black Horseman?" Gisella mocks.

Charlie tilts his head. "Okay, almost anyone."

He and Gisella go in first, and I make up the rear with Vicky. We keep our eyes open while we cross the bar to Charlie's favorite table in the back.

I spot Chloe immediately. She's sitting at the bar, alone, with two plates filled with pancakes in front of her. She's not eating any of it but staring at it as if they're her worst enemy.

I bend closer to Vicky. "Is she fighting the urge to eat?"

"I think so," she whispers back. "But I can't imagine she'll be able to resist for long."

I let my gaze travel through the bar once more in search of the Black Horseman, or anyone who looks suspicious.

"I don't think he's here," Vicky says as she leads the way.

We arrive at the table, but I don't sit down. If Chloe is fighting against the hunger, she might accept our help. "I'm going to talk to her."

"No!" Vicky pulls me back.

"Why not?"

"If he's watching her, he'll know we're back."

"So what? He probably knows already. And he also knows we'll come looking for Chloe."

"But maybe he thinks we're still in The Nothing. We can use that to trick him." She falls silent for a second. "And what about Trevor's threat? He said if we kept fighting, he'd make sure you'll never see your mother again."

The corners of my mouth move up a little. "Well, my premonition showed me something else, so I'm not worried about that anymore. But you're right about us being able to trick the Horseman." I lean backwards against the table. "So tell me your plan."

CHAPTER 21

I have to admit, I'm not convinced the Black Horseman is watching Chloe, but I agree being a little more careful can't hurt, which is why Kessley goes to the bar disguised as a young Asian woman. She will order us some drinks and try to talk to Chloe without drawing too much attention to herself. Meanwhile, we'll watch the other customers, see if anyone is watching the Mahaha. After all, we don't know if the Black Horseman is able to disguise himself too or if someone else is watching her.

I see Kessley-in-disguise leaning on the bar and ordering our drinks. Then she casually says something to Chloe, who looks up from her pancakes with a small smile. They talk for several minutes. Kessley gestures to our table, and Chloe nods. She stands up, and they walk toward us.

"Guys, this is Chloe. She's willing to listen to our

166

story."

The Mahaha nods at us in greeting. I try not to stare at her blue skin and hold out my hand to her.

She shakes it.

"Hi, I'm Dante."

"Nice to meet you."

I turn to introduce her to the others when Kessley tugs at my shirt. "We'll start without you. The bartender wants to talk to you."

I frown. "To me?"

She shrugs. "That's what he said. He sounded a bit scared."

The waiter arrives with our drinks, and I hurry over to the bar.

The bartender is taking an order, but as soon as the customer walks back to his table, he comes over. His gaze darts around the room and to the door and windows before he leans over to me, giving me a full view of the third eye in the middle of his forehead. "You're Dante, right? Dante Banner?"

It's impossible to hide my surprise. *He knows my name? How? Did Charlie tell him?*

He must sense my confusion, because he quickly explains. "There was a man in here, a couple of minutes before you and your friends came in. Shelton Banks, maybe you know him?"

My blood freezes in my veins. "Yes, I know him."

"He was looking for you. Asked me if I had heard of you or seen you. If I knew where you lived and where your favorite hang-outs were." He shivers a little. "He described some of your friends too. Of course I recognized the description, but I said I didn't."

"Why?" I ask before I can stop myself. I grit my teeth. "I'm sorry, I didn't mean to sound ungrateful."

He shoots me a grin. His extra eye moves back to the door for a moment. "It's fine, I understand." He scans the room again before continuing. "I've seen that Banks guy a couple of times before. Not in here, thank God, but in town, and on TV. There's something dark and sinister about him. I'd say I don't trust him, but that would be an understatement. So I told him I couldn't remember seeing anyone who matched his descriptions."

I relax a little. "Thank you."

"You're welcome." He turns away, stops mid-motion and leans back onto the bar. "Listen. I don't know what that guy is up to, but it can't be anything good. The good emanating from you is just as strong as the bad that comes from him, so…" he taps my hand amicably, "please be careful. Stay far away from that man."

He picks up a glass and starts rubbing it forcefully.

"Thanks," I tell him again, and I walk back to our table.

My friends fall silent when I join them.

"What was that about?" Charlie asks.

I pick up my goblin beer and take a huge swig.

"That bad?" Vicky asks, rubbing my back in comfort.

I take in Chloe, who's watching me with a worried expression.

"Don't worry, we told her everything."

"Really? In three minutes?" It comes out harsh, and I hold up my hand. "I'm sorry, that came out wrong."

Vicky keeps rubbing my back. "We told her the basics. She's willing to accept our help."

Kessley, back in her normal blonde form, leans against Taylar lazily. It annoys me, until I realize it's better to look like we're all relaxed and having a good time than to come across as worried.

Vicky uses her empath powers to make sure we're all a bit more relaxed.

"Tell us what the bartender said," she urges me when she's done.

I summarize his story, and when I finish, I'm not the only one who needs a drink.

Soon, all of the glasses are half empty.

"What else did he say?" D'Maeo asks, scanning the room over my shoulder.

"Nothing, except that we should stay away from Shelton Banks."

Charlie snorts. "That'll be easy once he's in jail."

The other half of my beer is not nearly enough to take away the unease that's been building up inside me. "Exactly. But he's not locked up yet."

"And he obviously knows who killed his trolls and pixies," Jeep adds.

"He can't know for sure," I object. "He can only

guess."

Gisella is playing with the shadows under our table, turning them into a mini tornado that makes the glasses rattle. "Unless he uses his magic to tell him. He might be strong enough to do that."

"Is he after me too?" Chloe interrupts.

Fear makes her face look worse than it already did. It stretches the skin tighter around her cheekbones and makes her eyes seem even more hollow. Still, her kindness shines through them.

Maël pushes her full glass away from her. "He works for the Devil too, which means it is better if he does not see you. We should assume you will only be safe with us."

The Mahaha drapes her thin locks over her blue face. "Maybe we should leave then, in case he comes back."

I try to give her a comforting smile, but with the bartender's messages still fresh in my mind, I fail miserably. "I don't think he's coming back any time soon. But I agree that getting out of here is a good idea. The Devil's accomplices might be getting restless and decide to check up on you, and frankly, I don't look forward to another confrontation with him." I stare at Maël's full glass longingly, and she slides it over to me.

"Drink it. I do not want it."

I empty half of the goblin beer before handing the rest of it to Charlie.

I wipe my mouth and turn back to Chloe. "Did

they explain the plan to you?"

She glances at the door that leads to the toilets. "They did, but I don't want Kessley to risk her life for me."

"Afterlife," Kess corrects her.

Chloe shrugs. "It's still a life."

Kess shoots her a broad smile. "I like you."

The Mahaha blushes deeply, her cheeks turning purple.

"It's really sweet of you to be concerned about us, but this is what we do," I explain. "This is our task. We're meant to protect you."

"I know, but still…"

"We'll be watching Kessley every step of the way while you go to Darkwood Manor with Charlie, Jeep and D'Maeo."

Kessley squeezes her hand gently. "I'll be fine. Really."

A heavy sigh escapes Chloe's lips. "Okay then."

Charlie puts down the empty glass and gives Gisella a quick kiss. "I'll go into the bathroom to open my secret door and send you a WhatsApp when the coast is clear."

I give him a high five and take my phone from my pocket.

"What about Ginda?" Chloe asks after a short silence. "Is she coming too?"

"She's waiting for us in the car. We might still need her help here."

Chloe's eyes fill with tears. "She's such a good

friend. I've been so stupid."

"Why?" Vicky asks gently.

The Mahaha dries her cheeks. "I should've told her what was going on, instead of thinking she would judge me. I should've told her I saw part of my death."

My mouth falls open. "You relived your death?"

She shakes her head. "Only part of it. I can block it out."

"How?"

She shrugs. "Practice. People have tried before to kill me." She lowers her head. "Because I'm a Mahaha."

I swallow. "That's horrible."

She shrugs again. "Yeah, well…"

"So that's why they sent the Black Horseman after you. Their first plan failed."

She lets out a sigh. "Yes, and Ginda wanted to help me. I don't understand why I ever doubted her."

"Don't feel bad about that," Vicky comforts her. "The Horseman has been playing with your mind, which has made you emotional and agitated. He wanted you to go through this alone. The doubts you had about Ginda weren't your own. And your friend will understand this."

My phone vibrates, and everyone tenses around me. I glance at the message that appears on my screen.

Ready, it says.

Send me another message when you arrive safely at

Darkwood Manor, I type back.

Will do.

I put my phone away, take a deep breath and turn to Chloe. "Okay, this is it. Jeep and D'Maeo will try to hide you from sight so you can slip into the men's bathroom. Kessley will change into you and leave the bar, followed by us. Remember to hold onto Jeep or D'Maeo at all times, since we don't know exactly when the distance between us will be enough for them to get pulled home. And don't forget to take Charlie with you too."

She nods tensely.

"Be careful," I tell all three of them. "I'll see you soon."

After a quick look around the room, they hurry over to the door that leads to the toilets. I can only hope no one is standing outside to see them leave.

I scan the tables around us and step in front of Kessley. "Okay, go ahead."

She changes into Chloe so fast that I can barely see it. I lean closer to her and squint at her skin, which is no longer see-through and has an unhealthy blue color. Her hair is still long, but it has changed into a dirty kind of brown, and it hangs stiffly around her sunken face, frozen. Her clothes stand out for the wrong reasons now. She no longer looks as if she's going to a party. She's now more like a walking corpse. She smells like it too.

"Well?" she asks.

"I can't tell the difference," I say genuinely.

"Well, of course not," she says in a cocky tone. "What I meant was, can we go?"

"Oh." I check for any left-over beer on the table and sigh when I can't find any. "Sure. The party's over."

"I wish we were at a party," Vicky says when Mahaha Kessley walks to the door and disappears outside.

"Me too," I agree, trying to act casual as I follow our bait.

"Do you think he will fall for it?" Taylar asks from behind me. Nerves trickle through his voice, and he pushes me forward when I pause at the front door.

"I don't think anyone can see through this disguise," I answer, peering into the street to find Chloe's double walking calmly in the direction of the Mahaha's house. "Except Satan himself maybe."

"I hope so," the white-haired ghost answers.

Gisella slaps him on the shoulder and closes the door behind us. "She'll be fine."

We set off after Kessley, keeping an eye out for the Black Horseman or anyone else following her. We've covered about two feet when a dark shape rises from the ground to her right.

Kessley must see him too, but she pretends not to, like we agreed. It's a wild guess, but we assume that Chloe wouldn't see much of the world around her if the Horseman's power fully worked on her.

Vicky, Taylar, Maël, Gisella and I dive into a driveway and hide behind the wall of the house.

It seems we guessed right. The Horseman stares at the fake Chloe with a content grin on his face.

He follows her at a relaxed pace, confident that she's going home. And she is, but he doesn't know she won't stay there for long. She'll be gone, and he won't know where she went. Especially since, of course, it isn't Chloe he's following at all.

"If only we could think of a way to take him out," I whisper to Vicky as we leave our hiding place.

We hurry over to the corner, and Vicky peers around it, invisible to everyone but us.

"For now, we should be fine," Maël says. "But if you want, I can try using the power of the black tree on him."

I hold up my hand. "No, don't do that unless you have no other choice. You don't know how to control it yet, and we have no idea what you can do with it exactly."

Gisella cracks her neck, as if she's getting ready for a fight. "We should find out in the protective circle. Nothing can happen to us in there. And I'd like to find out what else *I* can do with the evil powers within me."

"I agree," Vicky says, pulling back her head. "I'm confident that Maël will be able to control the parts of the tree from the Shadow World within her. After all, Gisella received a lot more evil powers from her aunt than the sliver that was left behind inside Maël, and she can do some awesome things with them."

"True."

Vicky peers around the corner again. "Okay, we're good to go."

We break into another quiet run until we reach the next corner.

When Vicky sticks her head around it, she ducks instantly and presses her back against the wall of the house.

"What is it?" I whisper. "Did he see you?"

A shiver runs along her body. "I'm not sure. It felt like it."

"But you were invisible, right?" Taylar says.

She shakes her head. "That doesn't mean anything. The Pale Horseman could see us in our invisible forms too, remember?"

I take her hand. "We should hide."

We run back, searching everywhere for a place where he won't find us. When I don't see a good spot, I keep running straight ahead, but Vicky stops me. "Wait."

I duck behind a car and drag her with me. "What?"

She checks the road behind us before answering. "What if he isn't coming this way? Kessley will vanish into thin air if you get too far away from her. He'll know something is wrong."

I press the sides of my nose. "You're right. She'll be pulled back to Darkwood Manor too soon. But isn't Chloe's house on that street?"

"It is, but she wasn't inside yet when the Black Horseman turned toward me. We should wait here to see if he's coming this way."

"But if he is, he'll find—" My breath catches in my throat. "He's coming."

I duck when the dark form of the Horseman steps around the corner.

"Great, now we're trapped," Taylar whispers.

CHAPTER 22

I slip under the car and move forward until I can see the Horseman. He scans the street and the houses. His skeleton fingers tap the wall of the corner house. He lifts his chin and sniffs.

"Yesss..." he says. The sound makes the hairs on my arms stand up. "You're here, aren't you?" He chuckles softly. "Dante Banner." He takes three steps forward and shakes his head, tutting. "You should've stayed in The Nothing. You were safe there. Now you're forcing me to think of a new plan, and I can promise you..." he cracks his knuckles, "it will involve pain. Lots of it."

My heart pounds deafeningly in my ears, but the Horseman's voice seems to come from within me somehow. It's as if he's speaking inside my head.

"This is your lassst warning, Dante. Stay out of this, or I will torture you for eternity."

With every word his voice gets louder until it reverberates through me, making me shake all over. I reach out to grab the edge of the car for support, but suddenly, everything is moving: the ground, the sky and even the car. My teeth chatter, and my elbows scrape the tarmac. Behind me, I hear Gisella groaning. When I manage to slide back out from under the car, anger has taken over her face. She stretches her arms out sideways and beckons the shadows to her.

"What are you doing?" I call out above the noise of the earthquake. "Don't!"

When she doesn't respond, I reach out to her, but she moves back and rises to her feet.

Seconds before her head becomes visible above the roof of the car, Maël pulls her down.

"Let me go," the werecat-witch grumbles.

I squat beside her and look her in the eye. "Listen to me. He knows we're here somewhere, but not where exactly, and he obviously doesn't have the power to haul us to him. Instead, he's trying to scare us into surrendering and into using all of our powers against him. If we do, we will have no surprises left for when we really need them, and we will probably end up in a place worse than The Nothing." I pause to let my words sink in. The trembling below us ceases, and with a last squeak, the car stops moving.

Gisella lowers her hands. "You're right. I'm sorry."

Maël lets go of her, and we sit still and listen for approaching footsteps.

"I wish I had a mirror," I whisper after a long

silence.

Vicky digs into her endless pocket and finds a hand mirror. She holds it out to me with a grin.

I blow her a kiss and slip back under the car. I'm not moving all the way to the front this time, in case the Horseman has come closer. I have a feeling I'll discover how heavy a car really is if he spots me. Instead, I move the mirror until I have a clear view of the pavement. I scan every part I can see but find no bony guy in black clothes.

I turn and scan the other side, but I already know he can't be there. We would've heard it if he had passed us.

I push myself back out from under the car and hand the mirror back to Vicky. "I think he's gone."

"Gone?" Taylar asks incredulously. "Why would he leave if he knew we were here?"

Gisella slowly stands up and peers over the roof of the car. "You're right, he's no longer there."

"Maybe he got called away," Vicky suggests, rising to her feet and wiping the dust from her black jeans.

I lean against the side of the car and smile. "No, I don't think that's it."

Vicky looks down at me. "What then?"

"I think, like us, he doesn't know exactly what we can do. He's probably wondering how we escaped The Nothing."

Taylar's face lights up. "He's scared of us."

I stand up and stretch my legs. "Scared is not the right word. Cautious might be a better description.

And maybe he thought we'd set up a trap from him."

"Like he did for us."

"Exactly."

Vicky taps her soft lips. "You know, setting a trap for him isn't such a bad idea. Maybe we can use the tree remnant inside Maël for it."

I nod. "We'll discuss that when we get home." I glance at a woman with two bags filled with groceries crossing the street. "I think Kess has had enough time to execute our plan, right?"

The others agree. By now, Kessley will have entered Chloe's home and disappeared into the bedroom with her hands full of food to ease the Black Horseman's mind.

"Let's get back to the car then," I say.

Scanning the street behind us every three seconds, we make our way back to the Winged Centaur, where Ginda is waiting behind a screen of flowers covering the windows of my car.

"Are you okay?" I ask, lowering myself onto the driver's seat.

She exhales slowly. "I'm fine now, but you took so long I thought something had gone wrong. And I heard…" she searches for words, "a sort of rumbling in the distance."

While Vicky explains what happened, I start Phoenix and drive out of the parking lot. There's a shadow at the end of the road, and I freeze, but when I blink, it's gone.

"Did you see that?" I ask the others.

No one did, but in case someone is following us, I take a detour.

Ten minutes later, we arrive at Darkwood Manor. The mansion looks quiet, and the crows are back in the trees, waiting patiently for us to make a mistake.

Ginda lets out a squeal of joy when Chloe appears in the window of the study. She opens her door, and I grab her arm quickly. "Hang on, we need you to create a safe passage to the front door."

She shuts the door, and a crow slams against it, hard.

"Eh…" She turns to me with a desperate look on her face. "I don't think they'll fall for the same trick again."

"Can you create a cage of branches around them?"

She frowns. "That would have to be a pretty big cage."

"True." I tap the steering wheel in thought. "What about a smaller cage around each of them?"

She turns her head to study the crow that's now watching us from the steps to the front doors. "I can try."

After a deep breath, she starts to move her hands again and to wiggle and twist her fingers. Two branches appear above the crow's head. Immediately, it spreads its wings and knocks them out of the way, only to land in the same spot seconds later.

Ginda tries again, this time from the side. She forms a flower next to the stairs and makes it grow higher and higher. Large petals sprout from the top.

The crow watches it all with interest. Meanwhile, vines creep up from its other side.

"That's it," I say softly. "Try hitting it on the head."

Ginda twirls the fingers of her left hand higher while she creates a new flower with her right hand. The crow carefully pecks at it, oblivious to the vine slithering closer from its other side. With a quick turn of her wrist, Ginda directs the vine over the crow's head and rapidly moves both hands down and up again. Branches sprout from the vine and close in around the bird. It shrieks so loud you would think someone is poking it with a hot stick. The other crows fly to its rescue, yanking at the brown and green cage that has locked their friend in.

Ginda's face slowly goes red as she tries to keep the cage intact with frantic movements.

This will never work. We'll need to think of another... My thoughts come to a sudden halt. "Ginda, can you move the cage to the trees at the side of the house?"

She grumbles something unintelligible, and her frown deepens. Slowly but surely, the cage starts to move. It hops sideways, making its prisoner shriek. As expected, the crows follow it, continuing their efforts to free their friend.

"Try rolling it, that might be easier," Taylar suggests.

Ginda takes a couple of quick breaths and shakes her hands loose. Immediately, the birds start to break through the vine bars.

Ginda raises her hands, wiggles her fingers and moves her arms forward with force. A large vine rises from the driveway and slams against three of the crows. They are catapulted toward the pine trees at the side of the mansion. The vine curls back to hit the other crows, and they fly for cover.

With calmer gestures, Ginda closes the cage up again and rolls it to the side of Darkwood Manor.

As soon as the birds realize the large vine isn't moving anymore, they drop back down to help their captured mate.

"Okay, on three, we run for the front door," I say.

"One…" I take the keys from the ignition.

"Two…" My hand wraps around the door handle.

"Three!" With force, I push the door open and throw myself from the car. In one movement, I close the door and make my way around the hood. Ginda is running to the front door with her eyes on the birds and her hands still moving like crazy. Gisella is right behind her.

Even though the ghosts can apparate into the house, they stay with us.

But there's no need for their protection. Ginda has got this. In the time it takes the crows to realize we've tricked them again, we're already halfway to the front door. When they rise from the lawn as one, Ginda ceases her efforts to keep the cage intact and focuses on the large vine again. It dances around like a drunk snake, lunging itself at the birds whenever they try to pass.

The front door swings open.

"Quickly!" I call out.

One of the crows manages to get past the vine. It soars toward us.

In my haste to get to safety, I trip over the last step and fall face forward into the hallway. Two people grab my arms and haul me inside while two others repair the salt line I disturbed.

The crow comes after me at full speed. I raise my arm and conjure a lightning bolt, but there's no need. The bird slams into an invisible wall and tumbles to the ground, stopped by the protection spell. The rest of the flock joins it, pecking uselessly at the air between us.

With my foot, I slam the door shut. Vicky helps me up, and I look around to check on everyone.

They all seem fine. Ginda is hugging Chloe, Charlie puts his arm around Gisella and Mona reaches up to kiss D'Maeo.

"Nice job, everyone," I compliment them. "And now we know they can't get past the salt lines."

Ginda wipes the sweat from her forehead. "I wasn't sure if I could keep it up long enough."

Chloe pushes her frozen locks from her face and beams at her friend. "You were amazing." She shakes her head. "I still can't believe you went to them for help."

Ginda shrugs. "What else could I do?"

"You could've left me to fight this on my own."

The chlorokinetic witch is momentarily at a loss

for words. "Are you crazy?" she says when the words finally come to her. "Of course I couldn't! You're my friend."

Chloe sucks in her breath, making her look even skinnier than she already did. Her shoulder bones stick out, and I can see every bone in her face. "I'm sorry," she says. "I should've trusted you." Her lips form a solemn smile. "I'm just not used to having a real friend."

Mona throws some sparkles onto her, and she looks a little less blue. "Get used to it, girl, because you've found yourself a whole bunch of friends now."

Chloe stares at the floor and shuffles her bare feet. "Why would you want to be friends with me?"

D'Maeo steps up to her, puts a finger under her chin and lifts her head. "Why wouldn't we?"

She blushes. "Because I'm an evil creature."

The old ghost tilts his head and raises his eyebrows. "Are you really?"

"Yes, I am." It comes out more confident than anything I've heard her say so far. "I've killed people."

"Good people?" I ask.

She nods. Sorrow pulls at her jaw.

Ginda strokes her back. "That wasn't your fault, and you know it. You were five, Chloe, and they threatened you."

The Mahaha shakes her head. "That doesn't matter."

"Sure it does," Ginda insists. "If you hadn't

defended yourself, they would've killed you."

There's a short silence. D'Maeo's hand moves to Chloe's cheek. "The fact that you mourn for the people you hurt shows the kindness in your heart."

"Few people are good or evil by nature," Maël adds. "Some powers may seem malevolent, but it is all about what you use them for."

Chloe balls her fists. "I want to use them to help people."

"Tell you what," I say. "If you let us help you now, we will gladly call upon your help when we need it. How does that sound?"

Finally, she manages to smile. "That sounds like a good deal." She holds out her hand, and I shake it. "Thank you."

Charlie claps his hands together. "Great. Now that that's settled, can we please sit down and eat? I'm famished."

CHAPTER 23

Chloe helps Mona prepare an extensive lunch. The smell of bacon and eggs soon fills the kitchen and makes my stomach rumble.

I open the Pentaweb on my phone and type in 'seven souls trapped in tattoos'.

Vicky leans over to read along. "What are you doing?"

"Trying to find information on those crows."

"Maybe Jeep can tell us something about them," she comments. "After all, he's the one that fought and trapped them."

Jeep is stroking the top of his hat, placed in front of him on the table. "Unfortunately, I don't know anything about them. I don't even know why they tried to kill my wife."

I scratch my head. "You never tried to find out?"

"Of course," he grumbles. "But I failed. And after

a while, I thought, what does it matter anyway? They couldn't hurt my wife anymore."

"True." I focus on my screen again. There's no match, so I try something else: 'ghosts that change into crows'.

"Here's something. *Bestia morphers can turn themselves into animals. A morpher can only turn into a certain kind of animal, while a shapeshifter can turn into any living being. Bestia morphers that turn into crows are usually malevolent. In contrast to real birds, morphers don't usually live in flocks. Therefore, a flock of magical crows is created in another way, for instance by a curse. Thus far, there have only been accounts of ancient mages able to turn people into birds, especially for longer periods of time. Young mages, no matter how powerful, will not be able to cast such a curse without inflicting harm to themselves. Older mages, however, can gain power over time and learn how to protect themselves against the backlash.*"

I look up from the screen. "That sounds like something Shelton Banks would be able to do. He's an old mage, right?"

Gisella holds up her hand. "Wait a minute. Now you're saying it wasn't me that turned them into crows?"

I shrug. "I think you helped a little, but Shelton Banks must have done something to them while they were still inside Jeep's tattoos. Otherwise, we'd be able to get rid of them with a spell."

Vicky sits up straight. "If that's the case, maybe we'll find something about it in one of the books we took."

Mona looks over her shoulder. "Do you want to take another look?"

"Yes, please."

The fairy godmother reaches into the air and pulls out one book after the other. I quickly get up and take them from her. Once they're on the table, Ginda gives them a curious look. "You stole these from Shelton Banks? That rich businessman?"

I nod. "He put a curse on Vicky, *and* he killed Taylar's brother, so we needed something to work with. I cast a spell that selected these three books."

"And did you find anything useful?"

With a sigh, I sit down and slide one of the books toward me. "Not yet. We can't read them."

Chloe puts the bread on the table and glances at the books. "Are they in Latin? Because I can read it for you if they are."

"No, I think he put a protection spell on them."

"Oh." She sounds disappointed. "In that case, I can't help you."

I flip through the book in front of me. I can see the pictures and drawings inside, but not a single word makes sense. "What if I take a picture and put it on the Pentaweb? Someone must know of a way to decipher this, right?"

Vicky grins. "That's a good idea. We can create a false account, so no one can track us here."

I freeze. "Speaking about tracking…" I get up and hurry over to the window in the study. The driveway is deserted.

"What is it?" Vicky asks from the kitchen.

With a frown, I walk back. "Isn't it strange that Shelton Banks hasn't shown his face here yet? Or the demons of the third circle? I mean, every enemy we have knows where we live. We've had visits from demons before, Satan sent us a zombie with a message, so why is everything so quiet now? Shelton Banks was looking for us; he wanted to know where we hang out. Why didn't he just come here? It's not as if our address is a secret."

Mona clears her throat and turns to face me. "Well, actually, it is."

A room full of confused expressions answer her.

"What? What do you mean?" I ask, placing my hands on the back of my chair for support.

"Ever since Susan was taken, I've been working on a way to get this house more protection. When I couldn't find a way, I went for a different tactic."

"What kind of tactic?" Charlie asks, tearing his gaze from the sizzling bacon behind Mona.

Mona puts her hand on her waist and lifts her chin. "I made Darkwood Manor invisible to anyone who wants to hurt you."

My mouth drops open. "You can do that?"

Her smile says it all.

"So, they can't see the mansion anymore?"

She turns back to the stove and throws some sparks around to help Chloe put the bacon on the plates. "They can't see it, and they can't find it. If they come near, they will be led away from here without realizing it."

"But what about the crows?" Taylar asks. "They found us."

Mona puts a plate in front of him. "That's because I only figured out how to do this after they arrived. But we won't be bothered by anyone else."

I sit down and lean back in my chair. "That is great news, Mona. Thank you."

Chloe and Mona hand out the plates, and we eat in silence.

We watch Chloe carefully to make sure she doesn't eat too much.

"It's so odd," she says with a longing look at my plate. "I always had so much trouble eating enough to stay 'alive'…" she makes quotation marks in the air, "… and now it's all I want to do."

I nod. "That's the Black Horseman's influence."

"Did you give in to the urge before we found you?" Maël asks, pushing half of her lunch toward Charlie.

Chloe closes her eyes in thought. "I did eat a lot more, but from the beginning, I knew something was wrong. Of course I knew someone had been trying to make me relive my death, but it also felt weird. The hunger didn't feel natural, and that scared me. So I ate, but not abundantly. With every hour, it got harder to fight the urge, which is why you found me staring at those pancakes. I'm not sure how much longer I could've contained myself."

I sigh with relief. "Good thing we found you when

we did."

"How does it feel now?" Jeep asks, licking the grease from his fingers.

She stares at Charlie's plate for a while. "It's still hard, but it's getting better."

Mona stacks the empty plates and puts them on the kitchen counter. "Now that you're far away from the Black Horseman, his influence must be waning. And he can't get close enough to use his powers on you again."

I wipe the crumbs from the table and grab the heavy book again. "I'll take some pictures and upload them to see if anyone in the magical world can read it."

I reach for my phone in my pocket and open the book with my other hand. Then I drop the phone. Everyone looks up.

I must be going pale, because Vicky shoots upright and follows my gaze.

"Oh my God," she says.

I beckon Jeep. "You're in here."

"Me?" He pops up next to me and stares at the drawing of himself.

Everyone except Maël comes to take a look. "This means it was not by accident that Jeep was taken to Shelton Banks' house," the ghost queen says.

I let out a frustrated groan. "If only we could read what it says."

Chloe frowns. "Why don't you use a spell?"

"Remember the crows outside? I cast a spell on

them, and it didn't work. Instead, they grew. So I'm afraid using my powers on the books will only make them harder to read."

The Mahaha tilts her head. "You think it's protected against white magic?" She sighs and walks back to her chair. "Too bad I can't do spells. It might have worked, since my powers are considered evil."

Gisella breathes in sharply. "That's it!" She holds out her hands to me. "Let me try something."

I slide the book over to her, and the others give her some room. She stretches her arms out sideways. The shadows in the corners of the kitchen respond instantly. They pull themselves free and dive down to wait for her orders. Gisella brings her arms down, and the shadows drop onto the book. The silence in the room is tense; no one even dares to move. Gisella's yellow eyes go completely black, and dark lines appear on her face and neck. She utters strange, single syllable words, and the shadows respond by crawling into the pages. The werecat-witch slowly brings her fingers up, one at a time. It's as if a shroud decorated with letters is lifted from the pages. Below it, there's more text, but I can already see it's English. *It's working!*

Gisella lifts her hands higher and higher. The pages of the book flip, and from each page, a veil drifts up to the ceiling. When all the pages have turned, the book slams shut, and the true title is revealed:

Whereabouts of the most powerful deceased mages and magicians that ever lived

The shadows crawl back to their corners when Gisella spreads her arms.

I can't take my eyes off the title when she slides the book over to me.

Jeep frowns. "I'm obviously not one of the most powerful mages that ever lived, so why is there a drawing of me in this book?"

The answer lies on the tip of my tongue, but I flip back to the page with his picture to check if I'm right.

"Seven mages were captured in the tattoos of a necromancer. It is said that this man will one day be part of the Shield of the chosen one. The souls trapped in his body will be even more powerful when released, since they will take part of the necromancer's magic with them."

My throat is suddenly extremely dry, and I feel dizzy. I'm afraid to look at Jeep and jump when he slams his fists onto the table.

"Great!" he yells. "Just great!"

Vicky hurries over to him and puts her arm around his shoulder. "Try to stay calm. You've still got magic, right?"

Jeep places his hand on his chest, as if he can feel the magic moving inside him. "Sure, but how much?"

"Try it," she says, rubbing his shoulder gently.

The tattooed ghost sits up straight, and Vicky withdraws her arm.

He cracks his neck and lifts his arms. He bends his

wrists, stretches his fingers and waves his hands in all directions.

After a couple of minutes, our focus shifts from him to the back door. Through the glass, I can see something drawing closer. It's hard to make out what it is. Something small, that hops closer.

"It's working," I encourage Jeep, whose forehead is wrinkled up in a deep frown. "Keep going."

He presses his lips together, and his gestures intensify. Soon, more small creatures move through the grass toward us. D'Maeo stands up and opens the door to let them in.

Then Kessley lets out a frightened shriek. Taylar's hand shoots out to comfort her. "It's okay, they won't hurt us."

"I know," she says, her voice trembling. "But they creeped me out for a second there." A nervous giggle escapes her throat. "I thought necromancers brought full bodies back to life."

Jeep stops moving, and the things he brought to life come to an abrupt halt.

"They do," I respond, scratching my head.

"Was this intentional?" I ask Jeep carefully.

The tattooed ghost seems to deflate in his chair. He slumps back, his shoulders hunched and his chin touching his chest as he shakes his head. "I can't do it anymore."

I gesture at the body pieces waiting patiently for his instructions on the threshold. "Sure you can. You called all of the pieces here. All you have to do is put them back together."

Vicky nods vigorously. "He's right. Come on, you can do it."

After a solemn sigh, Jeep sits up straight again, locks his gaze on the skeleton parts and lifts his hands. It takes some time and a lot of effort, judging by Jeep's grunts and repeated gestures, but finally the feet, legs, torso and head are in place.

"Where are its arms?" Kessley inquires.

Jeep wriggles his fingers some more and bends his wrists. "Coming."

In the silence that follows, the giant crows soar around the corner of the house and head straight for the open back door. The armless skeleton steps aside, bumps into the door frame and falls apart.

Taylar rises to his feet to close the door, but I stop him. "Leave it open. They can't get in."

"What if they've found a way?" Vicky says.

The first crow bumps into the magical protection I put up and screeches, in pain or fright, or maybe both.

"Then a door wouldn't stop them for long either," I answer. "But as you can see, we're still fine."

Two more crows attempt to get inside, but they retreat back to the trees after some dizzying hits.

"There they are!" Kessley calls out excitedly, pointing at the line of trees around the lawn.

"Who?" I ask, but then I see the arms walking our way. I say walking because they are upright, with the hands in the grass. They're a bit wobbly but steadily making their way to us.

Kessley cheers Jeep on until he has directed the arms into the kitchen.

"Great job," I compliment him. "It takes more effort than it used to, but I think with some training you'll be fine again."

Jeep stares at the skeleton pieces gloomily. "I hope you're right."

"Of course I am," I say with a wink. "Now rest a bit before you try to put it back together. We've got some more reading to do anyway." I gesture at the book in front of me. "So, thanks to this book, we know why Shelton Banks wanted to free the ghosts in Jeep's tattoos. He hoped he could make a deal with them. If he joins forces with them, he'll be unstoppable."

Jeep rubs his dark beard. "Can I see that page?"

"Of course." I slide the book over to him, and he bends over it.

Maël eyes the book warily from across the table. "What else does it say about those mages?"

Jeep scans the lines quickly. "The first one was a meteokinetic, like you, Dante."

"Only well-trained and a lot older," Gisella adds.

"Maybe we can trick Shelton Banks into a trade," Vicky suggests. "We'll give him one mage if he lifts the curse on me."

I shake my head. "And let another powerful mage run free? I don't think so."

"Shelton will be in jail soon," Taylar says. "So that

would leave us only one mage to fight."

I follow the edge of the table with my finger. "I'd rather have zero mages to fight."

"Besides," Gisella adds, "Shelton will be out in no time, don't you think?" She gives Taylar an apologetic shrug. "I mean, do you really think a bunch of bars and guards will be able to hold him?"

Taylar's face goes dark. "If not, why did we go through so much trouble to find evidence against him?"

Mona places a calming hand on his shoulder. "Because all prisons are equipped with magical protection on top of the non-magical, to make sure magical beings cannot rise above the system."

The young white-haired ghost relaxes again. "Good."

"There is something I am wondering about," D'Maeo suddenly says.

He has been quietly listening and observing, which usually means his brain is working overtime. I'm curious to hear what D'Maeo has been thinking about.

"What's that?" I ask him.

He entwines his fingers on the table in front of him as he leans forward. "What if Shelton Banks talked to the souls before we found Jeep?"

"He probably did," Maël agrees. "I think he told them to follow Dante and take him and all of his friends out."

D'Maeo nods. "Possibly. And that might mean

that the crows know about Satan's plan."

"We should try to find out what they know before we kill them," Maël adds, as if she and the old ghost have been discussing this in the past few minutes. Maybe they have. I'm not convinced I know about every single way they have to communicate with each other.

"You're right," I say. "If only we knew how to capture them."

"And how to kill them," Charlie adds.

Another thought floats up in my mind. "And how to turn them back into human souls. Because it might be hard to question a crow, right?"

"Yeah..." Charlie scratches his head. "I don't think any of us speak crow, you know."

"I can catch them," Ginda interrupts us.

"And I know a way to turn them back into their human forms." Mona stands up and throws around her sparks to take some glasses from the cupboard. "Drinks, anyone?"

CHAPTER 24

It takes us about half an hour to set up our plan, and after another twenty minutes, Jeep feels confident enough to act out his part. He manages to put the corpse back together and steer it around the table several times without it falling apart again.

"I think it would look more natural if you made it move a bit slower," Gisella suggests. "It will wobble less than."

Jeep gives it a shot, and it almost looks like a living person.

Vicky points at the ceiling. "I'll get some clothes." She vanishes and comes back with a pile of my stuff in her hands: trousers, a long-sleeved shirt and shoes. She walks over to the skeleton and starts dressing him.

"Hold up your arm," she says, as if the corpse can still move on its own.

Jeep raises two fingers, and the arm shoots up.

"Not that far," Vicky laughs, and Jeep drops his fingers a bit.

Lifting the legs is a bit harder because the skeleton starts to wobble on one leg. But with Kessley supporting it, Vicky is able to dress it completely.

They both step back for a better look.

"All we need now is a hat." Kessley turns her head and holds out her hand to Jeep. "Lend me yours."

Jeep's hand flies to his hat. "What? Not a chance. This is a weapon. I'm not letting the crows tear it apart."

Kessley reaches out and grabs the hat. She examines it from all sides. "This is a weapon?"

Jeep stands up and snatches it back. "Yes, it is. Please don't touch it."

The sixth ghost draws back her arms and lowers her chin. "I'm sorry, I was just curious. I wasn't going to damage it."

Jeep's expression softens. "I know, leopard girl. I'll show you later, okay? Once we've captured the crows."

Kessley gives him a relieved nod. Then she turns back to the skeleton in disguise. "How are we going to hide his head?"

Mona steps forward and blows a cloud of sparks over it. Bit by bit, the skeleton changes into a real person.

Kessley watches the change with her mouth open.

"That's brilliant!" she says eventually.

Mona gives her a smile.

"Can you make it look like me?" I ask.

Charlie gives me the thumbs up. "Good idea. Then the crows will definitely attack."

Once the skeleton has changed into a copy of me, Jeep sends it around the table one last time.

Vicky rests her hand upon his shoulder. "You'll do fine."

"It's not me I'm worried about," he says. "A lot can go wrong here."

Ginda joins the skeleton at the door. "Don't worry about me," she says to Jeep before nodding at Chloe, who is clenching her jaws so hard they crunch.

"Ready?" I ask, standing up for a better look.

"Yes," Jeep and Ginda say in unison.

Jeep starts his intricate hand movements again, and the skeleton steps outside. It strolls leisurely toward the protective circle. Ginda raises her hands too, ready to take on her part of the plan.

Maël rises to her feet and takes her staff out from under her golden cape. "Here they come."

As one, the giant crows swoop down and land on the walking corpse. Jeep's hand gestures get more frantic as he lifts both the arms to chase the birds away. At the same time, Ginda's fingers weave their incomprehensible patterns.

At first, I think it's not working. There are no plants popping out of the ground. But then, the chlorokinetic witch pushes both hands forward hard, and seven flesh-eating flowers shoot up from the grass around the skeleton. With a couple more twirls of her hands, she instructs the plants to gobble up a crow each. Five of them are caught by surprise, wriggling inside to break free, but the other two flee into the air. Ginda's hand shoots up, and one of the flesh-eating flowers grows at dazzling speed, folding its giant mouth around one of the birds. With her other hand, she steers three plants up at once. But the seventh crow is fast and smarter than its mates. It flies out of reach and toward the trees. I stand up, walk around the table, and come to a halt behind Jeep and Ginda. Chloe and Kessley barely notice me passing them. They wring their hands and watch with their mouths open.

Jeep turns the skeleton around and sends it back to the house, probably hoping the crow will follow.

"It's not falling for it anymore," Gisella comments as the bird lands on the nearest pine tree.

"Doesn't... matter," Ginda pants. "I've got... this."

She brings her hands closer to each other, bending and wriggling her fingers fast.

The crow tilts its head, as if it's trying to figure out a way to free its mates. From behind it, I see two vines closing in on the bird. Another flesh-eating flower appears above it. The white petals grow out of a branch. It opens its mouth, showing two rows of tiny sharp teeth.

When the crow hops a little to the left, the vines reach out. One of them grabs the tail, but the bird pulls itself free, shrieking in anger. It takes off into the air once more, but this time, it doesn't get far. The white flower swallows it up, and silence descends on the garden.

Kessley hops up and down and claps excitedly. "Way to go!"

Jeep lets out a relieved sigh and lowers his hands. Immediately, the corpse falls onto its face.

"Hey, I washed those clothes yesterday!" Mona exclaims.

"Sorry." Jeep directs the skeleton onto its feet again, but when he tries to steer it toward us, it doesn't obey. After some careful gestures, he lets out a frustrated groan and opens his arms wide, nearly knocking Ginda over. The skeleton thrusts his arms out too with so much force that they fall off, taking the sleeves of my shirt with them as they tumble to the ground.

Now it's my turn to yell, "Hey!" I place my hands on my waist, but when I see the exasperation on Jeep's face, I grin and slap him on the back. "Never mind, that shirt looks better without sleeves anyway."

"Do not worry," Maël tunes in. "We will get all of your powers back."

Jeep's mood brightens a bit when Ginda steers the flesh-eating flowers into the protective circle. Then she relaxes and shakes her hands. "That went better than expected."

I frown. "What do you mean? You didn't think it was going to work?"

She blushes. "Well, I wasn't completely sure. I haven't tried this on anything so…" she searches for the right word, "… active."

Chloe walks up to her and nudges her gently. "I knew you could do it."

D'Maeo turns to me in his chair. "Then it's time to cast the spell for the cages, Dante."

I nod. "Yes, I'll get to work. You guys watch those flowers, make sure the crows don't escape. If anything out of the ordinary happens, let me know. And, Jeep, you go upstairs and rest. You need it."

To my surprise, he doesn't protest and vanishes with a tap against his hat.

Vicky and I go into the annex to prepare the spell. As she hands me a bowl and some salt, she leans over and gives me a long kiss.

It's only when I gasp for breath that she lets go.

"What was that for?" I ask, unable to hold in a wide grin.

She shrugs. "I needed a kiss." A blush creeps up to her cheeks. "Okay, and I think you're irresistible when you order us around."

"Am I now?" I put down the bowl and salt and wrap my arms around her.

I can almost hear the electricity between us crackle as our tongues touch. Tingles spread all over my body when her cold fingers caress the skin above my waist.

"We should be working on the spell," Vicky whispers when I pause for air.

I stroke the back of her neck. "I know."

We let go of each other and concentrate on setting everything up.

I must be getting better at this because I've drawn a circle and mixed the herbs, four handfuls of four different ones, in about two minutes. Vicky puts the candles in place and hands me seven glasses.

"I hope these weren't expensive," I joke.

Vicky steps back. "Do you remember the words?"

I snort. "Of course not. I'm getting better at everything, but my memory is still not the best." I grab the spell I wrote earlier, when we came up with this plan, from my pocket and read it twice. Vicky takes it from me, and I light the candles. Then I raise the tower of glasses above my head.

"Turn these glasses into cages,
able to hold the strongest mages.
Make them grow with every change,
however the molecules rearrange."

I take the top glass and hold it above the flame of each candle until it starts to change form. Then I put it down in the middle of the circle and repeat the process with the other six glasses.

Once they're all in a circle of their own on the floor, I carefully step in the middle with the bowl of herbs in my hands. I sprinkle them over the glass forms while I slowly turn four times.

"Herbs of power, four times four,

make these glass prisons secure.
No magic force, except for mine,
can free whatever is confined."

When the last of the herbs touches the glass shapes, there's a loud screech, like a knife scratching something into ice. The herbs go up in smoke and mix with the changing glass. Glass bars are formed on one side of the glass boxes they've turned into. Simultaneously, they open, as if inviting prisoners in, and the candles are blown out.

I rub the remnants of the herbs on my pants and carefully reach for one of the cages, which is only a bit bigger than a shoe box. It's not as heavy as it looks with its thick walls. There are little specks of herb dust on the walls.

"Try the bars," Vicky says, and I pull at them as hard as I can. They don't budge.

I close the door and pull again. "It's really solid."

Vicky steps up next to me. "How do you open it?"

I frown at the box. "Eh…" I try again, and now the door swings open without trouble.

Vicky takes it from me, shuts the door and yanks. Nothing happens.

I cross my arms over my chest. "What, you thought my spell wouldn't work?"

She grins and hands the cage back to me. "Just checking. We don't want those crows to escape."

We each pick up two boxes and walk back to the kitchen.

"We're ready," I say, and I nod at the annex. "Can someone pick up the remaining three cages, please?"

Taylar and Kessley immediately hurry to the annex, and we all file out into the garden. Jeep apparates next to me. I want to tell him to take a longer break, but I'm actually glad to have him by my side, so I swallow my words.

We keep away from the protective circle, all a bit nervous around those big flesh-eating flowers, even though they look kind of friendly with their mouths closed.

"What now?" I ask Ginda.

The chlorokinetic witch pushes her fluttering hair behind her ears and steps into the circle. "Hand me the cages, I'll put them in place."

I hold out both boxes, but D'Maeo's voice stops Ginda from taking them. "We should try one first, to see what happens. We don't want all of the crows to grow or mutate into something more dangerous, do we?"

I drop one arm. "Right. Good call."

Ginda takes one box from me, and we put the rest in a stack about two feet from the protective circle. My heartbeat quickens as the flower witch puts the cage between her and the nearest flesh-eating plant. She raises her arms and takes a deep breath. This time, her fingers move slowly and purposefully. The plant responds by bending forward. Little by little, the white 'head' disappears into the box. The stem doesn't seem willing to follow, but eventually, with some extra twists of her wrist, Ginda directs the whole plant into the cage. She closes it and pulls the door to make sure it doesn't open again.

"Ready?" she asks.

We all nod, unable to speak because of the tension. Who knows what kind of monster it will turn into if this backfires again.

Charlie must be thinking the same thing, because he is conjuring a large grease ball. Maël has her staff at the ready, and Vicky is holding up a sword. D'Maeo steps in front of Chloe with his hands raised, ready to use his powers of deflection. Mona is standing next to him, her sparks jumping up and down her arms eagerly. Jeep's hand grabs the edge of his hat firmly. Gisella throws out her blades, and Taylar holds up his shield after a sideways glance at Charlie. I'm not sure where he got it from so quickly, but that doesn't matter. I almost want to say 'well, thanks for the vote of confidence', but that wouldn't be fair. I'm afraid myself too. We're dealing with powerful mages here. I conjure a lightning ball and hold it up, ready to throw it at the cage.

Ginda takes two steps back but stays inside the circle. Her eyes are glued to the plant that is locked inside the glass cage. When she moves her hands and fingers again, she looks like an air pianist. Gradually, the flesh-eating flower starts to dissolve. Smudges of green and white linger in the air for a moment, and slowly the crow becomes visible. It starts thrashing around as soon as it has enough room to do so. It dives toward the bars, and I suddenly realize the space between them is too wide. *The bird will be able to squeeze through without trouble!*

Charlie sees it too, because he throws his grease ball at the cage. Inches before it reaches it, the bars grow wider, making it impossible for the crow to escape. The last of the plant vanishes, and the crow spreads its wings... only to hit them against the walls. It hops around, banging its head on the ceiling and slamming against the bars several times, while Charlie's grease slides down them.

"It didn't change, did it?" Kessley whispers.

I smile at her. "No, it didn't. Mona was right about the protective circle."

She shoves me gently. "Don't doubt yourself and us. This was a good plan."

"You're right." I shove her back. "But it's still magic, so you never know how it'll play out."

She grins. "True."

Ginda rubs her hands and flexes her fingers. "Can I start on the rest?"

"Yes but take your time. If you get tired or cramp up, we can take a break."

She swats my words away. "I'm fine. And I'll be careful."

Vicky, Gisella and Chloe put the other cages in place, and while Ginda steers the second plant into its box, I watch the crow that's already locked up. Its eyes are bright red and watch me with interest through the glass bars. It tilts its head, as if it is sizing

211

me up. Then it turns and starts pecking the wall like crazy. Tiny shards of glass fly everywhere, and I let out a panicked scream. "It's escaping!"

Ginda stops her gesturing for a second to glance at the crow. "No, it's not."

I step into the circle and conjure another ball of lightning.

"It can't get out," Ginda assures me again. She nods at the box. "Look for yourself."

I bend over. "There's glass everywhere. It's making a hole in the wall."

"No, it's not," Ginda repeats. She steps in front of me, picks up the box and holds it up. "See? The glass grows back in place instantly. It can peck all it wants, but it won't help."

I squint. "Are you sure?"

She blows hard, sending the glass particles through the bars. I wave my hand to get them away from my face. Now I've got a clear sight of the inside. The wall is still in one piece; there's not even a scratch on the surface.

The crow catapults itself forward and tries to peck us, but the bars get wider with every attempt.

"It will hold," Ginda assures me.

I let out a sigh, nod and step away to give her some room.

She takes her time to put the rest of the crows in their prisons.

After the fourth one, I sit down in the grass. Chloe lowers herself down next to me. "Are you okay?"

"I'm fine, just a little impatient," I answer. "How are you feeling?"

Her lips curl up with an icy crackle. "I'm okay, thanks to Ginda, you and your friends. You're a special bunch."

I follow her gaze as she takes in the people around us. A fierce but calm African queen in a dress that's way too fancy for a fight but with a golden cape that makes her look like a superhero and a staff with which she can bend time. Next to her, an equally calm gray-haired ghost in a black suit stealing a kiss from a fairy godmother with perfect looks. Charlie and Gisella are still completely focused on the remaining flesh-eating flowers, ready to jump into action if needed. Gisella, quite literally, with her cat-like moves and dressed in the red catsuit that matches her hair. Although she now also has those extra Black Annis witch powers, it's obvious she's more comfortable with her werecat skills. She uses the shadows only when her other powers won't work. Charlie's serious expression doesn't match his shirt full of colorful flowers. One of his hands plays with a gel ball while the other goes up to his mouth every few seconds, pushing cookies inside to keep his jaws occupied.

Then there's Taylar, our youngest ghost, with bright white hair. There's no trace of the darkness that bursts out now and then. His face is soft and kind. With his shield held in front of him, he moves closer to Kessley an inch at a time. The girl in the tight, short, leopard skin dress pretends not to notice, but each time he gets closer, her cheeks turn redder. Vicky is standing next to her, watching Ginda work with interest, but glancing at Jeep on her left every few seconds. She's the hottest girl here, with her blonde-tipped black hair and dressed fully in black. The combination of lace and leather she wears reflects her personality: tough and soft at the same time. Although Jeep is much older, in human as well as ghost years, she seems protective towards him. It used to be the other way around, but since we found the tattooed ghost in Shelton Banks' mansion, he's been gloomy. With the souls, he seems to have lost his confidence and wit. I hope we can give it back to him soon, along with the magic he lost.

When I turn my head back to Chloe, she's studying me. I try to imagine what she sees, probably the most ordinary-looking person of everyone here. Sure, I've built up some muscles since this crazy magical ride began, but other than that, I'm just a boring sixteen-year-old boy in jeans.

"I know what you're thinking," she says. "That you're the only one here that looks normal. But you're wrong."

I frown. "How did you know I was thinking that?"

She gestures at my face. "It shows. But really, anyone can see there's more to you than meets the eye." She pushes back the stiff hair that blocks her view. "You're special; you all are."

I chuckle. "We're weird. But you get used to us after a while."

"I don't think you're weird at all. To me, you're almost ordinary. But the way you treat me makes you all very special." She lowers her gaze, as if she's afraid she's said too much.

I pat her on the knee. "Trust me, we're very weird. And that's why I love every single one of my friends. They're all special in their own way, just like you. You fit in perfectly."

Her face thaws a bit, and the blue of her skin turns a shade more natural. "You really think so?"

"Absolutely."

Her eyes sparkle when she meets mine. "Thanks, Dante, that means a lot to me."

Vicky turns her head toward us and frowns. *Is she jealous? Afraid of some other girl stealing my heart?*

She winks and holds up her thumb. *Of course not, she can read my feelings. She knows I'm head over heels with her. And even if she wasn't an empath, she would still be too confident to worry about me falling for someone else.*

I want to ask her without words how Jeep is doing, but I'm not sure how to get the question across. Before I can figure it out, Ginda claps her hands, drawing everyone's attention back to her. "Done!"

I push myself up and help Chloe to her feet. Everyone gathers around the cages in the protective circle, where the crows are thrashing around so much that the boxes move.

"Well done!" I compliment Ginda. "I don't know what we would've done without you."

Ginda smiles shyly. "I'm sure you would've figured

something out."

"Maybe, but I'm glad we didn't have to."

Vicky picks up one of the cages, not even flinching when the crow inside thrusts itself at her. "It's time for the hardest part of our plan."

CHAPTER 25

Although the success with the cages has given me more confidence, I'm nervous about the next part. The fact that this spell worked before doesn't mean anything. With magic, you never know. Something at our destination might have changed. That's actually something I've been worried about since Quinn's last visit. *If Heaven is under attack, will our plan still work? Will it be safe for us at the gates of Heaven? What if we end up inside Heaven by mistake and can't find a way back? What if the glass cages disappear once we're there?*

My doubts force me to make a decision I'd rather not make. "We need to split up."

"What? Why?" Vicky asks.

I explain quickly, and D'Maeo and Maël nod.

"I wanted to give the same advice," the ghost queen says. "If something goes wrong, you need someone here to get you back."

D'Maeo paces up and down the protective circle. "I think most of us should go with you to Heaven though. If the crows somehow escape, we need a lot of firepower to trap them again."

"I'm coming with you," Jeep says. His tone of voice is clear; he's not changing his mind about this. "If all else fails, I can lock them back inside my tattoos."

"That's a terrible idea," Vicky voices my thoughts.

He crosses his arms. "It's better than letting seven powerful mages roam free."

"True," Gisella comments.

Charlie ties his blond hair into a ponytail and releases it again. Once, twice. "I've been wondering about something." He shoots Jeep an apologetic look. "Not that I question how powerful you are or anything, but…" He hesitates.

"Go on," Jeep says.

"How did you manage to lock seven powerful mages inside your tattoos? You're not good at spells, so…"

"That's a good question," Jeep says. He takes off his hat and turns it round and round in his hands. "The truth is, I don't know. It all happened really fast. My wife was attacked, and I did what I could to get them away from her. Once I got a hold of the first ghost, I pressed it against me. I remember thinking of a way to trap them, since I didn't know how to vanquish them. Then it started melting into my tattoo. Once it was gone, I did the same to the rest of them."

"You don't have any idea how that happened?"

Jeep rubs his hat. "I've thought about it many times, of course. The only thing I can think of is that my wife had some magic left inside her, and she used it to help me."

I recoil. "Your wife was also magical? You never told me that."

"She renounced her powers soon after we met. Said they were too much for one person to handle. She always believed great power should be divided, not given to one person." He stares at his hand moving over the fabric of his hat, but I think he doesn't see it. The memories floating through his head are so strong I can almost see them. "They tried to kill her to steal her powers."

"Sounds like she was a smart woman," D'Maeo comments.

Charlie shifts his feet uncomfortably. "Not to be a nag, but that doesn't explain how you did it. You and her against seven mages? I don't see how you could've succeeded."

Jeep lifts his hands in defeat. "Me neither. But we did."

Charlie removes a hair from his shirt and shakes his head. "No, it doesn't make sense." Suddenly, his hand freezes, and his breath catches in his throat. "The book. Maybe it's in there." He pushes past us. "I'll go check."

Silence descends on the back garden when he disappears inside.

Jeep is still rubbing his hat, lost in thoughts.

Vicky puts her hand on his to make him stop. "You'll see her soon," she says softly. "Once our mission is over, you'll be free to join her."

His grateful smile tells me that's a comforting thought. To me, however, it's like a stab in the heart. After all, it's not only Jeep that will move on once we complete our mission. I'll lose my whole Shield. I'll lose Vicky.

Pain shoots through my chest when I imagine going on without her.

"It's in here!" Charlie hurries back to us with Shelton Banks' book in his hands.

Gratefully, I grab the opportunity to focus on something else.

"Listen to this." Charlie comes to a halt and tries to control his breathing. *"The necromancer, Jeep, was aided in his attempts to defeat the seven mages by The Keepers of Life, who—"*

"What are The Keepers of Life?" Kess interrupts.

"Not what, but who," I answer. "They are the ones that protect the Book of a Thousand Deaths." I wink. "The real one."

"I see." Kessley nods at Charlie to continue.

"The necromancer, Jeep," he starts again, *"was aided in his attempts to defeat the seven mages by The Keepers of Life, who kept an eye on Charlotte."* Charlie looks up from the book. "Was Charlotte your wife?"

Jeep nods. Shock is written all over his face.

"It is said that it took ten Keepers of Life to lock the seven

mages inside Jeep's tattoos," Charlie continues. He flips a couple of pages. "That's all there is."

Jeep's words sink in only now. "Wait, did you say your wife was a powerful mage too?"

"A magician yes, a female mage. Why?"

I walk over to Charlie and start flipping the pages of the book. "She should be in here too then, right?"

Jeep turns his back to us. "If she is, I don't want to see it."

Vicky rubs his back soothingly while I keep searching. There might be important information on her page.

"There!" Charlie calls out, and I pause.

Charlie goes back two pages, and I take in the drawing of Jeep's wife. She looks sophisticated, in a long, satin dress and with a small feathered hat, but there's a mischievous glint in her eyes. Her hair is pulled back, but several stray locks touch her high cheekbones.

Jeep turns his head curiously when neither of us speaks.

"She's beautiful, Jeep," I say. "And a bit... intimidating."

I study her again. She reminds me of someone, with that playful smile and the kindness behind that glint in her gaze.

It's only when Jeep comments, "I always thought leather suited her better", that I realize the answer is staring me in the face. *So that's why he likes Vicky so much. She reminds him of his wife. She could've been their daughter.*

Kessley steps closer, leaning in for a peek. "What does it say?"

Charlie clears his throat. *"Charlotte was a powerful magician who used her powers to entertain people. She worked in a circus for years, where she met her husband Jeep, a necromancer. After a couple of mages asked her to join the Devil's army, Charlotte renounced her powers. Her magic can be summoned by a powerful mage, with the help of her husband, with whom she still has a strong connection. To harness these powers, one will need an empty body…"* Charlie gives me a sideways glance full of questions before he reads on, *"because only someone without magic will be able to hold all of it. A magical body will not have enough room to take in all of the power, and will, therefore, perish."* He licks his lips. "Well, that sounds awesome."

Maël points her staff at Jeep. "This means Shelton Banks did not only want the mages inside your tattoos, but also you. He wants to use you to transfer Charlotte's powers into someone he controls."

Taylar clenches his fists. "As if seven powerful mages weren't enough."

"Well, that settles it then," I say, turning to Jeep. "You're not coming with me to Heaven. You can't lock the mages inside your tattoos yourself, and if they escape, they'll try to take you back to Shelton Banks or to one of Satan's other accomplices. You'll be safer here."

Jeep grumbles something under his breath but doesn't object. He knows it's no use; the ghosts in my

Shield have no choice but to obey me.

Vicky lets go of Jeep and pulls her leather jacket tighter around herself. "You know, the Devil isn't the only one who could use a powerful magician's magic."

I breathe in sharply. "You're right. We could…" I shake my head. "No wait, we couldn't. We've all got magic."

Mona clears her throat. She's been so quiet I'd almost forgotten about her. "Not all of us."

As soon as I look at her, I know exactly whom she has in mind. I hold up my hands. "No, absolutely not."

She leans forward. "Listen, Dante, Susan is strong. If anyone can handle those powers, she can."

"Are you crazy? I'm not putting Mom in that kind of danger!" My voice rises with a mixture of fear and disbelief.

Mona remains calm. "She's in more danger now without any powers to defend herself with."

"Fighting by our side is something completely different than getting kidnapped by someone who loves her. Right?" I look at the others for support.

Charlie shifts his feet uncomfortably.

"What?" I say.

He fidgets with the pages of the book.

"Just tell me, Charlie."

"Well, I think it's a good idea."

"To put her in the middle of a battle against Satan?"

He tilts his head. "She already is, you know."

"Not like that! Fighting with us is much more dangerous."

Gisella snorts. "More dangerous than getting dragged through Purgatory and Hell?"

Mona paces in front of the glass cages. "Think of everything she's been through and how she handled it. She lived with those fits for years. She lost her husband, learned about magic, got kidnapped by the Devil himself, and still she's standing. If anyone can handle it, it's her. I think this was meant to be, Dante."

I cover my face with my hands and try to think. *Could they be right?* My heart keeps screaming at me not to even consider it.

"I can't," I whisper. "I need to protect her, not put her in more danger."

Vicky grabs my hand. "Maybe you should let her decide, once we've gotten her back."

I straighten my shoulders and look Mona in the eye. "She's been through enough already."

The fairy godmother nods with a sad smile. "You're right about that, but unfortunately, we don't get to decide what's enough. We can only make the best of it all."

"True, and the best is not to involve her more than necessary."

"You can't protect her forever, Dante."

A sharp pain goes through my heart at the thought, but I push it away. "She won't need protection forever. But as long as she does, I'll be there for her."

Kessley blinks wildly and sniffs.

"What's wrong?" Taylar asks, putting his arm around her.

"I'm sorry," she says, her voice choked-up. "Dante's concern hit me hard. Maybe it's the booze playing up again…" She clutches Taylar's hand and leans against him. "It made me think about my mother. I wish I had a bond like that with her."

"I understand," Taylar soothes her. "If I were Dante, I wouldn't give my mother those powers either."

"Sometimes the best decisions are also the hardest," Maël interrupts.

I stomp my foot and nearly kick over one of the cages. "Don't try to push me into sending my mother to her death!"

My voice is shrill and loud. Silence answers me, as well as shocked expressions.

Like a deflated balloon, I slump down onto the grass and grab my pounding head. "I'm sorry. I'm not mad at you guys, I'm mad at the situation."

"It's fine," Mona says. "I understand. We're all angry and frustrated, I think."

There are mumbled agreements.

Mona raises her hand. "Does anyone need sparkles? I've got plenty to spare."

After a short silence, Kessley clears her throat. "I do."

Mona turns her hand, and several yellow sparks leap onto Kessley, who sighs in relief. "Much better. Thank you."

"Anyone else?" Mona asks.

"Hit me," I say, spreading my arms.

With a smile, she brings her arm back and throws some sparks in my direction. While I let them do their work, the others give in too.

"Why don't you just throw them in the air and let it rain sparkles?" Kessley asks.

I open my eyes in time to see the mischievous expression on Mona's face. She takes a step back and starts to turn. Her hands rise higher with each turn, and when her arms are fully stretched, she brings them forward. The air above the protective circle explodes in fireworks. There are sparks everywhere, almost blinding us. Soon, we all light up like candles. Another shot of happiness spreads through my limbs, and I lean back to take it all in. A quick sideways glance tells me the sparks didn't hit the cages or the crows inside.

"We shouldn't do this too often, Mona," I say with a sigh once the feeling subsides. "This is like a drug."

"How would you know?" Charlie teases. "You've never tried drugs. Mr. Perfect."

I laugh out loud. "I'm far from perfect, mate." I grin when he shrugs. "Anyway, it's time for the next step in our plan. Me, Vicky, D'Maeo and Kessley are going back to the gates of Heaven, where, according to Mona, the crows will show their true faces, just like we did when we went there. They'll turn into human ghosts again, so we can question them about Shelton Banks' plans."

"And hopefully get rid of them for good," Jeep grumbles.

"We will," I assure him. I rest my hand on the shoulder of each friend we're leaving behind.

"Stay safe," I tell Maël.

"We will be here when you come back," she says confidently.

Mona tries to hide her fear behind a smile. She hugs me. "Keep an eye on D'Maeo."

I squeeze her, feeling guilty for asking the old ghost to come back to the place where he fought the Black Void within himself. "Of course."

When I pass D'Maeo on my way to say goodbye to Ginda and Chloe, I nod in Mona's direction discretely.

He takes the hint and walks over to her to say goodbye. I hope he can assure her better than I could. I understand her worries, but I've thought about this, and I want D'Maeo's power of deflection, in case the mages are able to use their powers on us. Deflection works much faster than bending time, and without it, I'm not sure how we will stay safe.

"I'm coming with you," Ginda says when I reach her and her friend.

Chloe opens her mouth too, but I cut her off before she can utter a word. "You can't come."

"What? Why not?" The Mahaha's blue face goes a

bit purple.

"It's too dangerous for you. Here, at Darkwood Manor, no one can find you. In Heaven, they might."

"No one's looking for me," Ginda objects.

"True," I say, "So if you want to come, I would be grateful. But I understand if you'd rather stay here."

She shrugs. "I'll come. You might need my powers if the crows escape."

"That's settled then."

D'Maeo joins us, and I step into the protective circle to set up everything for the spell to take us to Heaven.

CHAPTER 26

The thought that I've done this before doesn't calm my nerves one bit. Visions of everything that could go wrong flash before me. *What if something blocks us and we get stuck half-way? What if Heaven doesn't only transform the crows back into ghosts, but also dissolves the cages?*

"Take a deep breath," Vicky says calmly. She looks me in the eye, and I feel her powers calming me down. "We'll be fine."

I blink away the depressing images. "Okay, everyone. Make sure you stay inside the circle."

I light the three golden candles that I placed inside the herb circle I drew. Then I turn to the candles one by one with the remains of the herb mixture in my hand.

"Powers that be, hear my cry.
Open a gateway to Heaven up high.

Grant us safe passage but keep us alive.
Keep us together until we arrive.

Powers of High, hear my plea.
Keep us safe and keep us free.
Let us travel to the heavenly gate,
and please don't let this change our fate."

The spell seems to work faster this time. The candle flames reach up, and we're swallowed by light. I squeeze Vicky's hand hard until my feet touch solid ground again.

I'm surprised to find cold creeping up my legs.

With a frown, I look down and find snow and freezing slush. *Why doesn't this look the way I imagined it? There should be a road made of clouds.*

I'm a bit dizzy from the journey, and some of the visions of failure still cling to me, which is why it takes me several seconds to realize we've got company. And not of the good kind.

"Fancy meeting you here," a familiar voice sneers.

Hate rages through me when I face the man in the burgundy suit. His hair is a bit ruffled up now, but other than that, he looks the same.

"Trevor, how wonderful to see you again." Each word that comes out of my mouth is drenched in disgust. "You must be lost. Hell is the other way."

"I see you've picked up even more attitude in the last days," he answers.

"And I see your company hasn't improved."

The panda demons by his side produce deep-throated growls and crunch their teeth. From up close, they're even creepier than I thought. Their eyes almost pop from their skulls, and their lips are curled into snarls. The snow and slush we're standing in comes from their dripping bodies. Their long claws scrape over the rocky surface below.

"Where's my mother?" I continue when Trevor doesn't respond.

D'Maeo, Vicky and Kess tense beside me, ready to dive into battle. I also see the cages with the crows in them. They've grown quite a bit, and see-through human shapes move within them. *It worked. If only there wasn't an earth elemental with a small demon army messing things up.*

Ginda is moving her hands. Only low muffles come out of the mages' cages as she weaves plants over their mouths. Good. This means they won't give away the purpose of our visit here.

"Susan is safe," Trevor says, folding his arms. "Now tell me, how did you find us?"

I do my best to keep a straight face. *He thinks we're here to stop him. He thinks we tracked him down somehow. Let's keep it that way.*

I copy his stance. "What does it matter? We're here now. I brought reinforcements." I nod at the cages next to me. "Seven powerful mages who will do whatever I tell them to."

Trevor barely moves, but the slight twitch in his mouth tells me he's concerned.

We stare at each other for a while. The earth elemental is the first to speak. "You know I'm not the only one here, right? I've got my own back-up inside." He waves vaguely at the gates of Heaven behind him.

I take a bold guess. "Oh, you mean the back-up that was supposed to let you in already?"

He grits his teeth, and the demons take a step forward. *So, my hunch that he's been waiting here for a while was spot on. Hopefully, that means the angels are winning.*

Inside, I'm begging fate to give me what I need to bluff my way out of a fight or for some pleasant surprise to help me out. If it comes to a battle, Trevor could get his hands on the seven mages, and that could mean the end of the world, of *all* worlds.

He raises an eyebrow. "I must admit, I'm impressed. Your powers are growing."

"It's never too late to choose the right side."

He shakes his head. "The right side is the one that will change the world, Dante. I know you don't see it, but we can't go on like this. Every living thing will be destroyed if we do."

I scratch my head. "I do see that, actually. But I also see that yours is not the way to make things better. There's a reason Lucifer got kicked out of Heaven."

My words provoke more growls from the panda demons. They step closer again, but none of us moves. My friends understand as well as I do that we need to keep up the appearance of having the upper-hand here.

"You surprise me again, Dante," Trevor says, with a small smile. "You realize the world is broken. Bravo. But what will you do about it? Sit back and let others do all the work?"

"Not at all," I answer with a smile that's wider than his. "First, I will make sure the most evil creatures alive go back to where they belong, which is far under the ground."

"Do you mean dead or in Hell?" he inquires sweetly.

"That doesn't really matter, as long as they're not here." I gesture at the line of demons by his side. "And as soon as all these poisonous monsters are taken care of..." I tilt my head as if I'm thinking, "... who knows, I might use my powers to make the world a better place. But with love instead of hate, and with kindness instead of wrath."

Trevor unfolds his arms and claps in mock applause. "Nice speech."

I bow. "Thank you. I didn't even practice that."

He lowers his arms, that change into red stone. "Too bad love and kind words don't solve anything. And I can't let you get in the way of our plans again."

With an exaggerated sigh, I conjure a lightning bolt in my hand. "Same here."

Meanwhile, my mind is whirling with possibilities. Obviously I can't set the mages free. But if I keep them in their cages, Trevor will know I was lying. He probably knows where the mages came from already.

His rank is so high in the Devil's schemes that he must know about pretty much every single plan to strengthen his army. And if it comes to a fight, we can't kill Trevor, because that will leave Mom unprotected.

Suddenly, an idea rises in my mind. *If I keep up the pretense that we followed him here, he won't suspect a thing. I'll make him think I'm going for a new strategy.*

Words jump around in my head, and I quickly arrange them into a 'spell'.

I grin at Trevor and hope it's convincing. "You know, the mages are actually not here to fight." I put my hand into Vicky's endless pocket and think hard about what I want. When my hand wraps around it, I squeeze several times. Then, I sprinkle the pieces around me and blow what's left in Trevor's direction. As fast as I can, I say the lines I came up with.

"With these mages, one to seven,
I block Trevor's way into Heaven."

I focus on lightning to make this look convincing. What I need is a spark, and that's the only way I know of creating it without Trevor noticing.

But before I succeed, Trevor gives his demons the order to attack. Vicky, D'Maeo and Kessley jump in front of me, giving me time to conjure the flash of lightning.

It hits exactly where I was aiming, in the spot between us where the crumbs have landed. The panda demons shriek with surprise and come to a halt. And then, something miraculous happens.

The flash I created is followed by a loud rumbling. The ground shakes, and a metallic squeal drowns out all other sound.

I step back when the gates of Heaven tilt forward.

Trevor turns to see what's happening, and even the demons look back.

Vicky pulls at my shirt. "We should go," she calls out above the racket.

She bends over to pick up two glass cages, but they're too big.

"I'll take them," Ginda says, twisting her wrists. "You guys go ahead."

I shake my head. "No way, we're staying together. We'll protect you."

"No need to run," D'Maeo says calmly.

"What do you m—?" I look up and swallow the last word. The gates are coming down fast. They are pressed together by an invisible force, the bars bent as if they're made of rubber.

Trevor throws me an angry look before vanishing into thin air, followed by the demons only seconds later. The gates crash to the ground in the empty spot he leaves behind.

"Nice job!" Kessley smacks me on the back and hops up and down excitedly. "I didn't know you had a spell planned."

"I didn't," I say, scratching my head in confusion. "That wasn't even a real spell. I used cookie crumbs."

"What?" Kessley comes to a halt and frowns at the folded-up gates that are rocking slowly.

"Then how did that happen?" Vicky asks with a concerned frown, nodding at the folded gates.

A vague figure appears in front of us, and we raise our hands to attack.

"It's only me," a low voice says.

I squint at the shape. "Quinn?"

"Yep." In a blur, he moves closer. When he comes to a halt and places his hand on my shoulder, he becomes clear.

I slap him on the back. "It's so good to see you. I was worried."

"Things haven't been easy up here. Did you come to help?"

I blush when he looks at me. "Well…"

"It's fine. I know you're busy."

"Who is this?" Kessley interrupts casually.

"Oh right, you don't know each other yet." I gesture at Kess. "Meet Kessley, my sixth ghost."

Quinn nods at her politely.

"And Ginda, a good friend."

The flower witch gives him a shy 'hello'.

"And may I introduce Qaddisin, God's right hand, also known as my friend Quinn," I continue.

Kessley bows deep. "It's an honor."

The flower witch's long locks twirl in Quinn's direction as she smiles at him. "For me too."

"The honor is all mine," Quinn answers with a smile, and both Kessley's and Ginda's cheeks turn a bright red.

I'd almost forgotten the effect he has on women. It's an angel thing, so he can't help it, but he seems pretty pleased with it, as usual, judging by the glint in his eyes.

"You know I will help in whichever way I can," I tell Quinn, "but I'm not sure yet what I can do. Do I go in and fight the demons that entered?" *It can't be as easy as that, right?*

As expected, Quinn shakes his head. "I don't know either. Your role in this has not been written yet. It'll come to you soon enough, though. And you already helped today, casting that 'spell'." He makes quotation marks in the air and shows his white teeth in an amused grin.

"What do you mean my role in this hasn't been written yet?" I ask. "Doesn't God write it all?"

"If he did, we wouldn't need a chosen one to save us all, would we?" Quinn stares at me hard, and my cheeks warm up.

"Right, I hadn't thought of it that way. So…" I continue, "did you bend the gates? Because that was not my doing." *I hope Saint Peter is listening. I wouldn't want him to think I tore down his gates.*

Quinn looks over his shoulder. "Oh, that." He snaps his fingers. Immediately the gates are straight again and back in place. "That was an illusion."

"No way!" Kessley points at the gates and starts laughing. "That wasn't real?" She slaps her knee and nearly chokes with laughter.

Quinn frowns at me. "It's not *that* funny, is it?"

Kessley is cracking up. "You guys chased Trevor away with a fake spell and an illusion! After all I've heard about him…" She grabs her belly and takes a couple of deep breaths. "Sorry."

"Booze?" I ask her.

She nods and straightens her hair. "I apologize."

Quinn still has a baffled look on his face.

"She died drunk," I explain to him. "And sometimes the alcohol takes over."

Ginda winks at Kessley. "It was kind of funny though. I mean, did you see Trevor's face? He was so scared."

"And angry," I say. "Which can't be good for us."

Vicky shrugs. "Isn't he always angry?"

Kessley giggles and tries to hide it by slamming her hand against her mouth.

From the corner of my eye, I can see D'Maeo's serious expression faltering.

"So how did you come up with the idea for that illusion?" I ask Quinn.

"I was on the other side of the gates with two other angels thinking about a plan to keep Trevor and those demons from entering Heaven. We're still not sure how they manage to get in. Then you arrived, and for a second, I thought you had actually followed Trevor here. I was watching you and wondering how I could help if it came to a fight. As long as Trevor and the demons were out there, we weren't allowed to leave our side of the gates. Then you came up with that brilliant fake spell, and I knew what to do."

"It was very convincing," I say.

"So were you." He tilts his head, as if he hears something, and nods to himself. "I have to go. More trouble in paradise." He turns back into his vague form.

"Good luck," I tell him.

"Oh, I almost forgot." He holds out his hand. "The angel that was supposed to deliver these got held up, so I offered to take them to you. Now that you're here, there's no need to send them to Darkwood Manor."

I take the envelope from him and open it when he's vanished.

I recognize the contents immediately. "These are the next Cards of Death."

Vicky frowns. "Why would he give them to us? We already found the soul they want to use to open the third circle."

I turn the envelope upside down and hold it above my other hand. "True, but now we can find out if they've given up trying to get Chloe." The cards slip from the envelope. As soon as they touch my hand, they turn to ash.

I let out a sigh of relief. "One less thing to worry about."

Vicky bites her lip. "Unfortunately, it also means they'll be looking for the next soul soon. Couldn't Quinn have given us the next envelope too?"

"If he could, he would have," D'Maeo says.

"There is a time and place for everything. And I think all of the cards need to be delivered to Dante in order. One set will free the way for the next. That is often how things in Heaven work, or so I've heard."

Ginda moves her wrists, and the vine she created picks up a glass cage. "I think the right place for us to be is back at Darkwood Manor with these mages."

With a nod, I agree. "The ghosts should remain in their human form now, just like our disguises wore off when we got home from Heaven. Are you guys coming?"

CHAPTER 27

While we walk down the same path as before, leading away from the gates of Heaven, the snow and slush evaporate, leaving only clean, white clouds under our feet. At least, that's the way I see it.

Vicky, D'Maeo, Kessley and I are each carrying a glass box. Ginda's vines carry the other three. The ghost mages inside have settled down. They seem to understand there's no escape. And they keep quiet, although the plants keeping their mouths shut have vanished.

Mona comes rushing toward us as soon as we set foot in Darkwood Manor's front garden. D'Maeo sets down the cage he's holding and kisses her on the forehead. "I told you I'd be fine."

She doesn't answer but buries her face in his shoulder. I don't think I've ever seen her this emotional, and my heart breaks at the thought of the end of our battle with Satan, when the Shield will move on. We'll both have to say goodbye to the love of our lives.

Ginda pauses, and the vines come to an abrupt halt when she lowers her hands. "Back to the protective circle?"

I nod, and we follow her to the back of the mansion.

Charlie, Gisella, Maël and Jeep file out of the back door, looking relieved, although Jeep fidgets with the hat in his hands when he takes in the ghosts trapped in the glass cages.

I quickly fill them in on what happened and rub my hands. "It's time for some questions." My gaze falls upon the seven boxes lined up on the grass. "Who wants to go first?"

"I've got something to say," a voice from the second box on the left says.

I walk over to it and squat down. "Go ahead."

The ghost inside is that of a middle-aged man, with slick black hair and sunken eyes. His cheeks are unnaturally hollow, and his eyebrows scorched. He moves closer to the bars and shows me his gray teeth. "If you let me out, I'll spare you and your friends."

"That's not going to happen," I say with a patient smile. "I'll ask you some questions, and if you answer them truthfully, I won't torture you."

"Forget it," he spits. "I'm not telling you shit."

I shrug. "We'll see."

I stand up and walk out of the circle. "I'll be right back. I've got another spell to cast."

"Wait," Mona calls out after me.

She joins me at the back door. "There's no need to torture them. I've got something that will force them to tell the truth."

"You do?" The disappointment in my voice is audible, and Mona shoots me a concerned look.

"Don't go down that path, Dante. If you resort to torture, you'll be no better than they are."

"Sometimes there is no other option," I say, refusing to give in.

"But now there is. Please take it." She reaches into the air and pulls a thin stick out of nowhere. She holds it out to me. "This is a twig from a Truth Tree. Aim it at the person you're questioning, and they will have no choice but to answer truthfully."

With a sigh, I take it from her. "Fine. It'll have to do."

Mona stops me from walking away by putting her hand against my shoulder. "Seeing even part of you turn evil will give our enemies only more pleasure, and hope. Holding on to our kindness will hurt them more than any torture you can come up with."

"Okay." I plant a kiss on her cheek and walk back to the protective circle, where the others are waiting and where Jeep is still shooting the captured mages nervous glances.

"You're in luck," I say, squatting down again and holding up the stick. "It turns out we have a painless way of making you talk." Without waiting for a response, I aim the twig at him. "Now tell me, what do you know about the Devil's plans?"

The tip of the twig grows. It snakes through the bars and wraps around the ghost's forehead, even though he lifts his hands to ward it off. He struggles to tear it loose.

"Answer the question," I say, and he ceases his efforts.

"I know as much as Jeep does, because I heard everything that was said around him."

"So you also heard Shelton Banks speaking to Jeep?"

"I did not."

"Do you know Shelton Banks?"

"Only from your conversations."

"I see." I scratch the top of my head with my free hand. "Then there's only one more thing I need to know. If I release you, will you work with us or with the Devil?"

The ghost clenches his teeth and reaches for his forehead again, but the twig keeps its firm grip on him.

"I'm… on Luci… fer's side," he admits grudgingly.

"What a surprise," I mumble. The tip of the twig shortens, releasing the ghost, as if it knows I'm done with him.

Without paying attention to the curses rolling from the ghost's tongue, I move on to the next cage. I ask this one the same questions, and he gives me the same answers. By the time I reach the last cage, my hands are balled in frustration. *This was our chance to find out more about Satan's plans or about Shelton Banks. I was hoping one of them knew something about the curse he put on Vicky. I still don't understand why he chose to curse Vicky instead of me. What is so special about her ancestor?*

Wearily, I hold out the twig to the last mage, wait for the tip to fold around his head and start again.

"What do you know about the Devil's plans?"

"Nothing." He spits the word out angrily, and for a second, his head flickers, and the crow he was shines through. "Nothing more than the others."

I glance over my shoulder to where Mona is watching. "What's happening? Are they turning back?"

The fairy godmother shakes her head. "I think he's fighting the power of the Tree of Truth. He's trying to turn back into his bird form so that he can't speak anymore."

Hope flickers in my chest. "That must mean he's got something important to say."

I turn my attention back to the seventh mage. "Do you know Shelton Banks?"

The mage tilts his head to all sides in a robotic way, his beady eyes and beak appearing for milliseconds at a time. The twig holds on, no matter how often he changes, forcing the ghost to answer my question. "I do."

"How do you know him?"

He flaps his wings, that briefly return. "We were friends once, a long time ago."

"Why did Shelton Banks put a curse on Vicky?"

"I do not know."

My shoulders sag. I look around for help. *What else can I ask him? He must know something we can use.*

Mona walks up to me. "Ask him for Shelton Banks' true name."

"What do you mean his—"

"Just try it."

"Okay. What is Shelton Banks' true name?"

The mage lets out a scream of frustration, followed by a bird-like screech. He scratches the walls and shakes his head violently. Black feathers appear on his neck.

"Tell me!" I yell impatiently.

He presses his lips together, but the answer is pushed through them. "Clifford... Wilton."

Mona straightens up and claps her hands. "Finally, some useful information."

The tip of the twig releases the ghost's forehead, and he shrinks against the back wall of the cage, defeated. Only now do I remember what Mona once told me. 'Using someone else's name can sometimes give you power over them.'

I hand the twig back to the fairy godmother and rise.

"So now what?" I ask her, stretching my legs several times to wake them up.

"Now, we use his real name to get what we need."

She turns elegantly, and while she walks back to the mansion, she reaches up and presses the twig into

246

the air. It vanishes without a trace. "Come!" she calls over her shoulder. "We've got work to do."

Back in the kitchen, we all drop down into our usual seats around the table and wait anxiously for Mona to explain. She looks around the table with a satisfied expression. "With Shelton Banks' true name, you can find out everything you want to know about the curse he put on Vicky."

I scratch my head. "I still don't understand how this 'using someone else's name gives you power' thing works. What does that mean?"

"Well, there's two ways to use that power." Mona holds up one finger. "The first is to use a name in a spell, which makes the spell harder to counter or break." She raises another finger. "The second method is to find out someone's true name. This gives you more power over them than any spell."

Kessley shakes her head, making her bleached hair jump around her shoulders. "I don't get it. What is a 'true name'?"

"Some wizards and witches bind their name to the darkness. This increases their powers in exchange for loyalty. They are given a new name, and the real one is erased from history. Only a select few will know it. If these wizards ever 'stray'..." she makes quotations marks in the air, "... from the path of darkness, evil will find them and swallow them, using their true name to do so."

Charlie shivers. "What does that mean?"

"I don't have the details, but I think it means they will be tortured in Hell or some other evil prison for eternity."

"Lovely," Vicky mumbles.

Taylar's face distorts with malicious delight. "Can we trick the darkness into locking up Shelton Banks?"

Mona gives him a sad smile. "Unfortunately not. Or at least, I don't know how. But his true name doesn't only give power to the darkness, it gives power to anyone who knows it."

"But how?" I ask, my voice dripping with impatience.

Mona sits back in her chair and rubs her chin. "Well, if you are face to face with him, and you call him by his true name, he will have no choice but to answer all of your questions. You can ask him why he put that spell on Vicky and force him to lift it."

"So we can control him with his name?" I ask. "Make him do whatever we want?"

She lowers her hand and sighs. "Normally, that would be a yes. But with a powerful mage like him, I'm not sure."

Taylar throws his hands up in desperation. "What difference does it make? What good is his true name to us? He'll kill us all as soon as he sees us. We would be lucky to get one question or command out."

Mona's face lights up. I can almost see an idea forming in her mind. "There might be a way."

CHAPTER 28

After Mona has explained her idea, the atmosphere in the kitchen brightens up considerably.

Suddenly restless, because this could finally mean total freedom for Vicky, I stand up and pace back and forth between one end of the table and the other.

I glance at the row of glass cages in the back garden. "I think it's a great idea, but I don't feel comfortable leaving those mages out there, even if they're trapped. And I'm not taking them inside. So we need a way to get rid of them first."

"I agree," Maël says. "The sooner we eliminate them, the better."

I lean against the kitchen counter. "Any ideas on how?"

D'Maeo rises to his feet and turns to look at the cages. "It looks like their crow forms aren't returning. Shelton Banks' spell on them must be broken." He shoots me a sideways glance. "Your magic will probably work on them now."

I sigh. "I don't know, D'Maeo. Are we really willing to settle for 'probably'? What if magic makes them grow or mutate again?"

He smiles. "There aren't many guarantees in life. I think you should try it on one of them first."

Since I'm still not sure, I turn to the others. "What do you guys think?"

When they all start talking at the same time, I raise my hand. "Let me put it another way. Who thinks I should try a spell on one mage?"

All hands, except for Jeep's, go up.

"Why don't you want me to cast a spell?" I ask the tattooed ghost.

He rolls up his sleeves, and for a moment, the tattoo on his lower arm seems to move again. I blink to lose the image that must still be stuck in my head, the image of how Jeep used to look. These motionless tattoos are still odd to me.

"Forget it," he says. "It's a good idea."

"No, tell me what you're thinking. Please."

He rubs his arm in thought. "It's fine, really." He hesitates. "But… they've tortured me for so long." He rubs his arm harder. "I'm afraid it will feel like unfinished business if I don't take care of them myself."

As quickly as I can, I go over the possibilities. *Could he use his necromancer powers, or what's left of them, to vanquish the mages? Can they be killed with non-magical weapons? Since they're powerful, I would say no to both.*

A thought makes my lips curl up. "You know what? I think we can arrange that."

Jeep's face shows a mixture of surprise and relief. "Really?"

"Well, if we join forces, you can do the actual killing. Would that be enough?"

"That would be great."

"Wait, wait, wait." Vicky says from the other side of the table. "I don't think that's smart."

"Why not?" we ask in unison.

"You want to put Jeep's life in danger by putting him face to face with seven powerful mages?"

I chuckle. "Not at the same time!"

"Even one would be too dangerous."

Maël clears her throat. "I disagree. We will all be here to back him up in case something goes wrong."

Vicky lowers her gaze to the table. "I still don't like it."

I want to walk over to her, but Jeep beats me to it. He apparates to her and takes her hands in his. "I understand why you're worried, but we won't get separated again. We'll be fine."

Tears well up in her eyes, and she buries her face in his chest.

My throat clogs up, and I try to think of a way to soothe her. I walk to the table and lean on the back of Jeep's empty chair. "Okay, how's this…" Vicky looks up and wipes her cheeks. "I try a small spell on one of the mages first. If that works, I'll turn them all solid so that Jeep can kill them one at a time. We'll all stay close and intervene if something even appears to go wrong. What do you think?"

I can see the wheels turning inside Vicky's head. Jeep strokes her back but remains silent. So do the others. Everyone knows it's now up to Vicky to decide.

Finally, she nods. "Okay."

Jeep hugs her again and kisses her on her forehead. "Good choice. I wasn't looking forward to dealing with unfinished business."

I can tell by the relieved expressions around the table that the others are happy with Vicky's choice too.

She wastes no time with small talk and gathers some ingredients from her endless pocket.

"What's that?" I ask, pointing at some lime-yellow flowers.

"Those are flowers from the lady's mantle. You can use them for transformation."

Kessley stands up for a closer look at everything that Vicky puts on the table. "How come you know so much about this stuff? You're not a magician, are you?"

Vicky shakes her head. "No, but I've always been interested in spells. My mother was too. We read all kinds of books about spells and herbs, and about the use of candles. I'm pretty good at spells too, but mages and magicians are born with spell-casting powers, so I leave them to Dante."

Kessley's mouth falls open. "You can cast spells even if you're not a magician?"

Vicky smiles. "Technically speaking, sure. Anyone with magic can learn how to do it, but to do it well, you need talent. Without talent, things tend to blow up in your face, figuratively and literally."

"Can you teach me?"

"If we ever have the time, I'd love to," Vicky answers with a chuckle.

"Woohoo!" Kessley does a little happy dance before sitting down again.

"Anything else?" Vicky asks me, gesturing at the ingredients.

I nod. "I was thinking of adding hemlock, to paralyze the mages."

"Great idea." She adds some small, white flowers from her pocket and puts her hands on her waist. "That should do it."

I mix everything in a bowl and add some holy water. Meanwhile, my mind plays with words I can use. They dance through my vision, trying to find a spot in my spell. Slowly, the right ones slide into place, and I grab my Book of Spells to write the lines down.

As soon as I put my pen away, Vicky takes the four candles—black for banishment—and walks around the table to the back door. I follow with my notebook and the bowl in my hands.

I set everything up inside the protective circle and point at the glass cages. "Jeep and I will be inside the circle, and the mage we're starting with will be outside, otherwise we can't hurt him."

Charlie, Gisella, Taylar and Ginda place the other six cages at a safe distance.

"We should surround the first cage halfway, in case something goes wrong," I say.

Within seconds, everyone has taken their place. I nod gratefully at Ginda and Chloe, who are also part of the semi-circle.

The mages wriggle restlessly in their cages. Some of them are shouting things, trying to scare us or even bribe us into letting them go. No one listens to them.

"Everyone, take your weapons out," I instruct my friends. "If one of them escapes, hit it with everything you've got."

Vicky takes out the sword I had no idea she was hiding. "I'd love to."

I look at Jeep, who's standing next to me empty-handed. "How do you want to kill them?"

He tears his gaze away from the mages and blinks. "Oh... eh... with a sword."

"Do you have one?"

For the first time since I met him, a blush creeps up from his neck. "I'll go get one now."

He vanishes and apparates back in seconds with a sword in his hand.

I give him a stern look. "Are you ready for this? Are you focused?" It feels unnatural for me to ask a forty-something man this, but I need to know. If he screws this up, if he gets distracted or hesitates even for a second, we could all get hurt, or even killed. Of course, there is the spell to protect us, but I can't rely on that completely.

Jeep straightens his back and clutches the sword he got from upstairs. "I'm ready."

"Good, here we go."

With the herb mixture, I draw a circle around Jeep, me and the first cage. Then I place a candle in each wind direction and light it. I return to my place next to Jeep and pick up my Book of Spells.

"Take the mage inside this glass.
Turn it into a solid mass."

I step closer to the cage, take a pinch of the mixture from the bowl and drop it.

The candle flames flicker, and the herbs disappear into the cage. Coldness spreads from my foot to my leg, and I shake it before stepping back.

"Block the power of this mage,
until it breaks free of its cage."

A shiver runs from my waist to my neck. The candles burn brighter. *What were the next words again?*

I glance at the notebook in my hand.

"For this mage no man is safe…"

"Stop!" The book and bowl are knocked from my

hand. Vicky grabs my wrists and shakes me. "Wake up!"

I blink. "What are you doing?"

"You're saying the wrong words. You're giving him power."

"No, I'm not." The cold crawls across my cheek and goes back down on the other side of my body. I want to rub my arms, but Vicky has me in a death grip.

"Look at his cheeks," Jeep says.

Kessley's voice is shrill with panic when she calls out, "Did it backfire?"

Gisella breaks the circle and drops down at my feet. She pulls up my pant legs and grinds her teeth. "Just what I thought. Look."

They all gather around me and look at my leg.

"What is going on?" I ask, trying to free myself from Vicky's grip but failing. The cold is getting worse, making my teeth chatter a bit.

Gisella lifts her head to look at me. "That mage touched you. It made you change the words of the spell."

"I feel cold."

Vicky rubs my bare arms, but since there's no warmth in her body, it doesn't help much.

Gisella rises and holds out her arms. "Let me do it. I can heal him."

Vicky lets go of me, and I sway on my feet. It's suddenly getting hard to breathe; the cold seems to freeze my insides.

"Sit down." Gisella gently pushes me onto the grass. She wraps her hands around my ankle, and heat shoots through it. I try to lean on my arms, but they're shaking so hard it's no use. My upper body falls backwards but is caught before it hits the ground.

Vicky is kneeling next to me. "You'll be okay."

I try to smile at her, but that only makes my teeth chatter more.

Another heat wave goes through me. It feels as if I'm floating. My limbs tingle pleasantly.

"Almost done," the werecat-witch says.

Calmness spreads from my feet to my neck, and I sigh.

"Better?" Gisella asks.

"Yes, thank you." Vicky pushes me in a sitting position, and I glance at the mage in the glass box. "How did this happen?" I wonder out loud. "Why didn't the protective circle keep me safe?"

"Because you stepped out of it with one foot," Taylar answers.

Vicky stares at the glass box. "He must have touched you when you sprinkled the mixture onto the cage."

I kiss her on the cheek. "I'm glad you realized something was wrong and stopped me."

Charlie kicks the bars hard. "Your plan didn't work, mate!" He turns his attention to me, stepping out of reach at the same time. "What now? Is there another way to vanquish them?"

I raise my eyebrows. "Now I undo the wrong

words and finish the spell the proper way."

"Are you sure that's a good idea?"

I grin at him. "As long as I stay inside the circle, I'll be fine." I pick up my notebook and wipe the sand from the pages. "Let me write down the wrong lines backwards."

As soon as I place the pen on the paper, I realize something important. "Eh... does anyone remember what I said?"

Chloe steps forward. "I do."

I hand her the Book of Spells, and she jots the lines down.

"Thanks," I say, taking the book back and scanning her writing. Coldness seeps into my veins again when I read the last line. *Vicky stopped me just in time.*

Quickly, I write the words down backwards, like Charlie taught me when I accidentally made every evil creature in the Winged Centaur go berserk. Then I scratch my head. "What do I do with the candles? Do I light them again and blow them out?"

Vicky shakes her head. "No, they're already extinguished. You're good to go."

"Efas si nam on egam siht rof.
Egac sti fo eerf skaerb ti litnu,
egam siht fo rewop eht kcolb."

With a hiss, the candles light up again. The cage shakes, and the mage shrinks into the corner.

Vicky holds up her thumb and gestures for me to continue the original spell.

I squat down to pick up the bowl, which has miraculously landed face up, keeping the mixture safe from contamination. Straightening up, I focus on the cage and say the correct words, loud and clear.

"Block the power of this mage.
Keep it trapped within its cage."

I hand the book to Vicky and take another pinch of herb mixture from the bowl. This time, I make sure I stay inside the circle while I release it above the cage. It falls through easily, and I read the last lines when Vicky holds out the book to me.

"This mage has lost all of his power,
and Jeep will end his final hour.
But before that he will get,
all of his own magic back."

"Sounds good to me," Jeep comments, gripping his sword tighter.

The candle flames are blown out, and I put down the bowl.

I bend over to get a better look at the mage. He has placed his hands against the sides of the glass box, and the herbs I dropped crawl over his hands and arms. He shakes his head wildly and grunts with the effort of fighting the spell, but it's no use. The herbs reach his face and disappear into his mouth. He makes a choking sound, retches and kicks his legs. Slowly, his face becomes solid, followed by his bare chest and then his legs and feet. His eyes, filled with hatred, meet mine. "You'll never win! We'll come back to get our revenge. You wait and see."

Without responding, I straighten up and nod at Jeep. "He's ready."

Jeep takes my place at the edge of the circle. He sits down on his knees so he can look inside the cage.

"This is your punishment for attacking my wife and torturing me for years on end," he says calmly. He waits for the mage to open his mouth to answer and drives the sword through the bars and straight into the man's chest. The mage groans in pain and slides down the wall when Jeep pulls the sword out. His head hits the ground, and blood trickles from his mouth while a stream of red leaves his chest.

A light escapes his mouth. It hesitates for a moment before shooting straight through the bars and into Jeep's nostrils.

He coughs and shakes his head, swaying back slightly.

Gisella's gaze moves from the cage to him and back. "That was easy." She sounds disappointed.

Jeep stares at the mage, who lets out his last breath. "It's fine. The only thing that matters is that I kill them. The how is not important."

She places her hands on her hips. "Don't tell me you wouldn't prefer a good fight."

"Normally, yes," Jeep admits. "But now…" He shrugs. "I'm tired. All I want is to finally get rid of the ghosts I fought for so long. I need my energy for the upcoming battles."

The solemnness in his voice pierces my heart. He has fought so many battles already. I don't blame him for being tired and wanting some rest.

He turns back to me and gives me a wary smile. "I think we can move on to the next one."

I peer inside the cage. The mage has stopped moving. He slowly becomes transparent again, until he is no longer visible at all. A second later, the cage goes up in blue smoke.

Kessley starts hopping up and down again. "You did it! He's gone!"

Jeep's face lights up when he smiles at her. "He sure is, leopard girl. One down, six to go."

I rub my hands together. "I think I'll cast the spell on all six at once, if you don't mind. It'll save us a lot of time."

"Fine with me," he answers, sounding a lot happier already. I think Kessley's hopping and wide smile have something to do with that too.

Taylar, Kessley and Gisella stack up the remaining cages inside the herb circle I drew, and I repeat each step.

Without the mages disturbing the spell, it takes only minutes to cast it and vanquish all six of them.

When the last bit of Jeep's magic disappears inside him and the last glass box goes up in smoke, the tattooed ghost stares at the empty spot with a mixture of relief and regret.

I grab his hand when he drops the sword. "What's wrong?"

"Nothing…" he says, but he leans on me slightly. "Nothing except…" His eyes meet mine as he whispers his next words. "This takes me one step closer to seeing my wife again. One step closer to the end of this battle that seemed to go on forever." He bows his head. "And now I realize… I'm going to miss all of you immensely."

Vicky, standing next to me, able to hear every word he utters, flings herself forward and into his arms. "I'll miss you too, Jeep."

I wrap my arms around both of them. "I can't imagine a life without you guys anymore, but we're not done yet. We've still got some time together."

CHAPTER 29

We sit in the protective circle together for quite a while resting and chatting. The weather is nice, not too hot and not too cold, with a clear sky and a bit of wind.

Charlie lays down on the grass beside me, with his hands behind his head. "This feels like old times but with some new friends, you know."

I turn my head to him, my right arm wrapped around Vicky. "I know what you mean. This could almost be a normal summer break. Chilling with our friends in the garden, having a drink."

He sighs. "If only staring at the sky didn't remind me of the battle raging in Heaven."

"And Quinn stuck in it," I add.

Vicky lifts her head from my chest. "We'll figure out a way to help."

Charlie plays with Gisella's long, red locks. "I hope

so."

We listen to the chatting of the others for a while, until Charlie speaks again. "Do you think the sky will change if it gets really bad?"

I frown and follow his gaze. "You mean, like, will it turn red?"

"Yeah, or will there be a large crack or something?"

I shrug lightly. "Hopefully we'll never find out."

"I'm going to make dinner," Mona announces from the other side of the circle. "Who wants chili?"

I join in the chorus of *me*'s going up. Maël and D'Maeo decline, but the other ghosts are in for some spicy food. Chloe pushes herself to her feet. "I've had enough food for a while, but thanks for the offer." She fidgets with her stiff locks of hair. "And thank you all for saving my life. I will never forget it."

I gently push Vicky off of me and sit up. "Are you leaving?"

Charlie chuckles. "You didn't expect her to move in here, did you?"

I shove him without taking my eyes off Chloe. "You can stay here for a while, if you like."

Her smile makes her lip crack. "Thanks for the offer, but I'd really like to go home. I'll be a burden more than a help here. But if you do need my help in the future, let me know."

"We will." I step up to her and hold out my hand. Then I change my mind and wrap my arms around her. "It's been a pleasure having you here."

She blushes, the warmth of her cheeks thawing part of her face.

Ginda stands up too. "I'm going with her. To make sure she's safe."

"The cards have turned to ash, which means the Devil has failed to get her. No one will come after her now. We stopped her from committing the sin of gluttony."

Ginda glances sideways at her friend. "I'd rather not take the risk."

Chloe's blush deepens.

I open my arms. "I understand. Thank you so much for all your help."

She hugs me and then the others. Chloe is shy at first, but my friends won't let her leave without a proper goodbye, and I can tell our affection touches her. By the time they leave, the Mahaha looks a lot warmer than when we first met her at the Winged Centaur.

"I'd better give them a ride." Charlie gives Gisella a quick kiss and takes off after them.

"Good thinking," I mumble. *I forgot we took them here, and it's a long walk to town.*

Vicky slaps my shoulder. "Are you coming?"

When I blink, I realize we're the only two still standing outside. *When did they all go inside?*

"What were you thinking? You were far away for a moment."

I put my arm around her. "I was thinking of all the special people we met recently. The world is so much stranger than I thought."

We start walking to the back door, and Vicky pokes me in the chest. "Of course it is, you're in it."

After dinner, we discuss how to use Shelton Banks' true name to get what we need. For a moment, our plan to make sure the vortex behind the portal in the silver mine can't reach Hell crosses my mind, but I decide it'll have to wait. If Satan was anywhere near succeeding, we would've noticed. Or so I hope.

I write down every question I need to ask Shelton Banks, in order of importance, in case we manage to get only one answer.

The first one is obvious: I need to get him to undo the curse on Vicky. Honestly, I'll be happy even if that's all he does.

We go to bed early, tired from a very long and exciting day.

"Are you nervous about facing Shelton Banks?" Vicky asks when I kiss her goodnight.

I play with the black lock that falls over her face because she's lying on her side. "A little. But I think I'll be safe. I'm actually more scared of not being able to get information out of him than I am of talking to him."

"He'll be furious."

"Sure, but he'll also be unprepared. He won't be expecting me."

"I think a mage as powerful as him is always—"

We both shoot upright at the sound of a loud

bang.

Without a word, we jump out of bed and hurry into the hallway. The others open their doors at the same time. Charlie and Gisella come running down the stairs from the top floor.

Another bang reverberates through the house before anyone can speak.

"It's coming from the secret room," I say, and I run around the stairs in the middle of the hallway. The doors of the built-in closet between Taylar's room and the storeroom tremble with another bang. I open the doors and push the top shelf. The other shelves drop down, and the back wall moves sideways. The next bang seems louder than the previous ones. *We're getting closer.*

"Where is it coming from?" Taylar asks as he follows me into the secret room.

I walk to the only place I can think of: the porthole into the silver mine. *Was it bad luck for me to think the portal could wait?*

The glass inside the porthole shudders with another bang. After a short hesitation, I pull it open and peer into the tunnel. The pulsing of the red symbols inside the secret tunnel gives me just enough light to see where the noise is coming from.

"The portal," I whisper. I could hit myself in the face. *How could I be stupid enough to think this could wait? It probably would've taken about fifteen or thirty minutes for me to cast a spell on it. But no, I wanted to sleep.* A low grunt escapes my lips. "Something is trying to get through."

Maël pushes me aside to confirm. A shocked expression takes over her face when she steps back again. "Get the Bell of Izme, quickly."

"Yes, of course."

I try to remember the spell to reveal it, but I can only think of half of the lines. I reach behind my waistband to consult my Book of Spells but find nothing there. Of course not, I'm in my pajamas.

"I know them," Vicky says. "I'll recite them for you."

It takes us about two minutes to reveal the Bell of Izme that Dad hid in here. The bell was made by the iele, a fairy kind, and can be used to keep the portal in the silver mine closed. Maël is keeping watch by the porthole, and she steps through as soon as I join her with the bell in my hands.

"Hurry!" she urges me. "Ring it, before it comes through."

Her words awaken a chill on my arms and back. *What if we're too late?*

"Ring it!" Maël repeats when I don't respond.

I lift my arm and start to move the bell. Before I walk into the secret tunnel, which no one seems to bother to close anymore these days, I look back to make sure someone is staying inside Darkwood Manor, in case we need our weapons.

I feel naked in my pajamas and without my notebooks, Morningstar and athame. That feeling only intensifies when I get a good look at the swirling black at the end of the secret tunnel. I've never seen the creature that's trying to get through, but for some reason, I immediately know who it is.

"This can't be," I mumble, swinging the Bell of Izme harder.

"What?" Vicky asks, way too close. "What is it?"

I hold my free hand out behind me. "Stay back!"

"Why?" she asks, naturally doing exactly the opposite of what I tell her to. She grabs my outstretched arm and breathes in sharply. "Holy crap."

"Stay back, babe. Please," I repeat.

"And let you and Maël handle this alone? I don't think so."

The bell is now moving completely on its own, my hand is a blur. The inaudible sound it produces slowly closes the portal, or at least, it tries to. But there is a hand, with flaps of skin hanging from it, stuck in the middle. Through the gap it has created, I can see a horrible face with shredded skin, a round mouth with small, pointy teeth and glowing yellow eyes. A face I'd hoped never to see: that of Beelzebub, Satan's strongest warrior.

CHAPTER 30

"Maël, can you freeze him?" I ask, without turning my gaze away from the horrifying creature.

"Already trying."

Vicky lets go of my arm and steps up next to me. "I'll try to get him to give up and retreat."

Now it's my turn to grab her. "Are you crazy? You're not looking him in the eye! Who knows what he'll do to you!"

Reluctantly, she steps back.

Maël's mumbling grows louder, but it doesn't seem to do much good. Beelzebub is still coming through. He's already managed to push his arm through up to his elbow. His gruesome face is getting closer. I don't even want to think of what might happen if he pushes through completely.

Suddenly, Taylar rushes past me. He stops inches from the arm, just out of reach, and pours some sort of liquid over it. The bones hiss, and the white-haired ghost steps back.

"What did you do?" I ask him.

He holds up the empty bottle. "Holy water. I've got more of it."

"Good, go get it."

Beelzebub isn't retreating yet, but maybe his arm will dissolve if we pour enough of this on it. At least the bell seems to be working better since Taylar used the holy water on the creature. The darkness is crawling up Beelzebub's arm and pulling at the tattered skin and bare bones.

While Taylar hurries back to wherever he got that holy water from, Gisella joins us in the secret tunnel. "Give me some room, I'll cut him up a little."

Although I'm not fond of the idea of any of my friends getting too close to this monster, I don't think we have much of a choice. Maël's time-bending powers have little effect on him.

Vicky, Maël and I take two steps back, and Gisella changes into a whirling ball of limbs and knives. Now that I'm not caught up in my own fight—the Bell of Izme does all the work itself—I can pay attention to the werecat's moves. Nevertheless, I lose sight of her after about two seconds. Then the yellow of Beelzebub's eyes is reflected in Gisella's blades. Even though she's moving so fast I can't see what she's doing, I can hear the slashing, and pieces of skin are thrown everywhere.

The hand opens and grabs Gisella by her hair. I

want to dive forward to help her, but there's no need. She performs a back-flip and lands safely out of reach. Deep cuts decorate the monster's arm, but they heal up quickly.

Vicky nudges me. "Try your powers on it."

I look at the creepy arm with the visible sinews and bones and try to think of the best way to attack. A lightning bolt is the easiest for me to conjure, so I start by throwing that at him. He blinks and growls, and electricity goes through him. That's all. *Okay, something else. Ice?*

I picture cold creeping up his arm and spreading to his face. A layer of ice forms on his skin, but he shakes it off without trouble. *Water then.* I envision a waterfall appearing above his head. In my mind, an endless stream tumbles down on all sides of him, but the water stays inside the portal.

"Great, keep going," Vicky says softly as the images in my mind become reality.

Beelzebub splutters and withdraws.

"Yes!" Kessley cheers from somewhere behind me.

That provokes an angry, animal-like growl from the creature. His arm moves a few inches forward again.

Meanwhile, my hand and the Bell of Izme are still a blur. I don't feel my arm anymore.

Vicky squeezes my free hand. "Keep focusing."

When I turn my attention back to the monster, the waterfall is gone. I quickly envision it again and make it fall down even harder.

"I'm back!" Taylar hurries past me and waits for me to pause the waterfall before emptying another bottle of holy water over Beelzebub's arm.

The bones hiss again, and I hit them with a lightning bolt. Immediately, I create hail the size of golf balls and make sure they land on his head. He knocks them away with his free hand, blocking his vision.

That's when Vicky lunges forward. When I reach out to grab her, she's already standing in front of Beelzebub, her back straight and her hands balled into fists.

"Please be careful," I whisper while I try to keep my focus on the hail.

Maël's mumbling grows louder, and her gaze is locked on the arm sticking out of the portal. Silently, I thank her. She's focusing on freezing only the arm to make sure he can't grab Vicky.

When I look at Beelzebub's head again, only a couple of balls of hail fall down on him. If I had time to kick myself, I would. *How could I lose focus again?* The giant man-monster lowers his arm inch by inch, fighting Maël's power, and shakes his head angrily. Then his gaze drops to Vicky. His eyes meet hers, and his expression changes from irritated to curious. His fingers unclench and his thin lips curl up in a lazy smile, showing the sharp ends of his teeth.

I stare at his face in amazement. *I shouldn't have doubted Vicky. She's strong; she can do anything.*

As soon as I think it, malice takes over Beelzebub's face. I expect him to grab Vicky, but he doesn't move. His gaze remains glued to hers.

Vicky's whole body stiffens. She stretches her arms and fingers so far it's as if an invisible force tries to tear them off. Then a shiver runs through her. And another. Her head jerks back, but the monster's eyes hold on to hers.

"Something's wrong."

Jeep's words barely register. I'm already flying forward and grabbing Vicky's wrist. But when I pull, she doesn't move. It's as if her body, rigid and unresponsive, has been nailed to the ground.

There's movement behind me. Jeep places his hands on Vicky's other shoulder and pushes. Still she doesn't move. Beelzebub's lips curl up unnaturally far. His unfrozen hand tries to break through the portal. My heart beats louder and louder as it gets closer to Vicky. *He can't take her. I can't let him!* Cold fear spreads from my feet to my head. It reminds me of the hail I created. *I need to block his vision, break his connection to Vicky. Before he fries her brain.* With my hand still firmly around her arm, I try to envision large balls of hail falling down on our enemy. It doesn't work. All I see is Vicky trembling like crazy. In my mind, she collapses. I drop down next to her and beg her to wake up.

Something moves on my left. Jeep is pushed aside, and in a blur, I see a shield rising between Vicky and Beelzebub. Behind it, there's a patch of white hair.

Vicky's trembling stops, and when I pull again, she tumbles sideways. Suddenly, D'Maeo is at my side, catching my girl and urging me to lift her with him. I support her head and shoulders while the old ghost takes her feet. As fast as we can, we walk out of the secret tunnel and lay her down.

I caress her cheek, which is more see-through than usual. "Please wake up, babe."

A panicked shout makes me look up. "Dante!" Kessley is waving the Bell of Izme at me. I must have dropped it. "I can't make it work!"

"Go," D'Maeo urges. "I'll take care of Vicky."

I'd rather stay here and let someone else handle that monstrous man, but I know it doesn't work that way. Apparently, I'm the one who needs to handle the Bell of Izme, and I need to do it before Beelzebub manages to enter our world. The portal is already opening further. He has pushed his other hand through. Taylar and Jeep have retreated, and Maël's mumbling is slowing down. Soon she'll be out of energy.

I take the bell from Kessley and call out to Taylar. "Use all the holy water you have and push him back through with your shield." My hand starts shaking the bell before I consciously tell it to. The darkness of the portal instantly wraps around Beelzebub's arms and drops down onto his head. It doesn't seem to bother him. He keeps grinning like the maniac that he is, but his eyes are now locked onto me.

"You cannot escape me, chosen one," he roars.

"No one can."

"We'll see about that," Taylar yells, and he empties another bottle of holy water onto the monster. Drops hit his face, and the skin hisses. The white-haired ghost raises his shield and dives forward. He hits Beelzebub in the waist hard, but the monster doesn't move an inch.

Charlie throws large grease balls at him, but they simply melt when they hit. Maël starts to sway on her feet, and Jeep rushes to her side to support her. *If the holy water doesn't drive him back, we'll need to come up with a new strategy.*

Taylar steps back, preparing to slam into the monster again, but Kessley stops him with a simple, "Wait! I'll handle it."

She changes into a minotaur as big as Beelzebub himself. She lowers her head, and when Taylar throws the last of the holy water into the portal, Kessley charges at full speed.

Beelzebub grits his sharp teeth with a grinding noise. His arm trembles with the effort of pushing further through to our world. Then the minotaur collides with him. The horns connect with the chest, and Beelzebub stumbles back. Kessley's momentum carries her forward, her head disappears into the portal.

"No!" I scream when I see Beelzebub's unfrozen hand reaching for Kessley's back.

But my sixth ghost is no fool. She throws herself onto her belly with her hands outstretched to give the man-monster a final push. Taylar drops his shield and grabs Kessley's hooves. While Beelzebub falls backwards, the minotaur comes to a halt.

I slow down the shaking of the Bell of Izme to give Taylar the time to pull Kess back.

"No, keep shaking as fast as you can," Gisella says. "I'll help Taylar."

I increase the speed again, and the blackness inside the portal becomes thicker. The gap starts to close. Taylar and Gisella free Kess while Charlie hits the monster with grease. Beelzebub throws himself forward again to grab her or to get through, or maybe both. Gisella lets go and jumps toward the opening in the darkness. Within a second, only a blur and the shimmer of her blades are visible. Beelzebub growls in frustration as he takes hit after hit. He tries to block the attack, but the werecat-witch is too fast. The monster has a hard time staying upright. Although I can't make out Gisella's hands or feet, or any part of her body at all, I can see where she hits him. He doubles up a bit each time she hits him in the stomach; his shoulder moves back, and a trickle of blood flows from his arm. Meanwhile, the gap in the portal gets smaller and smaller as the Bell of Izme works its magic. Soon, only a small part of Beelzebub is visible. He stretches out his arm to keep the dark void from closing, but Gisella keeps kicking it back.

Finally, the blur that is the werecat stops moving. Her blades turn back into hands as the blackness melts back into one piece. My hand slows its shaking on its own, and silence falls upon the tunnel.

"He's gone," Taylar says. "At least, for now."

I nod at him, Gisella, Charlie and Kessley, who has turned back into a blonde girl in a tight dress. "Well done."

Then I hurry over to Maël, who's lying on the cold ground with her head in Jeep's lap. She's not moving.

I squat down next to them. "Is she going to be okay?"

The tattooed ghost nods. "Yes, all she needs is some rest."

"Good." I turn and walk out of the secret tunnel with a pounding heart. My worst fears are confirmed when I see D'Maeo holding Vicky's hand while she lays motionless and almost invisible on the ground. I slide down onto my knees and grab her other hand. "Babe?"

"She's not responding."

CHAPTER 31

The fear in D'Maeo's voice is like a kick in the stomach. "What can we do?"

"Take her home and let Mona have a look."

"Okay." I slide one hand under her neck and one under her knees and lift her. Then I turn toward the porthole and step through carefully, making sure I don't hit Vicky's head against the side.

Mona is already waiting for us. One look at Vicky's fading form makes her eyebrows go up. "Put her on a bed, quickly."

I hurry across the hallway and into Vicky's room, where I lay her down gently. Mona practically shoves me aside, but I don't mind. I've seen my girl in a terrible state several times before, but this looks bad. I can barely tell the difference between the air and her body. Another minute and she'll disappear. It's like what happened to Taylar because of his unfinished business, except much worse.

I kick the wall so hard it leaves a small hole. "I told her to stay away from him. Why didn't she listen?"

Yellow sparks light up the room. I lean against the wall and watch them wrap around each other until they've formed a large, pulsing cloud. My restless feet start moving again, but while I pace up and down the room, I only pay attention to Vicky and the light that hovers above her. I only realize the others have joined us when Charlie places a hand on my shoulder, forcing me to come to a halt.

"She'll be fine; she's in good hands."

It sounds reassuring, but the words don't have the desired effect.

Charlie rolls back the desk chair and pushes me onto it. "Sit down and take a deep breath."

I do as he says. My breath is shaky, and I only notice the trembling of my legs now.

When I look up again, Mona moves her hands down slowly. The cloud of light obeys and eases into Vicky, who becomes less transparent instantly.

I breathe out slowly. Relief washes over me, even though her eyes are still closed. Mona drops her hands and sighs. "We'll let the healing sparks do their work for now." She walks over to me and smiles, but I can't find a trace of hope on her face. "I'll go get Mrs. Delaney. She'll be able to find out if there is a disturbance in Vicky's molecules."

I swallow the sourness rising to my throat. "Disturbance?"

The fairy godmother fidgets with the hem of her shirt. "Listen, honey, I'm not sure what that monster did to her. He changed something inside her when she tried to influence his emotions. I saw it happening through the porthole. But I couldn't help, I was the only one left in the house. I couldn't risk all of us getting stuck in the silver mine. And you were all there to help her. She wasn't exposed for very long, and she's fighting it, but I don't think she's strong enough to win this on her own."

I wrap my fingers around the edges of the seat so tightly it hurts. "But your sparks can heal her, right?"

Mona looks away. "I'm not sure. I've given her all the help I can give. I'm bringing in Mrs. Delaney, just in case."

"Okay." I nod and bite my lip when she vanishes with a soft whoosh.

Charlie is still standing next to me. "She'll be fine," he repeats. "Mona and Mrs. Delaney are powerful, and if they can't help her, Quinn will."

I smile at him. "You're right. We should keep the faith. We're a great team."

"Great?" Kessley repeats incredulously. "Brilliant, you mean! We fended off Satan's right hand!"

Jeep rubs the goosebumps on his arm. "For the time being, sure."

D'Maeo shakes his head. "No, Kess is right. Although Vicky is down, we have accomplished a lot."

I frown. "Really? We were only able to drive him

back because the portal wasn't fully open. If it hadn't been for the Bell of Izme, which we'll need to give back soon, in case you forgot, we wouldn't have won."

D'Maeo straightens his shoulders. "We don't know that, and we *do* have the bell." He starts pacing, but much calmer than I did a moment ago. "What you need to realize, is that Lucifer is getting desperate." He raises a hand when I snort. "No, hear me out. First, he tried to get you to join him. Not because he likes you so much, but because he knows you are strong and that you are a great threat to him. When you refused, he sent two Horsemen to kill you. They failed, which must have enraged him as much as it worried him." He stops pacing and looks up. "We expected him to send his right hand, Beelzebub, only if it ever came to a huge battle. As a last resort. But he sent his greatest warrior now, even though he has a back-up plan to get the souls he needs to open the circles of Hell. He's desperate, Dante. He wants you, or rather all of us, out of the way before we sabotage his plans any further."

Jeep nods thoughtfully. "Sound plausible."

It does, and we talked about him getting desperate before, but somehow, that doesn't really comfort me.

I rub my arms, that tingle unpleasantly at the thought of a desperate Satan. "Somehow I doubt this is good news for us. A desperate person will do anything to get what he wants; he'll even do things he normally wouldn't. In my mind, that makes him all the more dangerous." The itch spreading through me drives me crazy now, but scratching doesn't help. Instead, I try to shake it off.

D'Maeo starts pacing again. "In a way, you are right. But Lucifer has been struggling to get what he wants for decades. He has done things he normally wouldn't already. And now he has shown us his highest card: Beelzebub. And we drove him away."

His look of satisfaction chases the itch away. "True," I agree, dropping my arms. "But we haven't beaten him."

"Not yet, but we will."

I look past him at the still figure lying on the bed and sigh. "I hope you're right."

Charlie touches my arm. "What do you want to do now?"

I throw up my hands. "Find a way to defeat Beelzebub, of course."

"Yes, but how? It's not as if he comes with a manual, you know."

"Maybe there's something about him in the books we took from Shelton Banks' library," Gisella suggests.

I nod, walk over to the bed to give Vicky a kiss and to whisper 'keep fighting' into her ear, and leave the room. With an empty feeling inside, but all the exhaustion vanished, I walk down the stairs and into the kitchen. It's not until the others are all sitting in their usual spots around the table that I realize we don't have the books. Mona put them away.

"We should find a better place to hide the books," I say. "A place where all of us can get to them. In case we get separated or…" I'm afraid to finish that sentence, so I don't. "Which reminds me, did anyone put away the Bell of Izme? And where is Maël? And is the porthole properly closed?"

"Don't worry, we took care of the bell and the porthole, and Maël is resting in her room," Charlie answers.

"Good."

A tense silence follows in which we're all absorbed by our thoughts, judging by the pensive expressions all around.

After several minutes, I hear movement upstairs. I rise from my chair, but D'Maeo holds up his hand. "There's nothing you can do, Dante. Let them work in peace."

Reluctantly, I drop back onto my seat. It seems to take forever, but eventually Mona appears, surrounded by sparks.

I jump to my feet again. "How is she? Did she wake up?"

Mona gives me the calm smile that normally comforts me but gets on my nerves now. "Mrs. Delaney needs some time. Try not to worry too much, she was looking much better already." She walks over to D'Maeo and sits down on his lap.

"Can you get Shelton Banks' books for us?" I ask her.

The fairy godmother keeps smiling. I feel like

punching her until her lips curl down, but I know she means well, and I'm not actually angry at her, just at the whole situation.

Mona reaches into the air and pulls the books out one by one, placing them on the table.

I rise to my feet, pick up the two books that are still written in gibberish and take them to the annex. Gisella follows without a word with Kessley on her heels. The blonde ghost blushes when I raise my eyebrow at her. "I thought maybe you could use some help, since Vicky normally…" Her gaze drifts down, and she bites her lip.

Warmth floods through me. "That's really sweet of you, Kess. I don't think Gisella needs any help, but it can't hurt for us to stay close, in case something goes wrong."

She nods eagerly, and I feel a bit better now that I can focus on Gisella's moves. Without trouble, she lifts the protection from the first book. I let her hand it to Kessley when she's done, and she flips through it eagerly and looks up with a wide smile. "It worked. I can read everything."

"Great, take it to the others, please," I instruct her.

Gisella places the second book on the floor in front of her and repeats her moves. The shadows crawl into the pages, and once again, a shroud is lifted when she raises her hand slowly. But when the werecat-witch lifts her hands higher, the shroud doesn't obey. It drops back into the book, and no matter how frantically Gisella moves her hands, nothing happens anymore.

Kessley walks back into the annex and watches Gisella's attempts for a while.

Finally, the werecat steps back and shakes her hands.

"Maybe there's an extra layer of protection on this book," Kess suggests.

I hold back a sigh. "There must be. But how do we lift it?"

"Try a spell?"

I shake my head. "I'd rather not do spells on anything we took from Shelton Banks anymore. If he protected this book the same way he did those crows, I would only make it worse. I think what we need is more evil power."

Gisella cracks her neck. "Don't worry, I've got more inside me."

Kessley bites her nails. "If you use more, wouldn't that be dangerous? What if your dark powers take over?"

"They won't," she answers, but I can hear the hesitation in her voice.

I turn on my heels and make for the kitchen. "Wait here a moment, don't do anything yet."

As soon as Mona looks up, I beckon her. "Can I borrow you for a minute?"

She tries to hide her worries while she walks up to me. "Sure, what do you need?"

I explain the problem to her, and she frowns. "Using more dark powers doesn't sound like a very good idea to me."

I throw up my hands in despair. "I know, but what other choice do we have?"

"Okay, you're right. Maël has some dark powers inside her. Maybe she can help. Then we can at least spread the risk; not burden one person with all the evil we need."

"Yes, but we decided not to use that power. We don't want the Devil and his accomplices to know what she can do."

Mona smiles at me. "There's no need to worry about that as long as we're in here. Evil cannot find us here, remember?"

That brightens my mood. "I hadn't thought of that. I guess it's okay to ask Maël for help then."

The African queen appears beside me so suddenly I jump back. "Did I hear my name?"

She's standing up straight and proud again, as if nothing happened. I search her face for traces of pain or fatigue. "Yes, we were talking about you, but if you need more rest—"

"I am fine," she interrupts.

"In that case, maybe you can help Gisella lift the protection from the book." I gesture at the werecat watching us from the annex and repeat Mona's explanation.

"I will see what I can do."

Gisella explains what happened and asks Maël if it is possible to put some of the evil from the remnants of the black tree inside her into her time bending powers.

"I can try," Maël answers.

She takes her place on the other side of the book and pulls out her staff.

"Please be careful," I warn them. "Stop immediately if you feel like the dark is taking over."

"Of course," they say in unison.

I glance at Mona standing beside me. "If anything goes wrong, can you heal them?"

A frown appears between her eyes. "I'm not sure."

I bite my lip. *Maybe this is a bad idea. Is that book really worth the risk of losing two of our friends to the dark side? Sure, Kasinda's dragon egg should keep Gisella on our side, but dark forces can be tricky. And Maël has just recovered from a tough battle.*

"Wait!"

All heads turn to me.

"It's too dangerous. We'll think of another way to read this book, and if we can't, we can always try this, but we'll need to find a way to protect you both before we do."

"We'll be fine!" Gisella's voice rises as she continues. "I don't need your protection, Dante, even though I know you mean well. I can handle this."

For a moment, I believe her, but then I see a flicker of red in her irises.

CHAPTER 32

Mona sees it too. She raises her arm and sends a small cloud of sparks her way. Gisella wards them off with a flick of her wrist that calls more shadows to her, forming a wall the sparks can't get through. "Don't do that." Each word comes out as a low threat.

There's movement behind me, and I quickly step aside as Charlie rushes past me. He veers around the wall of shadows that tries to block his way and takes Gisella's hand. "Gis, listen to me. This isn't you. You are brave and kind, you know. You would never use your powers against our friends."

"I wouldn't if they would just let me do this. With Maël's help, I can lift the protection." Her voice is rising again. She takes a deep breath to continue, but Charlie grabs her face and presses his lips onto hers. A stunned silence follows, and slowly, the shadows blocking most of our view float back to where they belong.

When Charlie lets go, Gisella's lips curl up. She touches his cheek gently. "You chased away the evil inside me."

He grins back. "I sure did."

Before anyone can change their mind, I pick up the book. "Let's sit down and have a snack, shall we?"

With gratitude written on her face, Gisella slaps me on the back. "Splendid idea. I'm starving."

We return to the kitchen, where Mona digs into the cupboards in search of food again.

The sight of nachos lifts my spirits. *We can do this; we'll find a way. And Vicky will be okay,* I tell myself, and I almost believe it.

The others are bend over the two books that Gisella managed to change back to English.

"Did you find anything useful?" I ask.

Jeep flips to the last page of the book with the list of the most powerful deceased magical people and shakes his head. "Not really, unless we find a way to get these mages and magicians on our side."

D'Maeo taps the leather cover. "There are some useful parts in here if we find ourselves face to face with one of them. The book mentions some weak spots too."

"Great," I respond in a sarcastic tone. "So we'll need to memorize all nine hundred pages or take it with us and ask for a break in the middle of a fight."

D'Maeo chuckles. "Okay, maybe not so useful then."

I place a hand on my forehead. "I'm sorry, I didn't mean to be so rude."

"Don't worry about it."

I nod gratefully and tell them about the extra protection on the third book. "It must contain some valuable information. But we'll look at that later. Have you found anything about Beelzebub in that other book?"

"Not yet," Taylar says, already bent over the book again.

"Okay, holler if you find anything useful. Meanwhile, I'll—"

Mona turns around and throws some sparks on the table. "You'll not do anything yet." The lights land on the edges of the books and carry them over Gisella and Jeep's heads to the kitchen counter. "You all need a snack first." She waves a warning finger at me. "You too, Dante. You need your energy."

Immediately, my thoughts jump back to Vicky, and my appetite vanishes. There is, however, no use in arguing with a fairy godmother, so I sit back and try to keep the disgruntled look on my face while I stuff nacho after nacho into my mouth.

"You're such a cheater," I tell her when I find my plate empty too soon. "You put your sparks in it again, didn't you?"

Mona gives me a radiant smile. "Of course I did! You could all use a little optimism and joy." She doesn't say anything about chasing away the dark inside some of us, but I know she's thinking it, and

I'm grateful for her magic.

Taylar raises his cup of coffee. "I'm not complaining!" He throws Kessley a look that almost makes *me* blush. Kess giggles.

Mona's smile widens, and she winks at D'Maeo. I feel a pang of envy when I think of Vicky lying unconscious on her bed upstairs, but the feeling soon fades, and I relax a little. I know this feeling of ease comes from Mona's sparkles, but I lean into it anyway. *Stressing about Vicky won't do me any good, nor will it help her.*

Mona gives me some more nachos—she must have bought a ton of them—and when the salty taste fills my mouth, an idea pops up in my head. "What if I ask Shelton Banks how to defeat Beelzebub? That might be much easier than lifting that protection and sifting through hundreds of pages."

Everyone nods, and I get a couple of thumbs up, since everyone, even Maël, has their mouth full of delicious, magical nachos.

"Great," I say, digging into my snack, "we'll start as soon as I finish this plate."

It's hard for all of us to stop eating, but eventually Mona runs out of nachos, and Kessley helps her to clear the table. I rub my hands to drive out the sudden cold creeping into my fingers.

"Nervous?" Charlie asks.

I nod. "Of course, Shelton Banks is a powerful mage."

"So are you, you know."

"Maybe, but I haven't had much practice. Shelton has been a mage for much longer than me. What if he can hurt me, even though I protect myself?"

"He won't, because your spells work fine."

I shiver. "Except on the crows."

"Yes, but he put a protection spell on them."

"I can't leave you guys alone for a second, can I?"

I whirl around and nearly tumble over, taking my chair with me. Vicky is standing in the doorway, leaning against the frame with a small smile on her lips.

I manage to untangle myself from my seat and throw myself at her, wrapping my arms around her tightly. "You're awake! And you're not invisible!"

She seems a bit stiff when I hug her, and her arms hang limply down my back. I guess she's not fully recovered yet, but at least she's alive.

Mrs. Delaney comes down the stairs one slow step at a time. I want to hug her too, but I don't want to let go of Vicky, so instead, I blow Mrs. Delaney a kiss. "Thank you so much for your help."

"You're… welcome," she pants.

I hurry over to her, to support her, but hold on to Vicky with one hand.

Vicky pulls away. "You can let go of me. I'm okay now."

Without responding, I take them both into the kitchen and put them on a chair.

Vicky nods as everyone welcomes her back, then

turns back to me, leaning on the side of her chair. "You were about to cast the spell to contact Shelton Banks?"

"I was, but it can wait. Let's take care of you first. Mona?" I give the fairy godmother a questioning look. She prepares to hand out some more sparks, but Vicky holds up her hand.

"I'm fine, Dante. I've been hurt before. I can handle it."

"A few more sparks and a cup of hot chocolate can't hurt. You were in pretty bad shape."

She gives me a stern look, while she sits down. More than ever her eyes reflect her age, her real age, and I can read all the hurt and fear she's experienced in them. For the first time since I met her, I can feel the age gap between us. The decades that separate us seem to stretch further and further until I drop onto my knees. My hands fly forward and press her head against my shoulder.

"I know you can handle it," I whisper in her ear. "And I know you can do it alone. But you're not alone. I'm here for you. We all are." Gently, I kiss her temple. "Remember that I love you, even when you can't handle things for a minute."

I can feel her smiling against my shoulder. After a short hesitation, instead of pulling away, she wraps her arms around my waist and leans against me. It feels good to be the stronger one for once, the one who provides comfort.

"Okay," she says after a short silence. "I guess I

could use some hot chocolate. But I've had enough sparks for a while, really." She frees herself gently from my grasp and smiles at Mona and Mrs. Delaney. "Thank you both for your help. I don't think I could've come back without it."

"So next time you'll listen to me when I warn you not to use your powers on someone?" I ask, stepping back and lowering myself onto my own chair.

"Yeah, yeah, I'll listen." She coughs, and I can hear a soft 'maybe' in it. It only makes me love her more.

While Mona makes hot chocolate, we bring Vicky up to speed on what happened after she passed out. She's relieved to hear that we got rid of Beelzebub for the time being and agrees that we should ask Shelton Banks about a way to defeat him.

"Ask him that first," she orders me. "It's the most important question."

I disagree but keep my mouth shut.

I decline a cup of chocolate, because the nerves swirling around in my stomach make me nauseous again, and nachos and hot chocolate don't combine so well.

With a sigh, I push my chair back. "I'd better get started, before Shelton Banks gets the bright idea to put some more protection on himself."

Vicky downs her drink in one go and stands up too. "I'll help you."

I frown when she sways a little on her feet and grabs her head. "Are you sure?"

She straightens up and licks a brown drop from

her lips. "I'm sure. My head hurts a little, but I'll be fine. I'm going to put on something decent."

We walk to my bedroom, where I steal a kiss first. "I was so worried."

She pushes a finger against her temple and blinks a couple of times before answering. "Sorry, I had to try it."

I stroke her head softly, in hopes of easing the pain lingering inside. "You didn't, but I admire you for it anyway."

With a small grin, she backs up. "Enough about me. Do you have a spell yet?"

I shake my head while I put on my pants and grab my notebooks. "No, but I've got some ideas. Will you stay with me while I write them down?"

"Of course. And I can pick out the ingredients, if you like."

"That would be great."

We go downstairs. Vicky makes herself comfortable on the floor of the annex and starts collecting all kinds of herbs and spices from the supply in her pocket. I take the armchair and put my Book of Spells on my lap. Soon I'm lost in letters, words and syllables. They flow from my pen without trouble. Vicky is still emptying half of her endless pocket when I hold my notebook up triumphantly. "Done!"

I kneel down next to her and kiss her. "Need help?"

She points at some herbs, salt, a bowl and four

candles. "You can start setting this up for the protection spell. You did that one several times before, remember?"

"Of course. I just need to look up the words. You know how bad my memory is."

"I thought it was getting better?"

"So did I, but apparently, stress has a bad influence on it."

I take Dad's notebook from behind my waistband and flip through it. The book helps me find the right page, and I read the lines carefully. They jog my memory, and after one read, I can recite them by heart.

I mix the herbs, draw a circle of salt around myself and put the candles in the right places. Then I beckon Vicky. "You should step inside too. I'll be asking him to lift his curse on you, after all, so you can use some extra protection."

She doesn't object, and a couple of minutes later, we're done. We put away the candles and set up the other ingredients for the second spell.

My hands tingle with fear, and I bite my lip. *I can do this. I'm powerful too, and I have his true name. This is going to work.*

CHAPTER 33

I hop from one foot to the other and shake my arms to get rid of the uneasiness creeping up my spine.

Vicky hands me the herbs and spices she mixed and sticks her head around the door. "Are you guys coming? We're ready to contact Shelton Banks."

I can hear Mrs. Delaney sucking in air. "You are going to do *what?*" This is the first time I've heard panic in her voice. She appears in the doorway, shaking a bit. "Do you know who you're dealing with, son?"

"I do, Mrs. Delaney. Don't worry, we are well-prepared."

"We have his true name," Vicky explains.

Her face lights up. "You do? That is marvelous." Then she shakes her head vigorously. "But still, I can't be here when you contact him. I don't want to get near that man ever again."

I nod. "I understand. I wouldn't want to either, but we have no choice." Mona appears behind the old woman. "Can you take her home?" I ask her.

As soon as the two vanish, the others file into the annex. They all seem nervous, except for Kessley, who keeps smiling as if this is the coolest thing she's ever been a part of. It probably is. *I wish I could still have that kind of optimism. But maybe it's because she's already dead, and I brought her back. That changes things a bit, I suppose.*

"Hello?" Vicky waves her hand in front of my face. "Are you with us? You need to focus; this is important, babe. And dangerous."

I recoil. "What? I thought you said this was going to work? And I'm astral projecting myself because that's a lot safer, right?"

She bites her lip. "Yes, I did, and you are. Sorry, I didn't mean to make you even more nervous. Nothing in magic is a hundred percent safe. That's all I meant."

"Nothing in life is a hundred percent safe," Jeep mumbles.

"Okay, okay." I raise my hands as if to stop all the negative, faith-sucking comments from hitting me. "This *will* work."

This time, I draw a circle using black salt, which Vicky made with some charcoal, for extra protection.

To be safe, I draw another one around the first, in which I include my Shield. I put two silver candles in front of me for reflection, and one black one behind me to banish negativity and evil. Over the black salt of the inner circle, I spread basil leaves that aid astral projection.

I return to the middle, where I light the incense stick that Vicky hands me. Then I walk over to each candle and light it. The smoke from the incense follows me, creating a dark circle above the one made of salt. Once I'm back in the middle, I place the stick on the ground and dip one finger in the herb mixture that Vicky made. I press it against my forehead and glance at my Book of Spells, which Vicky holds up.

"Before I split my mind and form,
tie them so they can't be torn.
Keep both soul and body safe,
so I don't end up in a grave."

I hear Kessley chuckling when I say the last line, but I don't care. The most important thing about a spell is not the beauty of the wording, but the meaning and the rhyme.

The heat spreading from the herbs on my forehead proves that my words worked. I take some more herb mixture and spread that between the silver candles.

"Herbs of power, take my mind,
but leave my body here behind.
Clifford Wilton is the man I seek.
To him I safely want to speak.
Create an image for all to see,

at the place I want to be.
Leave me there in full control,
of both my body and my soul."

While the candle flames burn brighter, I pick up the incense stick again. The smoke curls up to the herbs on my forehead and then down to the line I drew between the candles. Smoke rises up in a straight line, creating what looks like a screen. I want to tell the others to keep their weapons ready, but the next thing I know, I'm drifting through the air towards the screen of smoke. When I blink, my vision splits. On the left, I find myself passing through the smoke, into darkness, while on the right, I'm still standing in the annex of Darkwood Manor, watching a blurry copy of myself vanishing. *I should've been more specific about me staying in control of both my body and soul. This can get confusing and, therefore, dangerous.*

I turn my head to look at my friends. They're all staring intently at the smoke, even though my soul is no longer visible. When Kessley's eyes wander back to me, she lets out a shriek.

"He's moving!"

I raise my hands in a reflex. "Calm down, I'm still half here."

Kess' hand flies to her mouth and Taylar rubs her back. "It's okay."

"Well, it is kind of creepy," Vicky admits. "But also convenient. You can keep us up to date on what's happening."

I nod. "And if anything goes wrong, I can use my powers to get myself back."

"Do you see anything yet?" Jeep inquires. He sounds a bit worried, which isn't very surprising, since he's met Shelton Banks in person. Even though he doesn't remember much from his time in Banks' mansion, he knows how powerful that man is.

"No, nothing yet," I answer, concentrating on the left side of my vision. "Wait… something's happening."

Ignoring the movement in the right half of my sight as best as I can, I take in my surroundings. I'm floating in the sky, descending slowly towards the roof of Shelton Banks' palatial house. *It's quiet here. I guess Shelton hasn't found new servants yet, or not a lot at least.*

"I'm going through the roof now," I tell my friends.

I land in the hallway. When I try to walk, I can't. For a second, I just hover an inch from the floor. *The spell must be searching for Shelton Banks.*

With a jolt, I start moving again. I glide across the hallway to what I remember to be the master bedroom. The door is closed, but I go through it. *Now I know what it feels like to be a ghost. It's creepy, but also quite handy.*

I swallow my nerves—or try to—when I come to a halt in front of the bed. Shelton Banks is sitting on the edge of it, engrossed by some sort of document. He's wearing a black suit this time and no tie. His hair is a bit ruffled up. *He's probably getting ready for bed, like we should.*

When he doesn't look up, I clear my throat.

His head snaps sideways so quickly that I can hear it creak. "Mr. Banner!"

Oh great, he recognizes me. Well, I guess that saves me some time.

"Mr. Banks," I respond, a lot calmer than he did.

He drops the document and rises to his feet. His eyes are fuming. "You killed my servants!"

It's not a question, but I nod anyway. "I sure did. And I will kill you too, if you don't give me what I need."

He throws his head back and laughs. Then he raises a finger and shakes it in front of him, as if he's talking to a toddler. "No, no, no, Mr. Banner. You may have caught me and my servants off guard, but that doesn't mean you will get that lucky again."

I cross my arms and ignore the sound coming from the other half of my vision. Someone's asking questions, but I have no time to answer them. "That actually didn't have anything to do with luck, Mr. Banks. We came prepared."

"I'm sure you did," he sneers, "but this time, my preparations are better than yours." He chuckles while he steps closer to me. "Stupid boy. You think you can take on a mature mage like me? You're just a baby! Chosen one or not, I am out of your league." He cracks his knuckles. "You signed your death warrant when you came here."

"I don't think so… Mr. Wilton."

He flinches when I call him by his true name and stops dead. He blinks several times and licks his lips. "What did you call me?"

"Clifford Wilton."

He shudders.

"Yes, I have your true name, and you will do as I say."

His blinking gets more furious, but he still doesn't move. It's as if saying his name has glued him to the floor.

"Don't worry, I don't plan on killing you." *Although I wonder why not. If I can make him take his own life, why wouldn't I? Better to get rid of him while I can.* "I only have a couple of questions, and a small request. If you co-operate, you'll be fine."

"If you think you can beat me by using my name, you're wrong, boy." His voice is deep and threatening, and I can hear the struggle in it. So far, his protests don't sound convincing, but I'll hurry up in case he does manage to free himself from his glued state.

"What's happening? Did you find him?" Vicky's voice asks from the other side of my vision.

"Yes, I'm starting the questioning now," I tell her.

On the other side, I start with the most important issue. "So, Clifford Wilton, first of all, I want you to release Vicky from the curse you put on her."

Shelton's face contorts with the effort of fighting my power over him.

"What… curse?" he pants.

"Don't play with me, Clifford Wilton!" I bellow. "When you touch her grave, Vicky gets pulled to the Shadow World." I point a finger in his direction. It trembles with anger. "Break that curse, Clifford… now."

The corners of his mouth twitch, and his hand flies up to cover his mouth, but the words spill out anyway.

"Break the curse upon the one,
that I want to make undone.
Touching her grave will do no good.
She will stay where she should."

He takes a piece of paper from his pocket and lights it with a snap of his fingers. It turns to ash in an instant, and letters swim in front of my eyes.

My concentration shifts back to my body.

Vicky's head snaps back, and a long string of black smoke escapes her mouth. It makes me feel relieved and scared at the same time. I reach out to support her, and she leans against me gratefully. When the last of the smoke leaves her body, she coughs and buries her face in my shoulder. I caress her back and whisper soothing words in her ear.

She straightens up and wipes the remaining smoke from her leather-clad body. She cracks her neck and looks around with a smirk on her face that makes me uncomfortable.

"Are you o-?"

"Well? What else do you want?" Shelton Banks' impatient voice interrupts us.

I send him a condescending smile. "I was just making sure you did what you were supposed to do."

"The curse is lifted. Now get on with it while you have the chance. I'd say you have about…" he stares past me, and the muscles in his face contract as he fights my hold over him, "… two minutes."

"We'll see about that. First, tell me why you put a curse on Vicky. Why is she so important to you?"

"To me?" Shelton Banks laughs out loud. "Come on, you can't be that stupid. You know who I work for."

"Fine." I grit my teeth. "You know what I mean. Why is she so important to Lucifer?"

"Because…" Shelton turns and tilts his head. His neck and jaws crack as he fights the pressure of the words that want to come out.

"Tell me the truth, Clifford Wilton."

"Well, I guess I can tell you now. Because she has inherited great power from her great-great-great…" he coughs and shakes his head, "great-grandmother." He wipes drops of sweat from his forehead. "Or however many 'greats' there may be."

I frown. "What do you mean? Who was her great-grandmother then?"

He stares at me with a mixture of hate and hurt.

I'd ask him what he meant by 'I guess I can tell you now', but I have a feeling I should hurry this up.

"Clifford... tell me who Vicky's great-great-great-whatever-grandmother was. And what powers are you talking about?"

He balls his fists; his face goes red. I fight the urge to step back. Then he throws his hands forward and opens his hands. A shock wave hits me, but instead of launching me, it travels through me.

I smile. This is exactly why I used a form of astral projection to speak to him. He can't hurt me, because I'm not really here. Or not fully, at least.

Suddenly, the image on the right side of my vision tilts, and I hear several outcries of shock and surprise. Two pairs of hands catch my body before it hits the ground.

Shelton Banks smirks at me. "I told you I'm stronger."

I raise one eyebrow and ignore the commotion around my body. "Are you now? I don't know what you think you've done, but..." I spread my arms, "I'm still here, and I'm fine. So let's continue, shall we? The sooner you answer my questions, the sooner I'll leave you alone."

Vicky's voice calls out, and I see her vague form moving in front of me. "Come back!" She sounds further away than before.

Jeep's voice comes through. "Ask him about Beelzebub first!"

"No!" Vicky yells.

I try to answer them, but my mouth won't open. Shelton Banks is breaking through my hold over him.

He is slowly freeing himself. I need to act quickly now.

What is more important? Finding out how to beat Beelzebub or getting rid of Shelton Banks?

I only have a second to decide, and I go for the former.

"Clifford Wilton!" I almost shout his name. "I order you to tell me how to kill Beelzebub!"

Vicky's voice drowns out my thoughts for a moment. "Dante, can you hear me?"

Shelton Banks raises his arms again, but this time, I don't wait for him to hit me with whatever he's got up his sleeve. I close my eyes and concentrate completely on my body. A blast of air hits me, but the invisible string between me and my body pulls me back at the same time. I shoot up through the ceiling and back into darkness.

* * *

Dante Banner returns in **The Eighth Mage** – Will Dante and his friends be able to keep their enemies at bay? Or will one of the Devil's allies finally find its way into their midst…?

Turn the page for a sneak peek! Or pre-order the book online NOW!

Make a difference

Reviews are very important to authors. Even a short or negative review can be of tremendous value to me as a writer. Therefore I would be very grateful if you could leave a review at your place of purchase. And don't forget to tell your friends about this book!

Thank you very much in advance.

Newsletter, social media and website

Want to receive exclusive first looks at covers and upcoming book releases, get a heads-up on pre-order and release dates and special offers, receive book recommendations and an exclusive 'look into my (writing) life'? Then please sign up now for my monthly newsletter through my website: www.tamarageraeds.com.

You can also follow me on Facebook, Instagram and Twitter for updates and more fun stuff!

Have a great day!   Tamara Geraeds

Found a mistake?

The Seventh Crow has gone through several rounds of beta reading and editing. If you found a typographical, grammatical, or other error which impacted your enjoyment of the book, we offer our apologies and ask that you let us know, so we can fix it for future readers.

You can email your feedback to:
info@tamarageraeds.com.

Preview

Cards of Death book 8
The Eighth Mage

CHAPTER 1

Faint voices are coming from one side; the other has gone silent.

While my astral form flies through the air, all kinds of thoughts go through my head, barely audible above the pounding that bounces in all directions. *I should've known it would be too dangerous to approach Shelton Banks, even if it was only in the form of an astral projection. Why didn't I put more safety measures into my spell? What if he damaged my soul somehow?*

My astral form slows down, and the voices go quiet. I open my eyes. My vision is still split, but only the left side, the eye of my astral self, has visibility. I try to make my body open its eyes. It doesn't respond. It's as if we're no longer connected.

I gulp for air, even though my current form doesn't need oxygen. *Don't panic. Don't panic,* I tell myself. *I'm not completely lost yet. There are still two visions, so some part of the connection must have remained intact.*

I take in everything around me, and when I blink several times, the incoherent shapes start to make sense.

I've returned to the annex, where my body is lying on the ground. Several shapes are hunched over it.

"Vicky," I whisper.

The shady person starts shaking my body. She can't hear me.

I send several commands to my body. *Move! Open your mouth. Open your eyes. Do something!*

Of course, it doesn't obey. It lies there, looking disturbingly empty.

When I drift closer, everything around me gets hazier again.

Suddenly I'm hovering near the ceiling. I reach out to grab something before I disappear in the next room. There's nothing to hold onto, even if my hands weren't see-through.

"Help!" I call out. "I'm here!"

The shapes below me move around the annex. None of them look up.

And then, I see something strange.

The people below me are all shapes of light, but some of them have black spots. One even has tufts of black crawling through them. *Evil?* I try to make out who they are. *Must be Gisella. She's the only one of us with evil powers. Although…*

I narrow my eyes at the figure standing behind the werecat-witch. This one is holding a staff. *Maël.* A

7

small sliver of black moves inside her chest. *Nothing to worry about. That's the remnant of the black tree in the Shadow World. It's only a tiny bit of evil, which she can control.*

I try to find D'Maeo to check if the Black Void has really left him. My gaze falls on someone with a bowler hat. *Jeep.* His body shows not even a single speck of dark. The person moving his hand to his mouth over and over beside him must be Charlie. He's also clean. Kessley is no different. Her body seems to glow a bit more than the others. *Probably her cheerfulness. Or the booze running through her veins.*

My gaze moves along. And freezes, along with my astral body. The person standing next to Kessley, with his arm around her, must be Taylar. His misty form is a weird mixture of dark and light. The black and white slivers swirl around each other as if they're performing an intricate dance. You'd think it was a battle between good and evil, but the twirls and dives don't come across as hostile. Playful is a better description.

I'm so mesmerized and stunned by the intricate pattern the slivers inside Taylar weave that I don't notice myself drifting through the ceiling until it blocks my vision.

I throw my head forward to get a glimpse of Vicky's body. Too late. My astral form keeps floating up. There's no use in struggling. I can't grab onto anything, and none of my movements have any effect.

Soon, I don't hear my friends' voices anymore.

The air around me gets warmer as I keep ascending. It's not until I spot a light in the distance, getting bigger and bigger, that I realize what's going on.

I start to struggle against the force pulling me in. "No! Let go of me!"

This can't be happening. Not like this. Not now that we're so close.

Again, I search for something to hold on to. I try to use my powers to turn back. Lightning, ice, water, sunshine…. nothing works. I'm defenseless.

Eventually I stop fighting. It's better to save my strength, because I will not accept this fate. So far, I've accepted all of it. I was meant to lose my father, to see my mother suffer from fits and torture, to fight Lucifer, and to lose the girl I love. If that is my destiny, then so be it. But I will not leave this battle so close to the end. I will fight for my life and for that of everyone on Earth.

Now that I have stopped resisting, I'm pulled into the light fast. I close my eyes and wait.

The light gets brighter, but it's not painful. It's soothing and warm. It makes me want to lie down and forget about everything going on below.

I shake my head. *No, don't forget. They need you. Mom, Vicky, Taylar, Jeep, D'Maeo, Maël, Kessley, Charlie and Gisella. Even Mona. I can't leave them.*

"Welcome," a soft voice says as the light dims.

I open my eyes. A glowing man in a white robe is standing before me. Ginger hair falls upon his shoulders, and his face is covered in freckles. His huge reddish wings seem too big for his slender body. His smile is sweet, and he gives me a small bow. "Welcome to Heaven, Dante."

I straighten my shoulders when my feet finally touch solid ground again. Or almost solid, since the road consists of clouds.

I bow back to the angel and answer him with a simple, "No."

His smile falters. "What do you mean?"

With my arms folded, I look him in the eye. "I don't accept this. Send me back, please."

"Your time on Earth is up, Dante. I'm sorry."

I take him in from head to toe and step closer.

He frowns but doesn't move.

"Listen," I say. "We all want the same thing here. Heaven and Earth are under attack. I'm the chosen one; I can save them both. But I don't have time to return as a ghost and learn how to move stuff. I need to be alive. So send me back."

"I know who you are, but there are rules. Unfortunately."

I cock my head. "Is there anything in the rules about someone taking over Saint Peter's duties at the gates of Heaven? Because I met him, and he didn't look anything like you."

The angel's cheeks turn red. He stares at me with his too bright eyes, and I stare right back. I don't believe for a second that the normal rules still apply, and I'm pretty certain this angel has the power to send me back.

Finally, he licks his lips and opens his mouth. "You want to keep fighting, even when I don't return you to your body?"

I roll my eyes at him. "Of course. I'm the chosen one. That's my job. I keep fighting until Satan's ass is kicked."

He chuckles but pulls a straight face so fast I wonder if I imagined it. "The task of the chosen one ends when he dies. A new one will be appointed."

My mouth falls open. "You're joking, right? That's it? You give up, just like that?" I shake my head. "Well, I'm sorry, but I can't do that. That'll take way too long." I turn and start walking away from him. "If you won't help me, I'll find my way back myself. I've been here before, after all."

A stunned silence answers me.

I've taken five steps when I'm lifted off my feet again and drift back to the gates of Heaven, that are now visible behind the ginger angel.

I give him my foulest look and try to conjure ice above him. It doesn't work.

After another long stare, he finally nods. "Fine. You're right, everything has been turned upside down here. To be honest, I thought you'd be relieved to pass on the baton. I expected you to beg for your life; instead, you beg for the lives of everyone on Earth and in Heaven. You leave me no choice but to honor your request."

I grin at him, and he raises a finger. "However, if you fail again, there will be no turning back. No turning into a ghost either. That will be the end. Do you understand?"

I wave his words away as if they don't mean anything, although I feel the weight of them pressing on my shoulders. *This will be my last chance. I cannot fail again.* "Fine, fine. Just hurry, please."

"One more thing." He slams his hands together and a book appears between them. He flicks through it at dazzling speed, then nods and slams it shut. "Yes, I thought so."

"What?" I ask impatiently.

He throws the book over his shoulder where it vanishes into thin air. "There is a rule I would like to honor."

"What rule?"

"Your choice to keep fighting Lucifer in order to save everyone grants you a reward." He paints a large circle in front of him with a swipe of his hand, and seven familiar faces pop up inside it. "If you beat Lucifer, one of these people can stay with you on Earth until their time to move on comes again. Who will you choose?"

My eyes almost pop out of my head. "For real?"

"I do not make jokes, Dante. Choose the one who will not move on if you defeat Lucifer."

WANT TO READ ON?

Order the next book now, on Amazon!

SNEAK PEEK

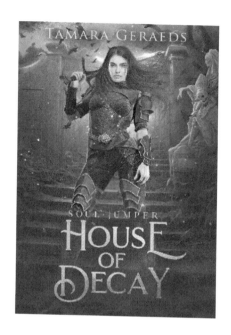

SOUL JUMPER
HOUSE OF DECAY

Welcome to Vex Monster Tours.
Please press PLAY to watch this video.

PLAY

Loading….

Loading….

Loading….

"Hi there, and welcome to Vex Monster Tours. If you're looking for an adrenaline-filled adventure, you've come to the right place. My name is Vex and...

You're laughing, aren't you? I don't blame you. I would too if I were you. But it's not my fault that I'm called Vex. My parents had a great sense of humor, or so they thought. They were both Soul Jumpers, of course, like me, and thought it was ironically funny to name me Vex, since they trained me to be a nuisance to any kind of monster.

Anyway, in case you don't know what a Soul Jumper is, I'll explain it to you briefly.

A Soul Jumper is a human with special powers, born and trained to kill monsters. We are stronger and faster than regular humans and have more endurance and agility and some other extras. When we touch the last victim a creature killed, a connection is made with the next target of that monster. When that target is attacked and about to lose the battle with the monster, our soul jumps into the target's body. From that moment on, our natural strengths are doubled, as are our senses. This gives us the power to defeat the monster before it kills another person. While we're inside the victim's body, they have no control over their moves but can still feel everything and talk to us. If they die, we jump back into our own body, which is protected by a flock of birds. Hawks, in my case. We have special Soul Jumper battle outfits, like I'm wearing now, connected to our souls to make them jump with us. They have some neat gadgets as extra back-up.

So, where was I?
Oh yes, Vex Monster Tours offers you the chance to see and fight any evil creature up close. To increase your chances of winning without my help, you get a day of training. That doesn't sound like a lot, but I'll give you a cupcake that contains a special mixture. It will give you the ability to pick up everything you learn a lot faster, and it builds up muscle at triple speed.

A blood vow is made between me and the monster of your request in which we agree not to attack before the arranged time. I will protect you the best I can while letting you fight the monster for as long as possible. Sounds cool, right?

But why, do you ask, would a monster agree to fight two people? Well, for one, most monsters are cocky, and two, these days, there are so many hunters roaming the streets that they have a hard time finding a quiet place to attack. They think they have a better chance for a meal when they're just fighting you and I… but we'll prove them wrong.

Have any questions? Feel free to email or call me!"

CHAPTER 1

I sense something off even before I see it. My muscles tense at the feeling that I'm not alone, like I should be.

Custos lands quietly on my shoulder while I peer left and right. Everything seems normal. There are no odd sounds, no footprints on the path or in the earth around the trees.

Then I notice it. The door to the training barn is ajar. It's just a crack, and there isn't enough wind to make it move, but I know something is wrong.

Custos cocks his head when he notices it a second later. He nudges my neck with his beak, as if to say, 'Go check it out!'

Slowly moving closer, my mind whirls around the possibilities. *Did I fail to properly close the portal after the last training session, making it possible for the monster to escape?*

I shake that thought off. Even if I didn't close it completely, the portal only lets monsters cross halfway. It's not really a passage; they can't get through to this world.

With narrowed eyes, I watch the creak in the door. My ears try to pick up a sound, any sound, that could give me an indication of what to expect. When they finally do, just as my hand moves to the doorknob, I freeze.

Custos lets out a disrupted croak as the pained whimper drifts toward us.

"That sounded human, right?" I ask him quietly.

He nods, and I wrap my fingers around the doorknob. "Good. That rules out the worst."

Before I get the chance to pull the door open, the leader of my protective kettle pulls my hair.

"Ouch," I whisper. "What was that for?"

The hawk swoops down to the ground and pulls at my pant leg.

A smile creeps upon my face. "Oh yes, good thinking, Custos."

I pull out the short blade hidden in my boot and wait for Custos to settle back on my shoulder.

"Ready?" I ask, and his talons dig into my shirt.

With one fast movement, I pull the door open. It takes me a millisecond to realize I won't need my weapon. No one is jumping out at me. The whimpering has stopped, but there's no doubt where it came from. Several of the traps that line the walls have been set off. Whomever broke into my barn managed to avoid the first trap, judging by the three arrows lodged into the wall on my right. Dodging them slowed him down enough to get doused with flammable liquid and set on fire.

I scan the floorboard in front of me. Yep, burn marks. The trail of black spots leaves no room for doubt about the intruder's next move. He dove for the bucket of water on my left, that has tipped over and is still dripping.

"And there it is," I say manner-of-factly.

Three small steps take me to the edge of what is normally a pretty solid wooden floor with no more than slits showing the dark void below. Now, the boards have moved aside and down, creating a large hole with a view of the endless blackness. Inches from the tips of my shoes, bloodied fingers are straining to hang onto what remains of the floor.

I lean forward so I can see my unwanted guest. "Hello there. How can I help you today?"

The man attached to the fingers is about nineteen years old. He has black hair covered in grease and green eyes that look up at me with a mixture of relief and despair. Scorch marks decorate his arms and face, and there are burn holes all over his shirt.

I study him shamelessly while he searches for an answer.

Custos scurries over and softly pecks at one of the fingers.

With a squeal, the man pulls back his hand, swinging dangerously by the other before wrapping it back around the floorboard five inches further to the right.

"Help me, please," he finally manages.

"Sure!" The fake smile on my lips almost hurts.

I squat down in front of him. "But first, I'd like to know what you're doing here."

One finger slips, and he groans. "I'll tell you everything. Please help me up."

"I will," I answer, examining my fingernails, "after you tell me."

"Fine." His voice goes up a couple of octaves. "I was hiking in the forest when a bear attacked me." My gaze drops down to his green shirt, which is streaked with red between the holes. There's a gash in the side that could've been made by a bear's claw, but it could also be the result of climbing the fence around my premises.

I frown. "Where's your backpack then? Did you drop it?"

"I did." He nods. His dark eyebrows are pulled together when he sends me a pleading look. "It fell into the pit. Please don't let me fall too. Please."

He sounds convincing, yet something about his story is off.

"Tell me exactly what happened with the bear."

He groans. "Please pull me up first. I can't hold on for much longer."

I stand up and take a step back. "I'm sorry, but I don't trust you. Your story doesn't make sense."

"Why not?" he exclaims. "I encountered a bear; I swear! I've never seen one so big in my life."

"What kind of bear?"

"A black bear, of course; it's the only one that lives here."

"Hmm." Anyone could know that.

And then it hits me. The thing that doesn't add up in his story.

"Bears never come close to my home. They sense

the monsters that visit frequently."

The muscles in his arms are starting to shake from the effort of holding on. "Please… I don't know what it was doing here. I'm telling you, it attacked me, and I figured climbing over your fence was my best shot."

I tap my lips with my finger. He is so full of bull that it's almost funny. Even if a bear would come close, climbing over the fence would trigger my alarm. *What are the odds of a bear approaching and my alarm failing on the same day?* And I'm not even counting the tripwires set up everywhere.

I cock my head. "You don't seem surprised to hear that monsters visit me on a regular basis."

He focuses on his fingers, trying to get a better grip. His breathing is fast, and sweat trickles down his temples and over the stubble on his cheeks. "Monsters are everywhere, why would that be a surprise?"

"No…" Slowly I shake my head. "You know who I am, what I am. You know what I do."

He clenches his teeth. "I swear-"

He yells in panic as his other hand slips from the edge. I drop back down quickly and grab it.

"Didn't your mother teach you not to swear?" I say. My voice is low with repressed anger. My patience has vanished. "Now, tell me the truth, or I'm throwing you in."

"All right, all right!" He swallows and licks his lips. His weight pulls at my arm, and I grunt.

"You better hurry."

"I know who you are. You're Vex Connor, a Soul Jumper, *the* Soul Jumper." He gives me a sheepish grin. "Everyone admires you. I just wanted to see how you did it all, you know. What kind of tools you use, how you live…" His voice trails off, and he breaks eye contact.

After a short silence, I shrug. "Well, that still sounds crazy but much more plausible than your other story." I grab his arm with both hands and haul him up.

He collapses on what remains of the floor and clutches his hands to his chest.

Custos shrieks, and I nod at him. "Yes, turn off the traps for a minute, please."

The hawk flies to the other end of the barn, close to the ceiling to avoid the booby traps that are higher up on the walls. I block the intruder's view as Custos picks up a rope, drops the loop at the end around the handle of the device I built and pulls.

With a sound like a collapsing bookcase, the floor boards pop back up until the black void below can only be seen through the cracks.

I stick out my hand. "Let's go. I'll give you a cup of coffee before you leave. You can wash up while the water boils."

* * *

Want to read on? Order this story on Amazon now!

IMPORTANT NOTICE

All *Soul Jumper* stories can be read in random order. You can start with the story that appeals to you most. It is, however, recommended to start with Force of the Kraken.

I hope you enjoy them!

ABOUT THE AUTHOR

Tamara Geraeds was born in 1981. When she was 6 years old, she wrote her first poem, which basically translates as:

A hug for you and a hug for me
and that's how life should be

She started writing books at the age of 15 and her first book was published in 2012. After 6 books in Dutch she decided to write a young adult fantasy series in English: *Cards of Death*.

Tamara's bibliography consists of books for children, young adults and adults, and can be placed under fantasy and thrillers.

Besides writing she runs her own business, in which she teaches English, Dutch and writing, (re)writes texts and edits books.

She's been playing badminton for over 20 years and met the love of her life Frans on the court. She loves going out for dinner, watching movies, and of course reading, writing and hugging her husband. She's crazy about sushi and Indian curries, and her favorite color is pink.

Printed in Great Britain
by Amazon